Patrician

BOOK 2
SECRET OF ALBA

Lindsey Winsemius

Get an exclusive sneak peek of
Outsider, Book 3 in *The Secret of Alba Series*
by visiting

www.lindseywinsemius.com/my-books

Published by ApogeeINVENT
www.apogeeinvent.com

ISBN 978-0692598672

First Edition January 2016

To my father, who showed me that kindness is never weakness, and life is not about what happens to us, but how we react to what happens. Miss you and love you always, Dad.

And to my mother, who was my first fan. Thanks for your unconditional support. Love you, Mom.

Part 1 Betrayal

There are two kinds of people in this world: Those who run away from trouble, and those who run towards it. Pray you never have to find out which kind you are.
    – From the Journal of Cecilia Delacroix

1

Aerina woke with a gasp, the terrifying crack of a mass ElectroMagnetic Weapon fading into her subconscious. The sound of rain pounding on the roof, and the innocent flash of lightning, reassured her that it had only been a dream.

Her eyes fell on the dark head resting on the pillow next to her. Joy settled in her heart, tempered by pervading sorrow. Sleep was a painful blankness, and each new waking forced her to again remember the anguish of the previous day. Would she ever be able to listen to a summer storm without remembering the devastation of their city? Without thinking of Stephen's lifeless body? Of the crushing pain in her heart that had been echoed in Lina's eyes?

The wave of grief threatened to overwhelm her, and she struggled to breath past the lump in her throat. Not wanting to wake Marcus, she turned to slip her legs over the side of the bed. A muscled arm slid around her waist, stopping her.

Without a word, Marcus pulled her down beside him, enfolding her in his large frame. As she broke into sobs, he kissed her head, stroking back strawberry-colored curls. He always knew what to say without saying anything.

As the tears subsided, Aerina looked up into the familiar stark features. He was waiting, lowering his head slowly to capture her lips with his. Aerina grabbed at the comfort offered in that kiss, returning it with passion.

Their joining was more than just passion; it was a celebration of life. Comfort, sorrow, and love all entwined in a painfully beautiful love-making.

Marcus rolled to his side, bringing Aerina with him until she rested on his hard chest. Both were panting, bodies replete.

"I love you," Aerina murmured against the soft hairs of his chest. She closed her eyes and fell back into a dreamless sleep.

Lina Rhodes sat listlessly in her mother's Serenity Garden. The sun was shining and the flowers bloomed, their essence floating on a light ocean breeze.

She hated it. She wished for the return of the grey haze and rain that matched her dark mood. Her slender hands curled into fists. She caught sight of the hedge-clippers left on a bench by the gardener, and she itched to take it and cut the blooming shrubs. To destroy their superficial beauty in the same way her life was destroyed.

Balance and serenity bring peace. The meditation only served to heighten her anguish; feeding her anger. She would never know peace again.

The ceremony for Stephen had been long and agonizing. Her mother and father had represented their class well; composed, stoic, they'd stood with the gathered crowd of Patricians to celebrate the great man their son had been. To recognize the great sacrifice he had made that saved their city from destruction.

She knew her parents had been embarrassed by her own lack of control. Weeping in great gasping sobs, Lina hadn't cared about her smeared makeup or swollen eyes. Stephen had been her only real family. The facsimile of care performed by her separated parents was limited to meeting basic needs. Stephen had been the one to kiss her hurts, listen to her concerns, and offer advice.

And now he was gone. Forever.

The scene following the ceremony played in her mind.

"Lina," her father had snapped after the mourners left. "You've embarrassed our family with your unrestrained behavior!"

"What family?" Lina had replied apathetically, noting the familiar dangerous anger rising in her father, but for once, not caring.

Her mother gasped, and her father's eyes narrowed. "Don't think because you're almost an adult that you can get away with impertinence. You're not too old for me to teach you respect." Lina knew her father wasn't bluffing. Beneath the numbing pain that permeated her core, she felt a frisson of fear.

"Richard, is this really a good time?" her mother had begun pleadingly.

"Quiet, Rachel!" Her mother subsided into frozen silence. "The next time I see you, young lady, I expect the correct decorum. Don't embarrass me again."

Lina had remained mute as her father strode towards his new model e-car without a backwards glance.

"Let's go, Lina," her mother said sharply, the sting of her estranged husband's words still etched on her tight features.

"I'll walk home," Lina had replied quietly, absently straightening her white coat.

"Fine. Don't be long. Senator Caius has invited us for dinner."

Lina had intentionally lingered, waiting until she knew her mother would be forced to leave without her. She wanted solitude; needed time to process her thoughts. It would be impossible for her to force any semblance of normalcy.

Not that their family had ever been normal. The dysfunction had drawn Stephen and Lina together, forcing them to depend on one another for survival.

And now she was alone.

Dropping her head into her hands, she let new tears fall. Just when she thought she couldn't cry another tear, her body produced a new torrent from an untapped source deep within. The salty drops stung a path down her already red, chapped cheeks, raw from numerous swipes with hand and cloth.

Would the tears ever dry up? Would she ever be able to feel joy; to feel normal?

The scuff of a boot had her lifting her head. The gardener had entered the back gate. Her swollen eyes met his blue-green gaze. Like many Aggies, he was brawny and tanned from outdoor labor. His light brown hair had streaks of blonde bleached by the sun, and creases lined his eyes where he smiled frequently. Cords of muscles made his chest and shoulders large, his entire body coiled strength. He would be frightening in all his strength, but his light eyes seemed to twinkle with inner mirth, as if he knew a joke the rest of the world was not privy to.

Before Stephen's death, she had spent many hours in the garden surreptitiously admiring the new gardener. She'd kept the growing infatuation secret even from her closest friends, even Aerina, who'd had her own relationship with a caste outside of their own. Desiring an Aggie seemed so forbidden, even admitting it aloud had seemed illicit. Now, the emptiness pervading her soul had her dark eyes sliding away in disinterest.

Nothing mattered. Certainly not her girlish crush on a gardener.

The object of her thoughts walked forward slowly, his booted feet making barely a sound on the walk.

"I'm sorry about your brother." His low voice, unexpected, made her jump. Her eyes met his enigmatic gaze. He'd never spoken to her before, and surprisingly, she felt a small rush of…something.

She looked at her feet, shod in dirty white ballet-style

shoes. "Thank you." Her voice was barely above a whisper, cracking lightly.

His hand, rough and blunt, caught a large tear that trailed down a well-worn path on her cheek. She instinctively jerked back at the contact, her eyes jumping to his again.

His light eyes were searching; curious and apologetic at once.

The chime of the front door interrupted the strange moment. The gardener — she wasn't even sure of his name — turned away, scooping the large pruners that had been sitting on the bench. The same pruners she had almost used to desecrate her mother's prized roses.

Lina reluctantly walked to the front door, not wanting to face any more well-meaning sympathizers.

Aerina stood on the other side. Lina felt pain in her heart, fresh and sharp. Anger engulfed the pain, her brown eyes darkening.

"What do you want?"

"Can I come in—"

"Just say what you came to say," Lina interrupted. She refused to notice Aerina's own swollen eyes and bright red nose. She couldn't give in to the desire to hug her close. The strange and unfamiliar anger burned too hot.

"I loved Stephen, too," Aerina said quietly.

"That is what you came to say?" Lina asked disbelievingly. "As if that makes any difference now. If it hadn't been for you, he would have never been involved. He would have never died!" Unable to face her former best friend, Lina slammed the door shut. Leaning back against it, she slowly sank to the floor, great sobs bursting from the bottomless well inside her.

Jay trimmed Magister Rhodes' hideous topiary, listening to the young Alban walk slowly up the stairs to her room. In spite of himself, he felt sorry for the girl.

She'd been cute; always finding excuses to be around

when he was working. Watching him covertly. He knew she was attracted to him, and had stored that information away for future use.

Her brother's death had changed her. Gone was the sweet, gentle girl with a woman's body. She was now withdrawn; bitter. Angry. He supposed it wasn't an unusual grief response. Everyone grieved differently. He just wouldn't have expected it of the dark-haired girl. She'd almost seemed shallow when he'd first noticed her.

But the curvy Patrician, while an entertaining distraction, was not important. She wasn't part of his mission.

It was still a shock that the Albans had defeated the Southern Empire warship. He knew the Empire hadn't even considered losing their ship in all their contingency planning. Failing to find the Technology, yes. Retreating had even been outlined. But not complete destruction.

He wondered how the President took the news.

2

"We need to appoint a new Consul immediately!

"An interim Consul—"

"Someone to get the people through this tumultuous time—"

Marcus stood silently, his arms crossed lightly across his chest, listening to the Senators argue as they had the last few times he'd called them together.

"Why don't we hear what Marcus thinks?" Aerina's father cut into the argument, his deep blue eyes, just like Aerina's, impaling Marcus. He obviously didn't like his daughter associating with the Alpha Virmortus; the leader of the assassin and intelligence caste. Marcus didn't care what the Senator thought.

Aerina belonged with him. She'd made her choice, and

he wasn't going to let her go.

He just hoped the Senator wouldn't allow his personal resentment to compromise his decisions.

The group quieted, eight pairs of eyes turning on Marcus. Rejecting the Consul's vacant seat at the head, Marcus chose to stand at the foot of the meeting table. Everyone knew he held the power now in Alba, but he did not want to become the figure head for the state. He needed to focus on security, not pacifying the masses.

"The Armati are doing an excellent job of communicating with the people what has happened. We've cleaned up the area of the Pleb city that was damaged in the battle; the dead have been honored and buried. The injured are being cared for by the Medella. Commerce has resumed. People are going back to their daily lives." Marcus paused in his succinct recitation of what had been accomplished since the fierce battle with the Southern Empire, North America's most powerful territory.

"What about the Consul?" Caius asked. Marcus' gaze flicked to the slender Senator of Technology.

"Per the Law of Death, Consul Julius has been sentenced to death for his crimes. Without an heir, the Senators may appoint a new Consul." The rest of the Senators began nodding, pleased the Virmortus leader was affirming their own opinions. "However," Marcus continued, his voice going dangerously soft, "We are in a state of war. The Southern Empire will return. You may appoint a new Consul to appease your Laws, and the people. But know this: I call the shots. Whomever accepts this position must do so with the understanding that we are under Martial Law."

Silence fell over the gathered Senators. Marcus could read on their faces they did not like his stipulation. Too damn bad. This was reality. If they wanted to have a chance against the most powerful nation in the Americas, perhaps worldwide, Marcus needed to be in control.

"I'm going to have to disagree with you." Antony,

Aerina's father, rose stiffly from his seat. The other Senators nodded their heads in approval, but remained seated. Confronting a Reaper took more courage than many of them possessed.

Marcus raised one brow, waiting.

"Now is important to maintain our traditions; uphold our laws—"

The lights suddenly winked out, the meeting room blinds closing. All the holoreaders in the room turned on, drawing up the same image of a historical file. It projected from each reader an image of a President of the former USA in the assembly hall at Paulskirche, the speaker on each reader playing as one: "Change is the law of life. And those who look only to the past, or the present, are certain to miss the future."

The lights came on bright, then dimmed. The blinds flung back open, letting in the midday sun suspended high over the mountainside city-state.

"Do you want to uphold the Laws, or do you want to survive?" Marcus asked calmly, arms still folded loosely over his chest. The Senators looked uncertain; nervous. Aerina's father had sat back down, although his eyes burned hotly with resentment.

The Technology gave Marcus even more power than he'd already held as leader of the state's intelligence caste. He was a trained killer; now he was a trained killer with an impossibly powerful weapon.

And he was their only real chance of surviving the coming war.

"How'd it go?" Aerina asked as she met Marcus at the door to his villa. She had just returned from visiting Debbie and Portia, the two survivors of a town in the south hit by the Southern Empire. The visit had helped a little to distract her from the emptiness left by Lina's rejection.

"Fine."

"That good, huh?" Aerina replied sardonically. She was

never going to get used to Marcus' taciturn ways.

"They've been persuaded to see my perspective," he finally added dryly. Aerina smiled slightly at that. She could only imagine Marcus' methods of persuasion.

"How did your talk with Lina go?" he turned the topic.

Aerina remained silent, shaking her head quickly. It was her turn to be vague. His arm shot out, wrapping around her slim waist, pulling her in.

"It's not your fault."

Aerina took a shaky breath, letting her head fall back against his chest, comforted by his strength; the sound of his beating heart.

"She and Stephen were my family. I can't lose them both." Turning, she buried her head in his chest, letting the tears fall.

3

Lina sat slowly in Stephen's office chair, staring at the blank screen before her. Her brother's familiar scent wafted from the soft fabric; a faint sweet spice cologne he favored triggering the release of overwhelming emotion.

Impatiently swiping away fresh tears, she instructed the computer to turn on. It booted up quickly, the virtual keyboard appearing beneath her hands, a connected holoscreen popping up to the right.

Even with the tidal wave of sorrow threatening to overcome her, the familiarity of the keys beneath her fingertips was comforting. She'd always found joy in losing herself in the enthralling world of processors. Holocomputers, devices, code... It had been her comfort and her passion. A fascination she'd shared with Stephen.

Her long, elegant fingers flew over the keys, the light buzz of haptic feedback the only sound in the darkened room.

Her brown eyes scanned the screen as lines of information flew across.

According to Stephen's history, the Southern Empire had appeared on radar and hooked into the Alban network. They began collecting information from the shared Network, including each individual's ID chip. The Empire had sent a virus, which Stephen must have uncovered, and the Albans had shut the Network down. Then, hours later, they had rebooted the Network, again connecting to the Southern Empire.

And then the warship had exploded, and Stephen had died.

The facts with time and date stamps were here, but none of the answers Lina needed were.

Why Stephen? What had they been doing on that warship?

She sighed, resting her head on the redwood desk where Stephen had spent so much of his time. Idly, she began going through the drawers. The bottom drawer revealed something unexpected. A bottle of whiskey.

Lina pulled it out, setting it on the desk, watching the amber-colored liquid swirl. Stephen drank alcohol? Patricians didn't drink. What else didn't she know about her beloved brother?

A small glass was in the drawer with the whiskey. As Lina removed the glass, she saw a small object tucked in the back. She couldn't help but smile. Razorback, Stephen's old action figure. Many Patrician parents, particularly theirs, believed in only educational toys. The popular superhero action figures were not educational.

But Stephen, in a rare act of rebellion, had gotten one from a friend and kept it. He'd also gotten one for Lina, Waterspout Woman.

She still had hers, too. They'd played superheroes for hours in Balance Park, away from the angry shouting and occasional violence at home.

Turning the action figure in her hand, she poured some of the whiskey into the glass. Just a splash, then a few more. Picking up the glass, she gulped the liquid quickly.

Gasping and coughing, she felt it burn its way down into her stomach. The glass clinked as she set it quickly down on the desk, her eyes watering. How did people drink this stuff?

As she stared at the nearly-empty glass, she felt an unfamiliar warmth spread through her, beginning in her stomach and spreading to her limbs.

That at least answered the *why*. She took another sip, slowly this time. It went down a little easier, and the warmth continued to spread.

Jay heard the scuff of a shoe near the worker entrance to the garden, stiffening. He had stayed late to meet his contact in Balance Park. It was going to be their first meeting since the destruction of the warship, and he knew it would be tough. Security was tight in Alba now.

His hand hovered over the sica blade most Albans carried. The small, curved blade was often used for simple tasks but could easily be deadly.

A familiar dark head appeared through the back gate, followed by a tall, curvy body. Her heart-shaped face was elegant, large brown eyes framed by dark lashes and brows, her pale skin making her full lips even brighter red. And her body. Albans preferred slender, athletic figures, which this girl was not. Her hourglass figure was fit but far from slender, but where he came from, curves were highly desirable.

It was obvious she didn't have a clue how desirable she was. Her lack of confidence might be beneficial to him; make her easier to manipulate.

He couldn't help but grin at the normally proper Patrician as she tumbled towards the ground, her white clothes disheveled with a few dirt streaks and a grass stain.

He meandered over to her slowly, again smiling at her

exaggerated look of horror as he approached, her big brown eyes darting around as if searching for a place to hide.

She was a damn cute drunk.

"Let me help you." He offered a callused, dirt-streaked hand. She hesitated, her own soft hand taking his slowly. He helped her up, steadying her when she stumbled again. She leaned into him, brushing her heavy dark hair back impatiently. Then she looked up at him, her height bringing her face close, just under his chin.

He liked that. Most woman were dwarfed by his large frame. He met her gaze. Her brown eyes, normally bright and inquisitive, were cloudy from the alcohol, unable to focus for long.

"You're going to regret this tomorrow," he said, his hands gently but firmly holding her upper arms, afraid she would collapse to the marble path if he let go.

"No, I won't," she murmured, and suddenly her full, warm lips were pressed to his.

He stood, frozen in surprise. What she lacked in experience, she made up for in enthusiasm. He'd never taken advantage of a drunken woman in his life, but he couldn't seem to pull away.

He took control of the kiss, forcing her to slow down and relieve the pressure of her closed mouth pressed tightly to his. He moved his tongue gently along the seam of her mouth until she sighed with pleasure and he swept inside, tasting the inner folds.

She tasted like whiskey and mint, which she must have used to attempt to cover her illicit indulgence. He didn't know if it was the night, the forbidden, or the fact that she was the enemy, but he'd never tasted anything so amazing.

She might not regret this—hell, she probably wouldn't even remember it—but he was going to. Remember *and* regret this kiss.

4

Royce waited in the shadows of Balance Park. Jay knew he was there, but circled the jogging trail an extra time to be sure he wasn't being watched. He'd spoken briefly with two Armati on the way here, one of which seemed suspicious about an Aggie spending time in the Patricians' recreation area.

When he was sure he was alone, he approached his cohort. He'd had one close call weeks earlier, when he'd thought he'd detected someone on a nearby outcropping in the park. And that had been before the Empire had attacked. Before the war had begun, and the Albans had unexpectedly won the first battle.

"The Condor is in the nest," Royce said. Jay nodded, answering the "everything's good" code with his own, "The Wolf is in the pasture."

"How's Congress taking the loss?" Jay asked.

Royce shook his dark head. "Not good. They were so certain about the mission's success. The President is getting worried. I think she assumed we'd have time to experiment with the Technology before the European Alliance meeting in July."

"The pressure is on," Jay grinned. "Good thing I do best under pressure, eh?"

"Any progress?"

"I know where the vials are hidden."

Royce impatiently swiped a hand, dismissing that. "We always knew where the vials were hidden — in the Training Grounds. We also can't get in there." He rubbed a hand on his clean-shaven jaw, dark eyebrows drawn. For being stuck in the wilderness for months on end, the slender black man looked well-groomed.

"I might have found a way."

Royce stared hard at Jay's cheerful face, then shrugged.

"Alright. But we're running out of time. The General is riding us hard. If we can't complete this, we might as well not go back."

Jay nodded, his grin still in place. They all knew the price of failure.

But he never failed. It was why he was the Wolf. Why he'd been chosen to head this mission. When the Alban Technology had become a priority, the General had called him.

And he wasn't going to go home empty-handed.

5

Lina's head pounded, and the morning light felt like rays of fire, burning her eyes. She tried to roll over, but the slight movement made her stomach lurch.

She made it to the bathroom on weak legs, spewing the contents of her stomach. Shakily, she rinsed her mouth and managed to get back to her bed, pulling the covers up to block the morning sun.

The next time she woke up, the sun was higher in the sky, and she felt a little better. Her stomach was still uncertain, and a light headache pounded behind her eyes. She finally took notice of her attire.

Balance and serenity, she was in her underclothes. Vague memories of the night before jumbled in her mind. Drinking the whiskey at Stephen's, stumbling home.

Him. The gardener. She didn't even know his name, and she'd kissed him, for serenity's sake.

"Oh, no," she groaned, burying her head in the pillow. What had she done? Had she…been intimate with him? After the kiss where she practically mauled his mouth, she couldn't remember anything.

Now she knew why Patricians didn't drink. This was awful. The lack of control. The inability to remember what she'd done while out of control. The brief moments of euphoria she'd felt while intoxicated was not worth this dreadful punishment.

She had to know what had happened. Which meant she was going to have to ask the Aggie. A blush heated her whole body just at the thought.

It was still a few more hours until she felt like a real person. She dressed carefully in white slacks and a ribbed white short-sleeved shirt that hugged her upper curves. Since Stephen's death, she'd shed pounds quickly, further accenting the voluptuous curves Aerina had always told her were her best feature.

She refused to think of her *former* best friend. The friend who had used Stephen, convincing him to play hero.

To be a martyr.

Taking a shaky breath, she tugged uselessly on the tight shirt. She wasn't used to having such obvious sexual shape, and had to fight against hunching her shoulders forward to hide the curve of her breasts.

Shoulders back. Chin up. Step lightly. Patricians don't slouch. Her mother's words followed her everywhere.

Her small steps eventually brought her to the back Serenity Garden where the Aggie spent most of his time at their house. It was Tuesday. He generally came to their house every morning, spending his afternoons working elsewhere.

Maybe she'd missed him, she thought hopefully, a little ashamed of her cowardice. Butterflies erupted at the sight of a familiar broad back, repairing a few loose bricks. The muscles rippled with each movement beneath the fitted brown shirt, making her heart leap.

He hasn't seen me, she thought. *I could still go back inside and just forget it ever happened. If it ever happened.*

But she had to know. Had to ask.

She cleared her throat quietly. He didn't turn.

"Excuse me." Her voice came out high and breathy. Her face felt like it was afire.

He finally turned, taking his time. Her eyes couldn't help but take in the broad chest, close-cropped beard, and the firm lips she remembered pressed to her own. Her heart was pounding and her face felt so red it must practically be glowing.

"I'm-I'm sorry about last night," she finally stammered, looking at his chest. He began walking forward slowly and she fought the urge to take a step back. She clenched her hands together to keep from waving them uselessly in panic.

He finally stopped, and she couldn't look away from the chest looming before her. She started when his hand came to her chin, lifting it so their eyes met. Her brown eyes were like a startled doe, wide and panicked.

"What are you sorry for? This?" His low voice barely registered as his sandy head lowered, those lips she remembered so well pressing again to hers.

Her knees instantly buckled, her hands going to his arms to catch herself. She felt the corded muscles bunch as he pulled her close, his tongue running along her lips slowly before sweeping inside to tease hers.

He stepped back, his hands still holding her up.

"I-I..." she couldn't say anything, her mind complete mush.

"What do you remember from last night?" he asked quietly, his blue-green eyes crinkling at the corners. He was laughing at her, she thought in despair. This was all a big joke to him.

Wrenching free from his grasp, she stepped back. Straightening her back, unaware of how it pushed her chest out, she looked past his head as she answered. "Nothing, except that I *mistakenly* kissed you."

The Aggie smiled broadly. "It was the best mistaken kiss I've ever had."

Jay watched the Patrician girl walk quickly from the garden, her head held high. She was so damn cute, it was painful to watch. And certain parts of his anatomy found it painful, pressing tightly against his work pants as he watched her backside sway with each step.

Turning back to the wall, he couldn't stop smiling. Yeah, she was going to be an easy in.

6

Aerina was brooding.

Marcus watched her hover over the chessboard, her eyebrows drawn, her mouth piqued.

"We don't have to play," he said.

She looked up quickly. "What do you mean? I asked you to play."

"Yeah, to get your mind off Lina. I don't think it's working."

Aerina sighed, slouching back in the kitchen chair. She'd moved in with Marcus following the defeat of the warship, and didn't regret it for a moment. Even with Marcus the unspoken ruler of Alba and a recognized hero, the Patricians were hesitant to include her. She'd left her caste to be with a Virmortus. A man of death. It was unheard of.

The only relationship she truly mourned was the loss of Lina. Even after her first time being an outcast, after nearly being executed by Marcus, Lina had remained her friend. The two had been inseparable growing up, each depending on the other to survive broken families.

And Stephen. He had been a brother to both of them.

Tears sprung forth, trailing a familiar path down her cheeks.

Marcus sighed. Damn. He hadn't meant to bring this on. But maybe she still needed to work things out. Rising, he came around the table and pulled her into his arms.

"I'm sorry," she choked as tears streamed silently. He said nothing, just holding her closer.

"Lina is grieving. Anger is part of the process, and you are just the most convenient target. She'll move past it. And she'll come back to you," he finally said gruffly.

Aerina smiled through her tears. "For being a man of few words, you sure know how to pick the right ones."

7

Final Examinations had come and gone. Lina was shocked she had passed the Technology Sector exam, Senator Caius himself setting up a meeting with her, no doubt to recruit her.

She would have worked with Stephen, just as she'd always wanted.

Now the thought of working in the University labs, meeting with Engineers and recruits, just sounded dreadful.

She couldn't help but notice that Aerina's scores had been posted. Her friend had also passed with high honors, although Lina doubted anyone was going to recruit her now. Lina squashed the feeling of sympathy that rose, cursing the soft heart she'd been afflicted with.

Her thoughts were often on the Aggie she was forced to see every day. The man she'd kissed, the man she desired, but didn't even know his name.

She stayed out of the garden, but it was impossible to avoid him completely. Even more impossible to ignore him, although she vowed to do her best.

He was the one to approach her next. She stayed out of the garden, but he caught her on the sidewalk, forced to grab her arm to get her attention.

"Can we talk for a moment?" The question sounded

more like a command, but he tempered it with a quietly voiced "Please."

Lina nodded abruptly, refusing to meet his amused blue-green gaze.

He pulled her into the garden, gently pressing her down onto one of the white chaise lounges. She sat stiffly, her hands folded and legs elegantly crossed. Her mother would approve.

Jay smiled, watching the stiff Patrician. Just to test his theory, he settled a large, callused hand on her thigh. Yeah, she could get even stiffer. Red spread from her neck to her forehead, delighting him even more.

To his surprise, she didn't remove his hand, just sat silently, waiting.

"Nothing happened the other night," he told her, and was rewarded by her large eyes clashing with his. "We just kissed, and I helped you to your room."

She studied his face, relief crossing her features. His pride took a little hit, but he ignored it. Most women of his acquaintance would be delighted by his attention. But she was different than the women he usually spent time with. Softer, naive. And kind.

Too kind for her own good.

"Well, I did help you remove your clothes. You insisted," he added as her mouth opened indignantly. "But I didn't touch any more than necessary. At least, not much more," he added, his grin fixed in place.

Emotions warred on her face. Embarrassment, relief, indignation.

"Thank you for telling me," she finally said. "Can I ask..." He nodded encouragingly when she trailed off. "What's your name?

Jay laughed at the unexpected question. This girl couldn't be real.

"Jay."

"Just... J?" she asked hesitantly. He nodded.

"Us Aggies are simple folk," he said with gentle teasing,

hiding the mockery.

"It's lovely to meet you...Jay. I'm Lina." She gingerly picked up the hand on her thigh to shake it. Jay closed his hand around her long, elegant one. It felt soft and delicate, just as the Patrician looked.

"Lina."

He'd known her name, but he refused to use it until now. It made his job easier when he kept his distance from his targets. If he was going to use her to get closer to the Alpha Virmortus, he would need to get very close. Part of him was looking forward to it; probably more than he should be. More than was good for his mission.

"Well, thank you for telling me...what happened. I couldn't quite remember," she said awkwardly, casting him a small smile. Jay smiled back. This was going to be easier than he thought.

"I know I'm an Aggie and you're a Patrician, but if you ever want to talk... I lost my cousin in the EMW blast. It's a little different, but I'm a good listener," he lied easily, his hand still clasping hers.

"Oh. I'm so sorry," she said. She took his large hand in both hers, holding it tightly. "I suppose I've been so wrapped up in my own concerns, I haven't considered that others are grieving, too."

Guilt swept through Lina as she met the beautiful eyes of the Aggie she suddenly felt so close to. Closer than anyone. She'd been so selfish. She wasn't the only one grieving; the only one who had lost.

Her heart swelled with an unfamiliar emotion as she looked at the Aggie still holding her hand. She was rich and privileged, and he was still offering her comfort after he had lost someone he cared for.

"I feel so ashamed," she admitted quietly, looking down at their clasped hands. "I haven't thought of anyone else. Just my brother; my own loss."

"Tell me," he urged. "It might help to get it out."

"I just don't know how to...to let go of the anger I have. I've never held a grudge. And now... I can't seem to forgive my best friend, to find a way to move on and let go," Lina haltingly explained, not even sure of her feelings herself. She told him briefly about what had happened, how Stephen had been convinced to help the Alpha Virmortus, Aerina's lover, and somehow died on the warship. "I just wish I knew why; why did he do it, and how did he die?" she finished softly.

"Ask her; your friend," he said. "Ask her to tell you everything. Maybe it will help you understand and work through the anger."

Lina was quiet for a moment. "You might be right. Maybe knowing will help."

Jay stood, deliberately letting his hand trail up her arm. "I need to get back to work. But if you need to talk again... I'd like to hear it. To listen."

Lina also stood, smiling up at him, feeling better than she had since Stephen had died. The feeling of warmth where he'd touched her morphed into something more. A strange heat began to spread, making her legs feel weak and her stomach turn over. Jay looked at her for a moment, slowly lowering his head. She ached for what was going to come next; needed this contact. The reassurance that she was still alive, that she could still *feel*. His lips touched hers gently, a kiss of comfort as much as it was passion. Just as she sighed and leaned into him, he took a step back.

"Good luck," he murmured, backing away with a smile and wave. Lina returned the smile before turning away, a new sense of purpose driving her. Suddenly, she couldn't wait to find Aerina and talk to her.

8

Aerina opened the door to the light knock, shocked to

see Lina standing on the step.

"Lina."

"I understand if you don't want to talk, after how I've been acting. I just—" Lina's faltering words were cut off as Aerina squeezed her tightly in an embrace.

"I'm so sorry," Aerina murmured, tears falling onto her friend's shoulder. Lina stood stiffly, wanting answers, but not quite ready to fully let go of her anger.

"Come in," Aerina finally said, pulling back. Lina nodded, following Aerina inside. She scanned the room quickly, taking in the large open space of Marcus' villa.

"I've never been inside a Virmortus' home before."

"If you don't feel comfortable, we can go—"

"No," Lina cut her off. "I don't mean it that way. Truly."

"Can I get you a drink, or…?" Aerina trailed off. Lina shook her head negatively, sitting down on the divan.

"I wanted to ask you some questions, if you don't mind."

"Not at all," Aerina answered, sitting in a chair across from her. The silence stretched between them as Lina appeared to be gathering her thoughts, her hands twisting absently. Aerina was surprised to see the leanness in Lina's face. She'd shed some weight since Stephen had died.

Lina interrupted her thoughts with her blurted question: "What happened? To Stephen. And before. Why did he do it? I just need to know." Aerina met her friend's pleading gaze. She would have felt the same way, were someone she cared about killed. She'd need to know the truth. To know everything. Perhaps if she told Lina everything, she'd be able to get over her anger.

Nodding, Aerina began at the beginnig. She told Lina about going outside the city with Marcus and almost being killed by Southern Empire assassins. About the destruction by the Empire of outpost towns, and how Marcus had tried to cut Aerina out of the investigation and she had uncovered information herself, then Stephen had discovered a virus sent from the Empire.

She told Lina about the warship sent from the Southern Empire to discover their hidden Technology, and how Marcus and Stephen had injected themselves with the Technology to destroy the warship. How Stephen had been shot attempting to flee the ship before it exploded, and Marcus had brought his body to shore.

"What is this Technology that is so powerful?" Lina asked, brushing aside the ever-present tears impatiently. She'd already known Stephen had been a hero, but hadn't known how truly brave he had been.

Aerina hesitated. "I don't know everything myself, but I've seen Marcus use it. It basically turns the human mind into a computer. And it lets him control any Network or digital machine."

"He's the only person who can use it?"

Again, Aerina hesitated. "Please Aerina, don't shut me out again," Lina begged quietly. "You are the only person I have left."

"The Technology is injected; it must need to bind somehow. Marcus has several vials of it, hidden. In case we need it to fight the Southern Empire. Because they're coming back, Lina," Aerina told her softly. "They aren't going to give up. This Technology changed the world once. It could again."

Lina was quiet, thinking about Aerina's words.

"You can't tell anyone about this," Aerina warned. "People would panic. Promise me, Lina."

"I promise," Lina said absently. "The last thing we need is more fear. Can I see it?"

"The Technology? Marcus isn't going to allow anyone to see it until he's ready," Aerina told her friend.

"I know he's got it here. A man like that wouldn't keep it far."

Aerina stared at her friend, then smiled. "When did you get so suspicious? But you're right. I suppose it can't hurt." Getting up, she walked to the Dispensare, typing in a request.

The refrigerated food processer produced a vial, and Aerina held it up for Lina to see. "It needs to stay cold to remain viable."

Lina didn't try to touch it, just studying the amber-colored liquid as it swirled in the vial. Like it was alive. Cognizant.

She finally turned away in disgust. "Put it away. I can't think that...*that* was the reason Stephen died. Why so many people died."

A few beeps and clicks later and Aerina had returned to her side, sliding a slender arm around her shoulders.

"I'm glad you came. I've missed you."

Lina wanted to speak; to tell her friend she was forgiven. That she understood it had been Stephen's decision. But she couldn't push the words past the lump in her throat. The knowledge did help, and she found comfort in this first step in rebuilding a relationship with her friend.

It was a start.

9

"You seem...happier." Lina looked up quickly at the deep voice. She hadn't heard Jay come into the garden. For such a large man, he moved quietly.

Putting down her holoreader, she smiled up at the large man. Unable to stop herself, she threw her arms around his broad shoulders.

He stood stiffly for a moment before squeezing her back. "What was that for?" he asked gruffly.

Stepping back, Lina smiled shyly. "You were right. I feel so much...freer after talking to Aerina. I never would have gone to her if it hadn't been for our talk. For you. Thank you."

Jay returned the smile, his light eyes gleaming. "I'm

glad." Glancing around, he took her arm gently. "I'm done for the day. Would you like to walk with me?"

The thrill Lina felt at his invitation was tempered by a deep-seated hesitation to break etiquette. Different classes rarely mingled, particularly not socially.

Definitely not romantically.

As if seeing her hesitation, Jay brushed off his own question. "Maybe another time."

Lina looked up at him. Was he offended? Her stomach twisted as he turned away, picking up his gear carefully. She felt like a fool, standing there and watching him. He strode towards the back gate, turning and nodding with a slight smile before exiting.

Sorrow twisted as he disappeared, the strange comfort she drew from his presence gone with him.

She remembered the bottle of alcohol in Stephen's desk. How Aerina had told her of his illegal access of the Virmortus Network. Sometimes rules and expectations were meant to be shattered.

A strange force propelled her forward, through the back gate and down the narrow path Jay had taken.

"Wait!" she called. His distant form turned back, waiting. She caught up, boldly resting her hand on the taut muscles of his forearm. "I've got time now."

Jay smiled down at her. His dark brown clothes and dirt-streaked forearms revealed by rolled up sleeves contrasted with her own smart white dress suit. Slowly, he slid his work-roughened hand into hers, giving her the opportunity to pull away. As if daring her to change her mind.

She didn't.

Hand-in-hand, they walked towards Balance Park. They got a few strange looks from passersby, but most people ignored them. Lina wondered what her parents would think, were someone to tell them. Unfamiliar euphoria spread, and she realized in this moment, she didn't care.

Was this how Aerina had felt with Marcus?

"Your talk went well with your friend; Aerina, isn't it?" Jay asked, breaking the silence.

Lina nodded. "Yes. And yes. You were right. It helped to know what had happened. I guess it was easier to be angry at her for my brother's decision, rather than being angry at him."

"But in the end, you know he did the right thing, and you had to let the anger go."

Lina looked at him in surprise at his insight. "Yes. That is exactly right."

He gripped her hand a little tighter for a moment as they walked down the tree-lined trails of Balance Park. The day was silent but for the discussions of birds overhead and the light rustling of wind in the trees. "I've been curious. What did they use to destroy that ship?"

Lina hesitated, Aerina's words clear in her mind. *You can't tell anyone about this. Promise me, Lina.*

She was hardly giving away any state secrets…

"I guess they used some old technology. Something the Virmortus have kept hidden for years."

"That is a relief to hear. If the Southern Empire returns, we're going to need a secret weapon," Jay said, his eyes scanning the park around them.

"Yes, it is a relief to know Marcus is keeping it close. If anyone can stop the Southern Empire again, it's Marcus Trent," Lina commented absently. She gripped his hand a little tighter, enjoying the feeling of his callused palm pressed to hers.

"What kind of weapon is it?"

Lina tried to concentrate on Jay's questions, but her mind kept straying to thoughts of how to get him to kiss her again. To the feel of his large body so close to hers; his masculine features, deeply tanned skin, and gleaming eyes that were both welcoming and mysterious at once.

"Aerina showed it to me; some kind of liquid that is

injected. It doesn't look impressive enough to attract the attention of the Empire," she said, shrugging.

"It was there, at their villa?" Surprise was in his voice, and she thought his voice changed, the words rolling differently off his tongue, a little drawl at the end of each word.

"Yes, someone like Marcus would keep it on hand in case he needed to take it immediately. I'm sure he has a few hidden in different locations." She looked up at him, curious at his increasingly forceful questioning. His face was intent as he scanned the surrounding park, as if he were cataloging and analyzing her words. "What are you thinking?"

His face cleared, and a smile appeared that cut deep grooves in his tanned skin.

Suddenly he stopped, swinging her carefully around to face him. His other hand laced with hers, pulling her close.

"I've been thinking about this all day. Since the last time," he said softly, lowering his head slowly. Lina parted her lips in anticipation. Finally.

His mouth pressed to hers, gently at first then more insistently. He pulled her tightly against his hard form. She heard a gasping moan and realized it was hers. His tongue met hers as his hands moved slowly down her body until they came to settle on her full backside, pulling her hips tight against his. Heat swelled as she felt his hardness pressed to her core.

She pulled her hands free, running them up under his brown work shirt, feeling the ripple of muscle beneath. The muscles flexed beneath her palms as she ran them lightly over his chest and down to the lean waist that tapered above his pants. His breath hissed in through clenched teeth.

He lifted her up on her toes, pressing her even closer as his mouth moved over hers desperately, as if he thought this stolen embrace would end at any moment.

And then it did. He pulled back so suddenly she stumbled forward. He steadied her, then pulled her with him.

Through her desire-fogged brain, she registered the sound of approaching steps. They were no longer alone on the path.

Breathing heavily, she followed him around the next bend. He slowed his pace slightly to match hers and they continued walking. Her eyes met his briefly and they both smiled. Her heart warmed, that strange euphoria spreading again.

After feeling numb for so long, the force of emotion was unexpected and a little overwhelming. Maybe it was wrong to feel this way for someone like Jay, and so soon after Stephen's death. Guilt tried to rise, but she forced it back down. She'd feel remorse later, but she wanted to enjoy this moment, in case she never had another like it.

They walked back to the park entrance in companionable silence.

"I guess I'll…see you tomorrow?" she said, her eyes searching his for a sign of what he was thinking. For a moment they seemed coolly calculating, then he smiled and the blue-green orbs took on their familiar twinkle.

"Tomorrow, bright and early."

10

The next morning was cold and rainy, a complete contrast to Lina's mood.

"Good morning," she greeted her mother brightly. Her mother eyed her speculatively as she entered the kitchen.

"You seem more cheerful. I hope it isn't because of some Aggie."

Lina stiffened, her cheerfulness extinguished immediately by her mother's sharp words.

"What do you mean?"

Her mother typed her selection into the Dispensare. Her regular granola and milk appeared. "I mean, Ava saw you holding hands with some Aggie dressed in his work clothes. Honestly, Lina, a little discretion is required, in the very least."

Lina flushed at her mother's censure. Had she witnessed a Patrician walking hand-in-hand with another class, she would have thought the same thing. It seemed different with Jay somehow.

Lina picked at her own bowl of fruit, her appetite gone. She pushed it aside, rising. "Of course, Mother. I don't know what I was thinking."

Setting down the bowl of granola, her mother approached, patting her daughter's shoulder. "You've been through a lot—we all have. I know you are a good girl. You'll do the right thing."

Lina nodded, leaving the room quickly before the tears in her eyes began to fall. The small bit of joy she'd begun to feel was crushed completely, and the old insecurities returned.

I know you are a good girl. You'll do the right thing.

And she had always been good. Good enough to avoid her father's verbal and sometimes physical abuse. Good enough to make her embittered mother proud.

She was just so tired of being the good girl all the time. Did she have the courage to be bad?

Jay sensed Lina before she appeared behind the huge rosebush he was wrestling. He hated these damn roses. His own mother had a rose garden, and he'd never thought much of it. But when he returned home, he was never going to look at it, and the gardeners, the same way again.

"Meet me in Balance Park entrance tonight at nine?" Lina asked quietly, watching the garden. Jay smiled. He'd found a big smile to be the best form of deceit. Most people trusted others who smiled frequently.

"Nine it is," he murmured, trimming another twisted branch. A bead of blood appeared where it punctured his arm and he suppressed a curse. As Lina walked away, he couldn't keep the anticipation from rising. No matter how high the stakes, he was enjoying this little Patrician more than he thought possible.

He was playing with fire, but it just made the situation more thrilling, and his focus that much sharper. The months of boredom playing the Aggie were about to pay off.

11

Jay waited impatiently for Lina to arrive. Nine had come and gone, and it was now nearing ten. For someone trying to avoid suspicion, loitering here wasn't going to look good if a patrolling Armati, or a damn Virmortus, showed up.

He hoped cultivating her attention wasn't a waste of his time. She was so reserved; so desperate to please everyone around her, at first he couldn't imagine how she might be useful. She'd seemed like a naive, frivolous girl. But now he was wondering if she were smarter than she'd first appeared. And her ties to the defacto ruler, the Alpha Virmortus Marcus Trent, had grown closer when her best friend had moved in with the powerful man. But then the girl had cut off her friend, foiling Jay's hope at having an in through that route. If he could just help her repair the relationship…

The Virmortus had been impossible to infiltrate after the Consul and his son were neutralized. Trent had really tightened up his security, identifying and correcting any vulnerabilities in the Alban Network with surprising speed.

Damn Albans and their penchant for technology. It had always rankled the Southern Empire engineers that Alba came out with better technology much more quickly than they could match. But it didn't stop them from stealing and reverse engineering every bit of technology they got their hands on.

It's the innovators who run the world, son. His father's words echoed in his memory. His father, born a farmer in

Texaco, had coerced or fought his way to power. He wasn't just talking about technology. Innovation covered a broad spectrum, including intelligence-gathering. His father's specialty.

Jay swiped rain off his face as if mentally wiping away the memory of his larger-than-life father. Now was not the time to dwell on the past. He needed to be alert.

He finally caught a glimpse of her tall, curvy figure approaching, her white slacks and light jacket glowing in the dim lamplight. He ran a large hand through his damp hair, slicking it back. The rain had let up a few minutes earlier, but the air was still heavy with humidity.

Lina's heart-shaped face, dominated by her warm brown eyes, was tense with determination. He crossed his arms lightly as she approached, wondering what this was all about.

She didn't pause as she approached, her slender yet surprisingly strong arms wrapping around his neck and pulling his head down. Then her full, warm lips were pressed to his, her body plastered against him.

He instinctively closed his arms around her waist, pulling her back into the shadows of a nearby tree, his mouth remaining fused with hers.

She tasted as good as she had the first time. His mood immediately changed from irritation to hunger.

This certainly wasn't what he was expecting, but he wasn't about to complain. He loved it when he could combine business with pleasure.

The temperature between them rose so quickly Jay half expected steam to rise in the cool, damp air. She tugged and pulled at his shirt until his buttons opened or popped off, stripping it from his broad shoulders. Not bothering to remove it completely, she ran soft fingers lightly over the muscles of his shoulders and down the rippled expanse of his chest to his pants.

He wanted this; and it would certainly go a long way in

gaining her trust. He had no problem manipulating people to get what he wanted, but he'd like to think he still retained some of his humanity. While he might be a lot of things, he wasn't completely without a conscience. He caught her hands as they worked his belt, stopping them.

"Are you sure this is what you want?" he asked, his voice hoarse with the effort. "If we keep going, there's no stopping. You won't be the same innocent girl tomorrow."

"Exactly. I'm done being the good girl."

"No regrets?"

She was quiet for so long he began to worry she was changing her mind. Finally, she whispered "No regrets."

"Then I'm happy to help," he softly said against her mouth. He made quick work of removing her clothes, freezing for a long moment after the last strip of white cloth dropped to her feet. She was curved; perfectly rounded in all the right places. A true Roman goddess. *Bella Diosa*." His mouth quirked at the fanciful endearment before he proceeded to worship the beauty before him. As he kissed his way over perfectly rounded breasts, down her smooth stomach, she made sexy little whimpers that made his hands shake.

He attempted to make a blanket out of their discarded clothing as they collapsed to the damp grass, bringing her down on top of his bare chest. She straddled his hips, her mouth and hands learning him; exploring.

She was obviously determined to see this through, even though he sensed her nerves and inexperience. He tried to slow her down; to calm her by running his hands gently over her exposed back. That only seemed to increase her frenzied need.

"Please Jay," she begged, not able to put her request into words.

"Tell me what you want," he commanded. She shook her head mutely, her eyes huge with nervous need.

"I can't..." her voiced pleaded with him to take over.

He was only too happy to comply. Raising her gently,

he held her gaze as he set her slowly down on his erection. She wiggled, her teeth coming together hard as she tried to work him into her tight sheath. He had suspected, but found himself both surprised and inexplicably aroused to be her first lover.

"Are you alright?" he asked from between his own clenched teeth, his hands shaking with the effort to hold onto his control.

"Yes," she gasped, moving experimentally. He groaned at the feel of her, tight and slick, gliding over him. Another slow rise and fall of her body over his felt like torture. He wanted to pump himself into her perfect body, to lose himself in the rising pleasure. He clenched his jaw against the near-painful need, forcing himself to let her set the pace.

Her hands were braced on his chest with nails leaving half-moons on his skin; his gripping her hips with a force that would probably leave bruises. Neither noticed.

She began to move faster as the discomfort faded, and he put his hand between their bodies to stroke the tiny center of her desire. She gasped in surprise, breathing his name.

"Jay, I can't...I don't..." she sounded both desperate and uncertain.

"Close your eyes. Don't think. Just think about my hands, our bodies, and—oh god you're so perfect—about this." He moved slowly in her, running his hands down her smooth back. His jaw clenched as he tried to hold onto his control; to focus on her pleasure rather than taking his own.

Her eyes closed, her head fell back as she did as he asked. Her rhythm became more sure, the tiny whimpers and moans that escaped her lips pushing him over the edge. He lifted her hips to better meet his thrusts, both gasping out as the climax came over them.

Lina felt her heart begin to slow, her breathing less ragged. As the afterglow of passion slowly faded, reality came rushing in. She'd just had sex with an Aggie. Even now, his large hands were stroking her quickly-cooling back, his hard chest beneath her rising and falling with each breath. Those hands, the strong hands of a worker, had touched the most intimate parts of her; had driven her nearly mad with need and pleasure. She hadn't known it could be so intense; so soul-shattering.

She couldn't imagine every experience was like this. This had to be something special. Something more than just a moment of stolen pleasure.

She should be worried about what other Patricians might think. What had happened to others who formed relationships with those outside of their caste.

In this moment, she couldn't work up the energy to care.

Why should she worry? No one knew. And she hadn't done anything wrong. After all, Patricians visited brothels for this very thing all the time, and no one thought less of them.

Looking up into Jay's hooded blue-green eyes, she felt a pang of guilt about comparing their joining to what happened in the brothels.

"No regrets, remember?" he murmured, sitting up with her still in his arms. Lina shivered as the chill of the night cooled her over-heated flesh.

He helped her dress, her shaky hands unable to do the job themselves, before donning his own damp work clothes. She cast him furtive looks as they dressed, wondering what he thought of the encounter.

He hadn't said no. And yet…

"I'll walk you home," he offered. Lina hesitated, remembering her mother's earlier words.

You're a new person now, she reminded herself. *Bold, unafraid of judgement.*

They slowly exited the darkness of Balance Park onto the neat sidewalks of the Patrician Terrace. Lina resisted the urge to duck her head as she walked with Jay in his telling brown clothes. Thankfully, no one was out on such a cool, rainy night.

Her house along the edge of the terrace, overlooking the ocean, seemed much further today. She'd never felt such relief to see it, brightly lit in the nearby streetlamp, the interior lights glowing in the damp mist that hovered.

They entered through the garden door. The back walk was barely lit, and in the dark, he pulled her around to face him, lacing his hands with hers. The gleam in his eyes was barely visible in the low lamplight.

"No matter what happens, this is just about us. You and me. And some amazing chemistry." His voice was low, intent.

He was trying to tell her something, she sensed, but she wasn't sure what. Did he sense her nervousness about being seen with an Aggie? She scanned his eyes, looking for a sign of anger or hurt. All she saw was the hint of humor that crinkled the edges, creasing his tanned skin.

Finally, Lina nodded slowly. Uncertainty warred with euphoria. What now?

"*Diosa,*" she thought she heard him murmur the unfamiliar endearment again, his hands gripping hers tightly as if he was afraid to walk away.

He watched her closely for another long moment, kissing her swollen lips gently, then disappeared into the darkness beyond the garden.

12

Morning brought a tangled mix of feelings for Lina. The familiar crushing sorrow flooded her with the onslaught of awareness.

Stephen was dead.

Aerina was an outcast.

Lina was alone.

Then unexpected delight arose with the memories of the previous night, helping to eclipse the sorrow.

Jay.

It was Monday, his day off, which meant Jay wouldn't be coming to the Capitol Terrace to work. For the first time, she began to wonder where he lived; what his life was like outside of his gardening and general labor he performed for Patricians.

She realized she knew very little about the attractive man from the Agriculture class. Laying back against the white pillows, Lina closed her eyes and drew up a mental image of her new, and first, lover.

He was good-looking in a roughhewn way, his muscled form and hard features a contrast from the slimmer physique carefully maintained by Patrician males. The large Aggie's blue-green eyes gleamed with continual amusement, as if the world existed for his entertainment. He was quick to smile, and kind to her. His movements were easy yet meticulous. Each clip of a rose, shovel of cement, even his very stride, was perfectly coordinated.

A frown knit her brow as she considered how, oddly enough, his movements reminded her of Aerina's Reaper. Measured, controlled; leashed power contained in a large package.

She had a sudden desire to share her experience with her friend. It was an overwhelming relief to no longer have the burning anger towards Aerina, who was more of a sister than a mere friend. She might finally be ready to let go of the remnants of bitterness that still lingered.

And she had Jay to thank for that.

If anyone would understand her unexpected relationship with Jay, Aerina would. She had her own forbidden relationship with a Virmortus. The Virmortus were responsible for the security of the city-state. *If you see a Virmortus, death always follows* was the common maxim that had given the group the nickname of Reaper. Aerina had always been a little wild and impetuous, but the past year she had completely changed, breaking the Law of Segregation by working as a Pleb and nearly being executed by the man she now lived with, Marcus.

After the attack by the Southern Empire, her friend had completely rejected Patrician society and moved in with her Reaper. Everyone thought the Senator's daughter to be crazy for giving up such prestige and wealth for a dubious future, but Lina was beginning to understand.

Would she give up her status as Patrician to become an Aggie? To be with Jay?

She wasn't quite ready to explore that decision. But she couldn't wait to share her story with Aerina.

As it turned out, she was forced to wait to spill her juicy secrets. Her friend wasn't at Marcus' villa, and she couldn't reach her on her holoreader. She wasn't bold enough to call Marcus, even though his number was listed in the Shared Network.

It was early evening when Aerina finally returned her call, inviting her over to chat.

"Marcus is going to be at the Training Grounds late tonight," she assured Lina, as if sensing her friend's reticence at being in close quarters with a Reaper. The fear was bred deeply in most citizens.

"Can I get you a drink?" Aerina asked as Lina entered a little later.

"Sure, sparkling water sounds great."

Aerina turned to the Dispensare, entering in her request. The tension between them was still tangible, forcing Lina to fidget nervously before stepping into the living room. This villa was different from most of the Patrician dwellings. It was small, open, and had no garden or inner courtyard attached. It was also decorated in earthy tones rather than the unrelenting white preferred by the ruling class. Lina found the colors pleasing, although she felt oddly out of her element.

"What have you been doing lately?" Lina finally asked to break the silence.

Aerina smiled, although it was a little forced. "Not

much, to be honest. I finished exams with everyone else, but of course no one has recruited me."

Lina felt a rush of sympathy. Aerina hadn't really done anything wrong. She was smart and ambitious, and would be an asset to any sector that recruited her.

Patricians were just too intolerant. Everything was black and white to them; there was no middle ground. No room for error or deviation from their strict laws and social regimes.

"What will you do?"

"I've been helping at the Training Grounds on small projects. Perhaps I'll become a Virmortus." Aerina shrugged, but Lina could tell she'd been thinking the matter over.

"Aren't most Virmortus taken as children? The warrior lifestyle is inculcated from a young age. Would they take an adult?"

"Probably not," Aerina said wryly. "It wouldn't matter anyhow. Marcus would never allow it."

"Men can be funny about the women they love," Lina commented, garnering a funny look from Aerina. Where *had* that statement come from? What did Lina know about love?

Lina was settling onto the divan when a shadow moved on the stairs leading up to the roof. Fear made her stomach drop, her vocal chords frozen but for the high-pitched gasp that escaped.

Aerina turned quickly at Lina's gasp, but the masked shadow was suddenly before Lina, who had stood instinctively to flee. The intruder whirled the stunned woman around until she was a shield. The large hands and hard chest told Lina it was a man holding her, a man that was taller than her own curvy height.

"Don't touch the weapon," his low voice warned. Aerina froze as Lina felt something hard press up against the side of her head. Some weapon, she thought hysterically, her mind frantically trying to make sense of what was happening.

"Get the Technology vials," the man ordered,

unmoving. Aerina looked confused, her hands held out to the side.

"I don't have much time. I know they're here. I suggest you hurry," the man warned again, his voice barely above a whisper. The words came out in an unfamiliar cadence, different from the clipped, carefully enunciated speech of Albans. Who was he? Could it be someone from the Southern Empire?

Aerina shook her head, a white-slippered foot moving almost imperceptibly towards the bedroom.

Lina thought she heard a low expletive before pain exploded in her arm. She gasped, her knees buckling. Only the bands of steel that were the intruder's arms held her up. Her peripheral vision caught the hilt of a small knife protruding from her upper arm, and nausea rose in her throat.

He'd just stabbed her. *Oh please, oh please, oh please...*

Aerina's eyes, too, were fixed on the weapon embedded in her friend. "You're dead," she breathed furiously. "Who the hell are you?"

"Do as I ask or I'll select a more vital area to put the next knife," the man stated quietly, the arm around her chest moving quickly to produce another throwing knife. Lina bit her lip, unable to hold back a whimper. The man holding her seemed to stiffen for a moment before resuming his ready stance. Her heart pounded, and small dots appeared before her eyes. She was afraid she might pass out and the man would kill them both.

Oh please, oh please, oh please...

Aerina held both hands higher. "Alright. I'll get what you want. But you have to tell me who you are."

"You already know," was his only answer. A moment later, Lina felt burning pain in her side as the second knife slid in silently. Her mouth opened on a silent cry, and she began to wish she *was* unconscious for this. She clung to her composure with a strength of will she didn't know she possessed.

She heard Aerina swearing as if from a distance,

hysteria hovering.

"I suggest you move faster." The man's voice again, and through the painful haze surrounding her, she thought the voice sounded oddly familiar.

She watched Aerina move towards the Dispensare and begin typing in selections, cursing madly.

"I don't know the code," she said desperately, her small hands moving quickly over the screen.

"Then you aren't any good to me, are you?" That familiar voice again, and the pressure left her head for a moment, followed by a crack and pop. A nearly invisible blue light arced from the gun, striking Aerina, who dropped instantly.

Through her strange paralysis, Lina felt a surge of adrenaline at the sight of her friend dropping to the ground. Turning in the arms still around her, she swung an unpracticed punch at the masked face.

The man grunted in surprise or pain before tightening his arms, nearly crushing her. Pain spread in waves from the jostled knives. She continued to fight blindly against the man holding her, all the pent up anger, fear, and sorrow in her making her unexpectedly strong.

The man cursed again before a hand pressed on her neck and blackness overcame her.

13

Consciousness came slowly. Lina swallowed a groan, some sixth sense warning her to be silent. Her whole body ached, particularly her side and arm.

The man. The knives. Aerina.

Oh please no. Not Aerina too.

She lay frozen, trying to determine her surroundings. Trying to assimilate the situation. To determine where her attacker was.

She was outside in thick foliage. It must be outside the city, for it certainly wasn't the well-maintained park. From her position, laying still on the cool ground, she could only see bushes, trees, and a sliver of slowly darkening sky.

What in the name of peace was going on?

Low voices reached her, although their words didn't fully register.

"Why the hell did you bring her with?"

"We might need someone, in case they follow."

"Oh, they'll follow. And if you gotta bring a hostage, why didn't you take the leader's woman? Not this worthless aristocrat."

"Trust me, she'll be much easier to manage than the other one. She won't give us any trouble."

"I still say it'd be much easier if we didn't have any hoity-toity to deal with—"

"Are you questioning my decision, soldier?"

A long pause was followed by a stiff, "No, *sir.*"

Footsteps approached, and Lina tried to breathe evenly, her eyes shut.

"Rise and shine, *bella diosa.*"

Her eyes popped open at the endearment spoken by a familiar voice.

"Jay?" She could do nothing but gape up at the large man grinning down at her. Had he saved her? Was she on the Aggie Terrace?

Her mind refused to process the information before her. It was inconceivable that Jay was the enemy. She tried to sit up, feeling vulnerable in her prone position. Pain emanated in waves from her arm and side.

The knives. Panicked, her uninjured hand reached around, feeling the bandages on her upper right arm and side.

Her eyes met Jay's. He was waiting for the truth to sink in, and the fireworks that would follow, she realized.

He *was* one of them.

She'd slept with a spy from the Southern Empire. And he'd used her to get to Aerina. To steal the Technology Alba had kept hidden for a century. She'd broken Aerina's trust, and unknowingly led the enemy right to the secret.

The shame and unrelenting agony of betrayal consumed her. She wished he had killed her instead of dragging her here to learn of what she had done. Rather than the outburst Jay was expecting, perhaps hoping for, Lina shut down. Her eyes went blank, her features stiff.

"Damn." She heard Jay's curse from a distant place inside herself.

He grabbed her arms, hauling her to her feet. The pain from her wounds served as a reminder of her foolishness. Of his betrayal.

"Let's get moving, Lina."

She forced her gaze up to his. The familiar gleam, rather than sending a thrill of pleasure, filled her with loathing. In this moment, she wasn't sure who she hated more, him or herself.

She finally found her voice, needing to lash out somehow. "You." The word was both an expletive and an accusation. "You're one of them. You killed Stephen. And Aerina."

Jay's face tightened, the twinkle in his eyes hardening.

"Wrong on both counts. I can't claim either, as I wasn't even near the warship at any time. And I didn't kill your friend. She was very much alive when I left the villa with you in tow, just unconscious." His voice was still light, but Lina heard the dangerous undertone in the strange drawl that now altered his familiar voice. She felt overwhelming relief at hearing Aerina was still alive, but the burning anger continued to grow in her chest.

"You're still the enemy. I'm not going anywhere with you."

"Changed your tune pretty quickly, hmm?" The mocking words made angry red spread across Lina's face, the cruel taunt hitting its mark. "Unfortunately for you, you're no longer calling the shots in this relationship. If you want to stay alive, you're coming with me." His voice had become low and dangerous, and Lina knew he wasn't bluffing.

Her eyes took in the stranger standing before her. He stood, booted feet planted on the rocky soil, muscled arms crossed over his massive chest. Gone for the moment was the easy-going smile and friendly eyes, replaced by an icy stare that sent chills through her sadly battered body. Fear warred with the anger that burned so hotly.

"Here comes the cavalry!"

The shout interrupted their battle of wills. Jay gave up trying to get her moving. He moved swiftly, scooping her up and following the other man into the thick underbrush of the wooded mountainside. Instinctively she fought, pushing against his shoulders, trying to free herself from his unwanted embrace.

"Knock it off or I'll knock you out again," he grunted as she landed a blow to his chin.

Good, she thought. Then she wouldn't have to suffer through this.

A loud whir stopped her attack, and her disbelieving eyes took in some kind of airplane. She'd read of flying machines, of course, but had never actually seen one. Circular engines used forced air to hover above the ground. A man stood at the bottom of a small ramp that opened into the back, waving them frantically forward.

Lina heard other sounds of approaching engines, the Armati soldiers, or even the Virmortus coming to her rescue.

Jay practically tossed her into the plane, the momentum causing her to roll twice before catching herself. Despite her injuries, she jumped to her feet, desperate eyes fixed on the closing hatch. She stumbled towards the shrinking opening even as the aircraft ascended.

The hatch sealed closed with a final click, and the aircraft shot forward, causing Lina to tumble again to the ground.

Jay had made his way to the seat beside the pilot, buckling himself in, not even looking again at Lina. Her wide, terrified eyes took in the scene, noting two other men also buckled into jump seats.

Survival instinct took over. She managed to make her way to one of the identical seats across from the two uniformed men, her shaking hands fumbling with the buckles, unable to connect them.

"Brace yourself! Here comes the EMW strikes," the pilot called in a gravelly voice. The aircraft shivered like a dog shaking off water, the lights flickering. Lina's heart felt frozen in her throat, her breath unable to pass.

Another strike was followed by a sudden explosion.

"They masked the ballistic behind the EMW. Damn, the back engine's gone!" Lina wasn't even sure who was yelling, her eyes closed tightly. If she was going to die, she didn't want to see it coming.

Suddenly large hands were ripping at her seatbelt. Her eyes opened to see Jay's face before her. He grinned as he pulled her off the seat, keeping them both upright as the plane pitched hard to the left.

"I hope you can fly, sweetheart."

Lina didn't have time to wonder at that as the back hatch began to open, air grabbing at everything not tied down and sucking it out. The two men that had been across from her were strapping on packs she could only guess were parachutes before shoving a large carton attached to its own parachute out the hatch.

The jet lurched again.

"Everybody out. We're about to dive." The wiry little pilot hopped out of the cockpit, strapping on his own pack with amazing speed.

Lina stared dumbly, terrified eyes watching but not really registering.

She did notice that there were only four packs on the

hook. All being used.

The two first men were gone, throwing themselves onto the mercy of the wind and a thin piece of nylon without hesitation.

Lina met Jay's eyes. They were gleaming; he was enjoying this. One large arm grabbed her, swinging her around in a way she was becoming familiar with, her back pressed to his chest. He buckled a strap across her chest and waist.

"Hold on tight, *diosa*," he said, and then they approached the gaping hatch.

"Serenity and balance bring peace. Serenity and balance bring peace." Lina didn't realize she was muttering the calming mantra as Jay threw them both off the smoking aircraft.

Her stomach dropped as the wind whipped the breath from her. It rushed over her face, tearing at her thin white pantsuit. The ground drew closer at an alarming rate, patches of green and brown delineating into forest and open grassy areas.

Jay's arms closed around her, any words he might have said ripped away by the wind.

The ground continued to race towards them. Was he going to open the parachute? What was he waiting for? Then she saw a streak of blue lightening and new fear clasped her heart in its vise. EMW strikes.

Death by electrocution or splattering? She just hoped however it happened, it was quick.

Jay shouted something. Lina didn't even try to make out his words, just closing her eyes against the rising landscape.

A loud whoosh was followed by a painful jerk on her chest by the strap, and suddenly the swift decent slowed. Jay angled them towards an open area, away from dense trees that covered much of the terrain. A moment later they hit the ground. Jay attempted to absorb the impact in his large frame, but the hit forced the air from Lina's lungs.

She lay on the ground, still strapped to Jay, gasping for a breath. He made quick work of the latches, setting her aside as he rose, leaving the parachute where it had fallen.

"Let's go." His voice was low but urgent, dragging her to her feet.

"I'll just wait here," she gasped, surprised she could find her voice.

"Nope," was his only response, pulling her along. She dragged her feet, pulling back. He swung around impatiently.

"Listen. You're coming with. I can knock you out and carry you, but it'll slow me down. If the Albans close in, I might be forced to leave you behind. Are you sure you want to take the chance that they'll find you before dark, which—" he paused to look at an old-fashioned wrist device "—will be within the half hour. I've heard that wolves and mountain lions have made quite the comeback in this region. I'd hate to leave you here, unconscious and injured, for something to finish off." His voice was cold, as if her decision meant little to him. "It's your choice."

Lina froze, her eyes going to the thick underbrush surrounding them. She remembered the eerie howls and distant shrieks she'd heard from Balance Park, the sounds of predators on the hunt.

"You are not the man I thought you were." She couldn't stop the bitter words from bursting forth as an accusation.

Jay turned, rolling his shoulders as if shrugging off her comment. "That is probably the brightest thing you've said so far." The mocking remark pierced her already-fragile heart, turning her anger to the ever-present weight of depression. He was right. She'd been a fool; she'd done this to herself.

Slowly, she began to follow him through heavy forest, the late evening sunlight streaming eerily through holes in the canopy, barely illuminating the mossy rocks and thick shrubbery.

Shock had settled heavily, and her aching body now

acted solely on instinct; to survive. *One foot in front of the other.*

This was nothing like a hike in the well-maintained Balance Park. Her already blood-spattered, wrinkled white pantsuit quickly became unrecognizable. Her neat white moccasins, perfect for a stroll around the University or Capitol gardens, were no match for the thorny, rocky terrain.

Each step was more painful than the last, and Lina directed all of her agony and resentment at the broad back several yards before her.

Jay had been prepared, the brown Aggie work clothes gone. In their place, he wore dull-colored camo that blended well with the terrain. His lightweight boots were perfect for fighting off the brambles, the rubber soles gripping the damp, mossy rocks with ease.

He also now sported weapons, a large handheld EMW slung over his shoulder, two hand guns and a large blade tucked into the utility belt cinched around his lean waist.

With his military fatigues, small arsenal, shadowed jaw, and watchful eyes, he looked less like the easy-going, harmless Aggie gardener and exactly like a dangerous enemy spy.

Less like the handsome man she'd made love with, and more like the agent who had used her and betrayed her trust.

A Patrician is careful whom she favors, and expects respect. If her mother could see her now…dirty, injured, and a complete fool. She should have listened. Things like this didn't happen to the good girl she'd been.

Was he laughing at her? Had he told his men of the stupid Patrician girl who had a crush on him? Had they helped devise the plot to use Lina to get to the Technology?

Had the sex just been part of his plot to loosen her up; to get her to trust him?

Her stomach twisted at the thought, nausea spreading with the heat of shame.

She'd been a fool, and now she was paying the penalty.

14

Aerina paced the Tech Room of the Training Grounds. At times like this, she envied Marcus his perpetual calm.

"Any sign of them?"

"No," Marcus replied for the third or fourth time, his eyes on the screen in front of Simon.

"They're going to head towards one of the old highways through the mountain, but we can't watch all of them. We've only got the two drones, and their range is limited," Kendra, their new tech recruit, explained gently to Aerina.

"My guess is that they're going to use this route," Marcus said, pointing to a spot on the holographic map projected above Simon's station. "But they might anticipate our blockade and find another way around. They'll have several vehicles hidden, ready for this kind of situation. We just need to guess where they might place them, and the most likely route they'll take after acquiring them."

"A needle in a haystack," Aerina murmured in frustration.

"Chess," Marcus returned, sharing a look with her. She smiled slightly. She knew he was an excellent chess player.

"Keep looking," Marcus ordered, leaving the room. Aerina hurried after him.

"What now?"

"I need to ask someone a few questions."

15

It was about thirty minutes, although it felt like much longer, before they met the other three Southern Empire agents. The three men lounged, their alert eyes belying their casual stances. All got to their feet as she and Jay approached.

"Takin' a romantic stroll with your *diosa*?" the small, wiry pilot of the now-deceased plane asked sardonically. His drawl was so thick, the words all blended together. Lina flushed in renewed shame, looking away from the men. She felt Jay's eyes on her.

"We're heading to the secondary storage location to retrieve the tank," was his only comment.

"But that's twice the distance from the primary —"

"They'll be looking for us there. The secondary location is better hidden, and we can take the tank to the other side of the mountain range and call for an extraction."

"Won't they intercept the signal?" the pilot asked.

"Doubtful. Their Com reach is still pretty limited. Use the two-way to set up the new rendezvous point." He swiped a few times on the wrist device, perhaps setting their new trail, and began walking again into the dense foliage.

Lina looked down at her broken, dirty moccasins, wanting to cry but not having the energy. Her whole body ached, particularly the knife wounds in her arm and side. They throbbed with each heavy beat of her over-worked heart.

You deserve this. You did this to yourself. To Aerina. You are a fool. The mantra repeated in her head, the weight of her burden threatening to drag her to the damp ground.

It was completely dark now, small headlamps on each soldier the only illumination in the midnight forest. It was cold, the limited warmth of the day having disappeared with the sun. Gooseflesh covered her arms, the thin pantsuit no protection from the cool air and tearing fingers of the undergrowth.

The men grabbed their gear, preparing to follow Jay.

"Ladies first," the small, wiry pilot said mockingly. She was coming to hate that scruffy little man and his comments spoken in a gravelly, broken voice.

Chin up, stand tall and don't slouch. Ladies are composed, remain calm, and keep control of their emotions at all times. Her mother's stern words drove Lina forward, keeping the tears at bay.

The wild beauty of the forest at twilight was now a midnight nightmare, her imagination creating wild beasts with grasping claws under each bush; atop each rock.

They walked steadily towards the towering mountains of the east, each painful footfall taking her further away from Alba. Away from her home and further into the arms of the enemy.

She watched the dimly lit path carefully as it shifted with the bobbing of the headlamps each soldier wore. Her tired eyes could barely make out the ground before her. Each treacherous step was more difficult than the last. She was so intent on taking careful steps, she bumped into a solid form before seeing it.

She looked up, startled, to see Jay looming before her, his headlamp blinding her.

"Don't tell me I'll have to carry you," he said in an undertone.

"Keep your hands off me," she hissed. "I'm still walking, aren't I?"

His headlamp scanned her slowly, stopping on her dirty, torn moccasins.

"We'll stop here," he called out, turning away. Lina sank to a nearby boulder in relief, watching with dull eyes as the men quickly set up camp.

It wasn't much. "Can't risk a fire," Jay told her, tossing her some tasteless, dried meal wrapped in unusual packaging.

She couldn't eat. The shame, sorrow, and shock stole her hunger. It seemed impossible that this was actually happening. That she was in the forest with enemy spies, one of which had been her lover. She sat staring at the wrapped food as if it might provide an answer. If she would have followed the laws, heeded her mother's warning, she wouldn't be in this position. Jay might never have known the loathsome vials of Technology were in Aerina's house. He wouldn't have been able to take advantage of her vulnerability.

If only…

The first of the men was already snoring loudly, wrapped in some sort of shiny blanket. The night forest in winter was cold, as cold as her heart felt. Huddled on the wet rock, she wondered if, after everything, she was going to die from hypothermia. Perhaps that would be best. To just give in to the cold that started in her heart and let it take over her body…

"Come, I'll keep you warm," Jay offered quietly. In the one remaining light, she was unable to see his expression. Unable to see the mocking glint that was surely there; the knowing gleam.

"No, thank you."

"You're going to freeze in that thin little outfit," he said.

"I'll consider it my punishment for poor judgement and worse luck," she replied coldly.

Jay laughed softly, and she heard a soft rustling as he lay down to her left. The other men seemed to have all settled and dropped into instant slumber. Perhaps she could steal a weapon while they slept, and take out the lot of them.

And then what? Freeze to death or be eaten like some pitiful martyr?

It is better than you deserve, a cruel inner voice taunted. And what was left for her to live for? It was unlikely she'd make it back to Alba alive. Someone like her would never survive in the world outside. She was a coward; naïve and passive. She had always been different from her best friends; had always felt inferior. She wasn't bold like Aerina, or relentless like Helen.

Overwhelmed with self-pity and depredation, she gasped when strong arms grabbed her, pulling her down below a crinkly silver blanket. Heat engulfed her as Jay's arms closed around her chilled form.

It was heavenly. She wanted to fight; to push him away. To dwell longer in the state of self-punishment that she deserved. Instead, she let him settle her closer, feeling the warmth slowly spreading to her cold limbs.

"Goodnight, *diosa*," he murmured, and as her exhausted eyes closed, she could swear she felt his treacherous lips brush her hair.

16

"Did he talk?" Aerina asked as Marcus slowly left the interrogation room where Julius, the deposed former consul, sat slumped forward.

"They always talk," he replied. Aerina studied his face. He seemed tired. Almost sad. The Consul had been the closest thing to a father to Marcus, she realized. Locking him up and interrogating him must be difficult, even after the former ruler's betrayal.

"Perhaps Ramus should be the one to question Julius in the future…"

Marcus raised one brow questioningly, then his features softened slightly. "It's my job. Unfortunately, he didn't know much. His contact was known as the Wolf. He only met him once, and that was in the dark, in Balance Park. They communicated by handwritten notes left under the first park bench after that."

Aerina thought back to the night in Balance Park—only a few months ago that seemed like a lifetime—when she'd seen two men meeting. She'd been too worried about her own safety at the time to wonder further.

Could it have been the agent? The Wolf?

"Most of their communication centered around the Technology, which he told them was only in the Vault, and how to kill me," Marcus continued. "He knows nothing about the team that extracted Lina, and how they knew a vial was in my villa."

Aerina sighed in disappointment, turning away from the interrogation room.

Had Lina told the wrong person? How was it possible that Lina would have had any contact with an enemy agent?

"He does, however, know why they need the Technology," Marcus continued, falling in step beside Aerina. "They have a meeting with the European Alliance mid-summer. They want to show their power by using the Technology, and gaining the upper hand."

"I thought the European Alliance was nearly destroyed by the ETG."

"The Eastern Terror Group, which called themselves the Holy Army then, did control much of the Mediterranean for several years, but it sounds like the Alliance has regrouped and retaken much of their region back."

"We can't get caught up in this. It will be another Global War," Aerina said. Marcus said nothing, but she could see he agreed by the grim set of his mouth; the familiar darkness of his eyes.

Ramus looked up as they entered the Tech Room. "We've sent out the drones. We won't be able to communicate with them, since our ComTowers don't reach very far to the east, but we can view their imagery after they sweep the landscape."

Marcus nodded. "We need to gear up. It's time to go hunting."

17

Lina trekked slowly through the open field. The forest had become sparse, covered only by straggly grasses and rocky soil. She didn't know how far they had come, and didn't want to ask how much further they needed to go. She focused on putting one foot in front of the other

A low buzz sounded in the distance, making her freeze. She looked up to the sky, hope unfurling. Hope and fear.

"Get down!" Jay called, all the men dropping to the grass. Lina felt desperation building in her chest. As she crouched low, a burst of unfamiliar courage made her stand at the last minute, waving madly at the bright white of the odd-shaped object. Her eyes were fastened to the insignia of a small stag etched on the corner. Alba's symbol.

Jay crawled over, jerking her legs out from under her.

"That was stupid," he growled in her ear as his weight pressed her into the rocky dirt.

Lina said nothing, her heart racing as the drone swooped by, the soft whir fading away. Had it seen her?

Jay stood, pulling her up. "You'd better hope it didn't see us. Do you think the Alban Virmortus will care about your life if it stands in the way of stopping us?" He released her arm, turning to motion the men on. He and the other men began walking again, conversing in low tones. Lina stood unmoving, watching the sky where the unmanned aircraft had disappeared into the misty morning sunlight, the truth of his words settling in. Her wounds continued to ache, a constant reminder of Jay's betrayal. Of her own stupidity.

"Let's go, *diosa*." Her back stiffened at the endearment she now heard as mockery, and she reluctantly followed the men. What else was there for her now?

She was too exhausted to fight.

The night had been long; the ground hard, and Jay's even breathing and light embrace distracting beyond measure. The sounds of the night had kept her alternating between hope of rescue and fear of wild animals.

Her feet hurt. Her arm and side ached with each step. The early morning air was chilly and she shivered, even though Jay had given her an extra camo shirt, which hung mid-thigh over her formerly white pantsuit.

She watched the men in front of her, walking steadily through the clearing with sparse grass and broken, blackened trees. A fire must have cleared the ground a few years past, and the ever-resilient nature was reclaiming the devastated land.

Could she be resilient like that? As she put one aching foot in front of the other, she was amazed at her own ability to go on. The ability to function in the face of overwhelming knowledge that her life was at risk; that she lived only because of a flimsy use they had for her. At any moment, her usefulness could expire and they would kill her.

Each soldier carried a heavy pack and their weapons, but none of them faltered or slowed, just moving forward relentlessly.

Jay glanced back at her, as he'd done frequently throughout the early morning hike. Perhaps making sure she was still there. The familiar twisting of self-loathing filled her gut. How could she have been so stupid? So desperate for affection—to make a connection with someone—that she had chosen *him*?

Every word, every touch, had replayed in her mind on the seemingly endless trek. She'd analyzed the meaning behind his words, seen the truth of each practiced touch. The ulterior motive behind his actions and conversations were now apparent. Should have been apparent from the start...

He had used her, unapologetically become her lover, for the purpose of getting close to Aerina and stealing the Technology. The only weapon Alba could use against the might of the Southern Empire.

If she were a different person, if she were Aerina, she would fight back against these men. She'd try to escape. To steal back the Technology. To make Jay pay for his callous actions

But she wasn't Aerina. She wasn't brave and bold. She was terrified. She was beaten down. And she felt broken.

Stephen was gone. Her closest ally, her confident, her caretaker. And she'd slept with the enemy that had been responsible for his death.

Lost in her dark thoughts, sorrow weighing heavily on her, Lina barely noticed her surroundings. The wooded terrain thinned as they ascended the mountainside, and her eyes flicked disinterestedly over ruins that had once been entire towns before the wars.

When Jay finally called a break for lunch, Lina could barely put one foot in front of the other. Her white moccasins were unrecognizable, torn and filthy. Her pantsuit was in a similar condition, the grasping fingers of the undergrowth having taken bits and pieces of the delicate fabric.

She collapsed onto a slimy log, not caring the damp green moss was leaving green streaks on her borrowed camo shirt.

Jay settled beside her, holding out an energy bar. The nearly tasteless bars were what they had been surviving on the past two days. Even though her stomach felt hollow, her throat closed up every time she considered taking a bite.

"You should eat."

Her dark eyes darted to meet Jay's watchful gaze. His voice sounded surprisingly gentle; concerned. She opened her mouth with a snide retort, then closed it again. It would take too much energy to tell him off. Instead, she broke a small piece off the bar and forced herself to chew it, swallowing heavily. The dry, grainy bite stuck in her throat and she coughed, unable to force it past the lump.

Jay silently handed her his water bottle. The cool water helped and she handed it back, unable to stop the quiet "Thank you". It was difficult to ignore a lifetime of good manners.

The other men lounged around them; the small pilot had pulled his hat over his eyes and seemed to actually be sleeping. Their ability to catch a moment of sleep was amazing.

"How much further do we need to go?" she asked, reluctant to even speak to him.

"We should be at the rendezvous point soon," Jay answered, his gaze moving around the small clearing. He glanced down at the device on his wrist. "In fact..."

Lina gasped as a fifth man materialized from the rocky outcropping, jumping instinctively to her feet. The other men followed suit, weapons ready.

Her heart seemed frozen in her chest, and only started beating again when the largest of their group, Thomas, rushed forward and grasped forearms with the new man.

"Little brother! Glad you could finally join us," Thomas boomed, pounding the smaller blonde man on the back. "Enjoyin' your little vacation while the rest of us worked?"

"About time y'all finally showed up. I've been dyin' of boredom out here. The only action I've seen this past month was the mountain lion I spooked up. But I see you've been gettin' action of another kind." The blonde man's gaze went between her and Jay, whose hand had settled on her shoulder as if to lay claim. She stepped forward, shrugging it off. The man smiled at her. "Is this one to share?"

"You know I don't share, James," Jay said sardonically, his eyes going to Lina as if to dare her to respond. "Let's keep moving. They won't be far behind us."

The sickening heat of shame again spread through Lina's body at the man's crass words. Would she ever be free from its crushing weight? She had been desperate and pathetic. How Jay must have laughed at her; how his men must have joked about the stupid Patrician.

"Are you alright?" Jay's low voice broke through her morose thoughts. She jerked away, keeping her head down, unable to answer past the lump in her throat. Tears blurred her vision until she could barely see.

"You've already had her, boss, and she don't look too interested now," the rude little pilot rasped, spitting on the ground. "Although in the condition she's in, I ain't sure why you want the extra work of draggin' her with us. Might be best to put her outta her misery here. You'll have plenty of pussy waitin' back home."

"Stix, you might have better luck with women if you learned a little more compassion. Even a guy like me wants a challenge once in a while," Jay drawled carelessly.

"I'd love to have your way with women," Thomas laughed. "Just a chip off the old block, eh Jayden Jr?"

Jay grinned, but it didn't quite reach his eyes. He rolled his shoulders, as if shrugging off the conversation. "So everyone says," was his only response.

Lina's stomach turned at the words. Gone was the patient, kind Aggie that had listened to her troubles. This Jay — the real Jay — was arrogant, crass, and cared nothing for her.

Had anything about him been real? Even his voice had changed to the slow drawl of Confederates.

And he was wrong. She'd hardly been a challenge, throwing herself at him. She dismissed the rare moments of kindness she thought she glimpsed as her naive imagination. Jay was a cold-hearted killer who wouldn't hesitate to hurt her if it benefited him.

Lina watched the men packing up their gear, Stix checking his locator and leading the way back onto the seemingly endless trek.

She looked at the group of dangerous men and her world seemed to shrink until it was only them and this godforsaken wilderness. What was the point of getting up to torture her already broken body? They were going to kill or abandon her anyway.

It was what she deserved for her stupidity; her betrayal.

Stephen, I'm sorry. I'm sorry I'm so weak when you were so strong. I'm sorry I couldn't help you; didn't understand you. So, so sorry...

Jay saw the moment that Lina broke. Her glazed expression turned desolate, and tears began silently cascading. He waved the men on, turning to wait it out.

He'd known this moment would come; was in fact surprised it had taken so long. The little Patrician was more tenacious than he had expected. She didn't complain or curse him or rail against her fate. But he could tell she had been waging an internal battle, blaming herself for everything that had happened.

He knew he shouldn't give a shit. She was weak. Naïve. Too soft-hearted to survive in his world. Normally that would disgust him. He'd been raised to appreciate strength and independence; it was what his nation was built upon. What his parents had valued. And how he'd survived his own childhood, and become the leader he was.

But for some reason he'd felt sympathy for the quiet girl. And a growing chemistry that had caught him off guard. He couldn't help but feel...something. She'd seemed so genuine; so honest in her emotions and reactions. That was rare in his world, and it held a strange appeal.

Kindness was weakness, he reminded himself. He wouldn't let this girl, this tool, become more than just that. He'd keep her alive because he needed her.

That was all.

And perhaps if he kept repeating it, he'd eventually believe it, he thought ruefully. He sighed inwardly, dreading this confrontation; being the man that was expected of him.

Lina crumbled to her knees, nearly silent tears leaving streaks of dirt on her pale face. She bowed her head, and her dark hair fell forward, covering her face.

Jay felt an uncomfortable wrenching in his chest at the sight of her despair. He repressed the urge to reach out and comfort her; to pull her into his arms and tell her it was going to be ok.

Stop being so pathetic, he told himself. He'd obviously

spent too much time in Alba, with their strict ideals and unrealistic concepts of human nature. The side of him that was weak, that his mother had always mocked and his father cautioned him about, was too close to the surface.

Kindness is weakness.

This girl was dangerous; she could find the chinks in his armor. Not that she'd want to anymore. He needed to forget about anything romantic with Lina. *Anything sexual*, he corrected himself. He was the enemy now. The betrayer. The side responsible for her beloved brother's death. And there was nothing he could do to change that.

He didn't want to change it. This was part of his plan all along, he reminded himself.

"If you're done with your little pity party, we need to keep going," he told her. She stiffened, her head slowly raising. Incredulousness turned quickly to anger.

Good. It would give her the strength she needed to get through this. And it was about time she showed a little gumption.

Shaking, she rose to her feet. Every inch of her tall, curvy body shook with fury, her slender hands clenched in fists.

Damn, she was beautiful. If he had to pick someone to seduce, there couldn't have been a sexier woman. He grinned at her, turning his back to continue after his men, inviting her to take some kind of action.

She took it, as he knew she would. He heard her come up quickly behind him, turning to grab the raised arm holding a rock she'd picked up. Not bad, for a Patrician.

He twisted it quickly until the rock disappeared into the tall grasses, spinning her around and pulling her back against him.

She felt good in his arms.

She began to struggle, and he tightened his hold. She got in a good hit, knocking her head against his nose. He cursed quietly, holding both her arms crossed over her chest, tucking her body tight against his until she could barely move.

He felt blood trickling from his nose, and he swiped it away.

"Shall we call it even now?" he asked dryly.

"We will never be *even*," she hissed.

Jay sighed in response. "Lina, this isn't personal, it's war—"

"I don't want to hear it," she broke in, her body stiff in his embrace. "It was personal to me," she added nearly inaudibly.

He slowly released his hold. "Fine. Stay angry if it helps. We've got a long journey to get through. I'll take care of you, but you need to trust me." Lina huffed angrily at that. Ok, asking her to trust him was probably too much after everything he'd done to her

. "I'll keep you alive, that much I promise."

Lina said nothing as she followed, the anger burning in her chest eclipsing the feelings of sorrow and self-recrimination.

She was going to survive this, not because of Jay, but because she had decided to. To show that arrogant ass that she wasn't just a pathetic Patrician. To show his miserable crew she was more than an easy lay. And to show herself that she was more than the scared, naive girl who had left Alba.

18

Aerina woke to the sound of Marcus' holoreader buzzing. She strained to listen to his low voice as he conversed with the person on the other end.

"What is it?" she asked as he began to methodically dress.

"One of the drones returned with evidence of the

Empire's men."

"Lina?" Aerina asked, jumping out of bed and hurrying over to the wardrobe to select an outfit. She tapped her foot impatiently as she waited for the whirring of the bar to deliver her selection.

"Yeah, she's on the footage."

Aerina felt relief lighten her heart. Her friend was still alive. She'd been terrified the spies would kill or abandon her once they were away from the city and no longer needed a hostage that would only slow them down.

The short drive to the Training Grounds seemed like an eternity to Aerina. The large, unremarkable building loomed before them and then they disappeared into the underground garage.

The interior was brightly lit, and one wouldn't know it was night by the amount of activity inside.

Ramus waited for them in Marcus' office, the large Network Grid that tracked each citizen glowing brightly with several million dots. It had been quickly restored after each ID chip had been neutralized during the brief battle with the warship.

The tall, dark-skinned man barely nodded to them both before playing the drone footage. It was grainy, but Aerina could clearly see the lone figure standing in a small, grassy clearing. It barely looked like Lina. Her friend's clothes were filthy, hair tangled and windblown. She saw movement in the grasses and then her friend disappeared, as if prey taken down by a stalking predator.

Aerina shivered, drawing her light white coat closer. What was Lina going through right now? What were they doing to her? Was she ok? Aerina had witnessed the man stab her friend twice before he'd knocked them both out. Surely the wounds must be painful. How bad were they?

"That's it," Ramus said, retracting the holofile back into the device. Marcus nodded, pulling up a new file on his holocomputer from his seat at the long desk. They all stared at the projection.

"Here." Marcus zoomed in on a topographic map. "This was their location. The most direct route is going to be the old interstate through the mountains. That is where they'll head."

"It is still a huge area to cover," said Ramus, using his hand to zoom the grid out until Alba appeared on the map. Marcus hit a few more keys and a red trail appeared, marking the path the Empire's agents had followed.

"They're heading to old Sacramento. The perfect place to hide a large military vehicle. It's what I would do. Our drones would have a hard time detecting anything there."

Ramus nodded his agreement. "To Sacramento?"

"I'll go," Marcus said. "I need you to stay here and continue to oversee the Technology Project. I might be able to use the Technology to stop them before..." he paused a moment, looking at Aerina. "Before they elude us again."

"I'm coming," Aerina stated.

"Fine," Marcus agreed without argument, surprising Aerina. "We're leaving now."

19

Lina walked slowly through the ruins of a suburb of Sacramento. She stopped, staring at the metal steeple of what must have been a church. It was rusted and warped in a strange spiral, a large pine tree having pierced the center.

She stared for a moment, having never seen a church before besides in holofiles.

It was eerie to see how nature had reclaimed what humans had so carefully manicured. Had Stix, the dour pilot, not mentioned that this was the ruins of Sacramento, she might not have guessed it had once been a bustling metropolis.

"You ok, miss?" The newest member of their group, James, sidled up next to her, matching his stride to hers. Except for his diminutive size, he looked just like his older brother Thomas. Lina wasn't sure what to make of the lean blonde man. His first crude comments had made her wary, but he'd been friendly towards her since. Was he trying to be nice, or did he have an ulterior motive?

"I'm fine, thank you for asking," she replied coolly, keeping her eyes on her feet. Some of the rocks were sharp, and her battered moccasins were little protection. She'd wrapped them in gauze from the medkit, but it hardly helped. Shoes were an underrated commodity. She would never take them for granted again.

"Are all Albans like you? All proper and shit?" James asked, undeterred by her attitude.

"Many are. The Patricians value balance and serenity above all else," she replied, darting a look at him. His pockmarked yet attractive face seemed to be considering her words.

"The wealthy in our country are like that. Refined. They talk real good, like you. But they don't know shit," James finally said, his hand darting out to move a tree branch that would have snagged her already sadly battered pantsuit.

"Thank you," she murmured, curious despite herself about the nation that so desperately wanted Alban Technology. "Patricians are highly educated. Most attend school for many years, and never quit researching and discoursing. Education is important to running an efficient society," she concluded. "Every caste is required to receive an education, and must select an area to specialize in before they turn 21."

"What did you specialize in?" he asked her, solicitously helping her over moss-covered stones that looked as if they might have once been a very large building.

Lina was silent for a long moment, feeling Jay's eyes on her from his position in back of the small group. "I studied technology, like my older brother Stephen." Thinking of her brother brought on the familiar vise around her heart, a pain she was growing familiar with but not accustomed to.

James grinned. "A little hero worship, huh? That is how I got into special ops." He nodded towards his big brother, who walked in front with Stix. Fighting the depression threatening to descend, Lina shared his smile shyly, her eyes darting back to Jay. He watched them, his eyes narrowing slightly. She slid her gaze away, his disapproval making her lose the fight with depression. James glanced back at Jay, then as if sensing her sudden change in mood, he nodded to her and strode to catch up with the men in front.

"We're getting close!" Stix's raspy voice reached her just as Jay fell into step beside her.

"Stay alert. This is where they'll be waiting," he said. The other men fanned out in some kind of formation, their demeanors immediately changing, becoming hyper vigilant.

Lina stayed close to Jay, nervously scanning the overgrown ruins. She wanted to be rescued, but dreaded the battle she knew would ensue. Even with her extreme anger and feelings of betrayal, she didn't want to see anyone killed.

Well, maybe just Stix.

The minutes ticked by slowly, the only sound the scuffing of the men's boots and the occasional creak of rusty metal wreckage that littered their path.

She stumbled again over a twisted mass hidden beneath the undergrowth, barely catching herself. She stood a moment, staring up at a lone building that still stood. A gaping hole in the side was evidence of the battles that had ravaged California during the Civil and subsequent Global Wars. California, a key source of agriculture for the Northern Coalition, had been targeted first by the Southern Empire and then by the terrorist states that had ruled for a brief time.

Lina shivered, the ghosts of the dead seeming to inhabit the ruins, warning them to turn back. Why humankind insisted on continually seeking destruction was a mystery to her. Was peace and serenity ever truly attainable?

Her esoteric musings were interrupted by Stix's low voice. "They've locked on us. Tank's half mile to the left. Go!"

Jay shouldered his weapon and grabbed her arm, running low through thick briars to the left. Lina gasped as the grasping thorns scraped and tore at her clothes and skin. She stumbled after him, her heart beating heavily in her chest. Her ears strained for the sound of a vehicle or weapon, but only the sound of her pounding heart and heavy breathing filled her ears.

This would be her chance. Albans were nearby. If she could escape…

Digging in her heals, Lina twisted her arm out of Jay's grasp. He swung around, his expression incredulous. He certainly hadn't been expecting any dissension from her. He grabbed for her as she turned to run back.

His arm wrapped around her waist, swinging her around and pulling her into his side. She fought, thrashing and wriggling to get free. She managed to connect a few blows but he seemed impervious to her struggles, his arms bands of steel around her. Twisting in an attempt to get at his face, a searing pain spread from her side wound. Doubling over, she clutched at it. Jay used the opportunity to run the rest of the distance with her gripped in his arms.

They burst into a vast garage-like room with only three remaining walls. Vines and a small tree shared the open space with a large vehicle. The tires were almost as tall as Lina, the camo-colored sides oddly smooth with some coating covering them. It was completely enclosed but for two large front doors. Jay practically tossed her inside, following her in and shutting the door.

Lina was barely in the back seat when the large vehicle rumbled to life and rolled out of what she now recognized as an old airport hangar. It accelerated quickly, heading towards the skeletal remnants of a bridge hanging precariously over the Sacramento River.

Each bump and jostle had Lina gritting her teeth, her hand pressed to the side wound. The sharp pain had become a throbbing that pulsed in time with her accelerated heartbeat. A small tree stood in their path close to the ruins of the terminal and Lina closed her eyes, bracing for a crash.

They hit hard, the vehicle scraping through, the small tree toppling slowly to the side. The tank neared the bridge.

"We're close," Marcus said, his massive vehicle swerving to avoid a pile of cement with pikes of rusted rebar. Aerina clung to the front and top bars, having learned the hard way to keep her mouth closed to protect her teeth during each jarring bump. "I can see the signal from their tank."

"Can you turn it off?" she dared to ask, her teeth clinking together with another dip in the road.

"Not without the ignition code." Neither voiced the thought going through their minds. Stephen would have been able to get into the vehicle's computer without the code. The Technology was a powerful weapon, but more so in the hands of someone knowledgeable about networks and systems.

Marcus drew a weapon, his other hand on the steering wheel. The wind whipped through Aerina's hair in the open vehicle, the early morning sun already surprisingly hot.

"There!" She pointed excitedly as the large enemy vehicle came into view, speeding across a grassy clearing near the river. They hit a rocky hill, and she grabbed quickly for the bar as she bumped off the seat.

"Take the wheel," Marcus instructed, standing with legs braced on the seat.

Aerina cursed silently as she leaned over and grabbed for the wheel, holding it tightly to keep it steady as possible. Marcus began firing the ballistic weapon, one hand braced on the roll bar, the other aiming the long barrel of the weapon.

It looked like he had hit the enemy's tire, but it began re-inflating quickly.

"Anti-puncture technology," Marcus muttered, so low

Aerina could barely hear him over the engine's roar. He fired off a few more rounds before tossing the useless weapon into the back. It couldn't penetrate the tank or even take out the tires.

He pulled out a handheld EMW, the pop and arc shooting across the open clearing as they approached quickly, dancing over the tank's surface.

"Dammit. Protective coating." He tossed the EMW in the back, vaulting over the back roll bar to get into the storage compartment. Aerina slid into the driver's seat, swerving to avoid a tree that had grown mingled with a mass of tangled metal. A pre-war car?

Marcus pulled a large, long weapon from the back compartment. He also held a Com device.

The enemy tank was now making its way across the old bridge. The crumbling mix of cement and twisted metal quivered under the vehicle's large tires, pieces crumbling into the river far below.

They approached the bridge, the open grassy area near the river making it easy. The tank ahead of them fired off a few shots, the protective coating on Marcus' own vehicle absorbing and grounding the EMW. But their vehicle wasn't the only target of the Empire agents. The bridge glowed blue as currents shot through it, the metal turning red-hot, the stone exploding under the pressure.

Aerina slammed on the brakes as the bridge began tumbling into the river, the one remaining support tower exploding in a shower of cement and metal.

Marcus readied his next weapon, the large ballistic. He took aim at the vehicle that just cleared the other side as the rest of the bridge collapsed down into the slowly flowing waters of the Sacramento River.

"Wait, you can't destroy the tank. Lina's in there!" Aerina said sharply.

"We can't allow the Technology to get back to the Southern Empire."

"We'll have to find another way to stop them. You can't kill Lina!"

Marcus' finger tightened over the trigger, his eye on the scope. His jaw was clenched, face intent.

"Don't Marcus," Aerina said more quietly. "We don't need to have this on our conscience. We'll find another way."

Marcus cursed, changing the direction of the weapon at the last moment before firing. The missile launched, leaving a fiery tail as it flew over the now-impassable river and hit the ground just below the tank's tire. The explosion sent the enemy tank rolling once, twice, and the back tire arched into the air, landing in the river below.

"Move over," Marcus instructed curtly. "We've got to find another way across the river. My life was much less complicated before you," Marcus grumbled as he took over the wheel.

Aerina smiled slightly. "But not nearly as interesting."

Marcus gave her a sideways glance, and that was the last thing she saw before return fire from the overturned enemy vehicle was deflected a little late by their anti-ballistics and exploded much too close.

Lina slowly unbuckled the harness that had kept her in the seat as the vehicle had seemed to explode around her. Her hands shook so badly it took her several tries to release the latch.

Jay was already out of his seat, helping Thomas from the driver's seat. She saw blood pouring from the blonde driver's nose, but he was conscious.

Her stunned eyes moved over the other men. They all seemed fine.

"I think I caused some damage!" Stix shouted, tossing a large weapon to the bottom of the tank, adjusting his eye-set.

"Good, but let's not assume anything. They've got a second team not far behind. We've got to change the tire and get out of here before they find a way across," Jay ordered, throwing open the hatch and jumping out, his eyes scanning the bank across the river.

James and Stix scrambled out of the overturned but mostly intact tank.

"Out," he ordered Lina. His voice came from a distance, and it was if she were watching herself move painfully from the seat. Shock, she thought distantly.

She exited through the open back hatch, the ground rising to meet her too quickly. It took her a moment to realize she had practically collapsed out of the vehicle onto the ground. Jay sighed heavily above her, his booted feet hitting the ground an inch from her head. His hands gripped her arms, lifting her and pulling her unceremoniously out of the way of the men. "You've proven your worth today."

The statement didn't at first register. Her worth?

Jay turned away to help the men, who already had the large spare tire from under the vehicle, when he stopped, looking at his hand. He turned back, his eyes narrowed. Lina saw the red blood streaked across his palm.

Her blood.

He crouched before her, gently lifting the dirt-covered, oversized camo shirt she wore. The equally filthy pantsuit beneath revealed a slowly growing crimson stain.

Pulling out a small knife, he carefully sliced the ruined fabric of her pantsuit, exposing the seeping wound beneath. He cursed lightly, turning and jogging back to the vehicle.

Lina's eyes followed his easily loping form before looking back over the river. The acrid smell of melted metal from the demolished bridge wafted past her, making her nostrils sting. She squinted, her eyes watering as she scanned the distant shore, looking for a sign of the large Alban vehicle that had been firing on them. Had it been hit? Was Aerina's Reaper in it? *You've proven your worth today*. Jay's words echoed in her mind, finally making sense. Was she the reason they hadn't destroyed the Southern Empire tank? It seemed unlikely that a Reaper would hesitate to kill them all. She was just collateral damage at this point.

Jay returned with a medkit in his hands. He began carefully removing the bandage covering her stab wound — from *his* knife, she reminded herself — and cleaning away the fresh blood. Lina sat still, her jaw clenched, as he worked. His eyes darted to hers several times, as if gauging her reaction.

"Hey, I've got an injury you can tend to next!" Thomas called jeeringly from where he ratcheted the spare wheel on. The other men laughed as Jay raised his arm in a rude gesture. Lina looked back across the river, seeing nothing but the sun shimmering on the ruined city-turned-forest.

"Stix hit 'em with a ballistic, or at least he got close. There's the vehicle." Jay nodded his head to the far south as he worked, and Lina could see more smoke in the distance. Lina felt despair rising as she stared at the evidence of the hit. All hope of being rescued was slowly diminishing.

"I can do it," she told Jay sharply as he moved to apply liquid skin to glue the wound back together.

"I caused this. Let me do what little I can to make amends," he replied quietly. His blue-green eyes met her dark ones, their normal sardonic gleam absent. He seemed sincere. And perhaps a little regretful.

Lina felt his large hands gently applying the liquid, one hand braced against her ribs. It was large, callused, and warm. It seemed like a different life when those hands had been touching her in another way. In passion.

The memories rushed back in an unexpected tidal wave, overcoming her resolve to hate him. This moment of tenderness had the animosity she clung to wavering. She studied his tawny head as it bent close. Who really was this man? He had betrayed her, and she didn't know if she could ever forgive him for that. More than that, he was the enemy. The enemy responsible for her beloved brother's death. She knew she could never get past that.

And she didn't know if she could ever forgive herself for caring, even for a moment. The guilt and self-blame returned, renewing her resolve to hate this man, and she pulled back the moment he applied a clean bandage.

"Thank you." The words fell from her stiff lips of their own accord. She stalked away, her eyes on the distant bank where the Alban vehicle sat.

A loud crash had her swinging back around. The men had pushed the tank back over onto its wheels using some rusted rebar as leverage. Thomas hopped in, and a moment later it roared to life.

20

"Aerina."

Her eyes popped open to see Marcus leaning over her, a cut on his forehead dripping blood down the side of his fierce features.

"What happened?" she asked, putting her hand to her throbbing head.

"A ballistic exploded nearby," he answered shortly, his Com device already in his hand. "We both lost consciousness for several minutes."

Aerina sat up slowly, shielding the bright sun with her hand until she located her sunglasses. Putting them on brought minor relief. "Are you looking for another bridge?"

"No," Marcus answered shortly. "I've sent the other team after them. We're going back. The Technology isn't as useful as I hoped in the wilderness; not without the ability to access their vehicle's computer or surrounding technology. Their weapons are manual; nothing for me to access, either."

"But she's right there," Aerina said in frustration, zooming her glasses across the river. The enemy vehicle was already in motion, slowly making its way through the remnants of old Sacramento towards the east. "It's not like you to just give up."

Marcus said nothing, but she knew her words needled him. As they'd been intended to.

"I want nothing more than to follow them all the way to the goddamn Empire. But the leadership in Alba is precarious, and I don't trust those smug conservatives not to try and appoint a new Consul in my absence. The other team will be just as capable." His words were carefully enunciated, and Aerina felt a tiny bit of shame. He was right. As usual.

Frustration crackled between them; she over their inability to save Lina after coming so close. He was no doubt angry with himself for failing to retrieve the Technology. And angry at her for stopping him from completing him job.

She didn't care. They would find another way that didn't involve killing Lina.

He instructed the second team to continue after the enemy; to stay with them until the Empire if necessary. Then Marcus started up the vehicle, driving away from the river that separated her from her friend and back towards Alba.

Part 2 Victim

It is amazing, the human will to survive. The end of the world is Darwinism at its finest. Some choose to give up, while others choose to fight. And fight. And fight…
   - From the journal of Cecilia Delacroix

1

The next hour passed quickly as they cruised over the increasingly rocky terrain. The forest that had taken over old Sacramento disappeared into sparse mountainous terrain. The old interstate was surprisingly intact, and they seemed to be making good time towards the rendezvous.

Lina was brought out of a painful half-sleep by the sudden slowing of the hypnotic hum of the engine. Thomas, again the driver, brought the vehicle to a complete stop, cursing. "The road is completely covered. Looks like some rockslides over the years, and part of it dropped down into the river."

Jay unlatched his harness, sliding open the front hatch and dropping to the ground to inspect the blockage.

The Truckee River flowed to the right, the level surprisingly high, almost near the flat terrain that used to be the well-traveled Interstate 80. To the left, cliffside rose. It was just high and steep enough to make it impassable with the vehicle.

"What about explosives?" James asked.

"And trigger another rockslide, you ignorant cooyon?" Stix returned derisively.

"Like you have a better idea, you damn mountain

scum—"

"Looks like we're walking." Jay headed off the brewing argument with his quiet statement.

"How much time does this add?" Thomas' voice was muffled as he began gathering gear from the back.

"At least a day," Stix answered, looking at his device. "Damme, if I can't get this to work, we ain't gonna be getting an extraction. They won't come if they can't read our coordinates."

Jay studied the rocks with Royce. Lina had determined he was the engineer of the group. The slender, dark-skinned man was shaking his head.

"This isn't an accident. Someone put these here. To block the way." His quiet voice was certain, and it sent chills down Lina's spine.

"Grab what we can carry. I've got a map and an old compass. We should hopefully find our way to the coordinates. We'll have to leave the vehicle here and hike out before the Albans catch up with us." Jay didn't look at Lina as he gave the order. She had followed the men out of the tank, and now turned to take her own small pack that consisted of some food, water, and a shiny blanket.

In a few minutes they were all climbing around the massive rock slide, carefully picking their way over the boulders.

Lina walked as if in a daze, her normal clumsiness exaggerated by exhaustion. Her legs felt heavy, and it became increasingly difficult to maneuver the rocky terrain. Jay stayed close, but thankfully didn't offer to help. She didn't feel very receptive to any compassion at this moment.

Stix no longer lead the way, his angry curses over the broken device he held making her blush. She'd never heard such foul language. She had to admit, some of the terms were quite creative.

When they were again on flatter terrain, Lina walked closer to Stix, trying to get a better look at the device he carried. Curiosity, and her natural interest in technology, overcame her shyness.

The small device looked just like Alban technology, a simple geo-locator that used tower triangulation to find a destination or track something with a similar signal.

"Can I see it?" she finally asked quietly. He looked at her in surprise, as if the rocks had formed mouths and spoken. Lina stiffened slightly, regretting the impulse that had driven her to offer assistance. Stix glanced at Jay, who shrugged, and slowly held out the device.

Lina turned it over, her fascination already outweighing her reticence to interact with the enemy. "Do you have a —" Stix produced a demagnetizer before she finished. She took it, opening the back, carefully removing the energy cell. Her dark hair fell forward, concealing her concentrated features.

Royce, Jay, and Stix crowded around while Thomas and James continued to scan the horizon for danger.

"I don't know how, but this is the very same device created years ago by Alban engineers. There is no way two devices from different nations could be so similar unless they were engineered by the same people," she said, as if talking to herself.

"Look." She showed the men a tiny button beneath the powercell, quickly removing and using her earing to press it. The device suddenly powered on.

"What did you do?" Stix's gravelly voice was incredulous.

"The device was built with an anti-EMP feature. Its default setting is off to save energy. I'm sure you recall how during the Wars, electromagnetic pulse weapons were employed in an attempt to destroy enemy technology. And, I'm guessing, to kill anyone using the pre-war version of Alban Technology. So our engineers spent years developing a force field that protects devices against an EMP weapon.

"The EMP feature I just activated also protects against

basic signal jammers. Which was why your device wasn't working — someone was blocking the signal," Lina concluded, impatiently pushing her hair back, offering the device back to Stix. She met three pairs of fascinated eyes. "What?"

"I thought all you over-educated types were just talk," Stix said.

"You were wrong." Lina met Jay's eyes, seeing the gleam of approval. She tried to pretend she didn't care, but she couldn't hide the light flush that spread over her cheeks.

"Alba has some of the most brilliant engineers in the world," Royce spoke up unexpectedly. "I've reverse-engineered some of their inventions."

"How did you get our inventions? Are there more spies in the city?" Lina asked.

Royce shrugged. "I'm not privy to that information." Lina looked over to the other men. Jay turned away, motioning to Thomas and James. She studied his face, wondering how much he knew about the Southern Empire's access to Alban technology. Probably much more than he was letting on.

"Lina fixed the locator. Apparently someone is jamming local signals. Let's get out of here before we find out who."

"Their signal is showing up on your locator; we're getting closer," she told him quietly, her gaze on the hills to the north. Jay followed her gaze, scanning the hills himself. A tiny beacon blinked in the holographic projection that had reappeared on the repaired device.

"Hopefully their signal is all we see of them. Nice work," he finished, his light eyes scanning her upturned face. She again felt the quick rush of pleasure at his approval, trying hard to keep it tempered with caution. His meaningless flattery had won her over the first time; she didn't want to fall victim again.

Stix took the lead, scanning the sparse, rolling mountains around them.

Lina fell in step behind the group. She was still exhausted, her side throbbed, and her feet ached in her tattered moccasins. But her heart felt a little lighter. She might be clumsy and naive, but she knew technology.

They walked for almost an hour before taking a break. Needing to relieve the pressure on her bladder, Lina slipped behind a grouping of bushes. The river rushed quickly just south of her position. She wandered along the high river bank, the water looking inviting after going unwashed for several days. She didn't even want to think about how she must smell.

But there was no means or time for a bath. Sighing, she splashed her face with the cold water. Then she filled her canteen, dropping one of the purifiers in as Jay had instructed her.

As she stood, her eyes fell upon a green, open area. Unlike the surrounding hills, it was flat and the grass thick and well-groomed. Flowers bloomed in tidy rows around carefully etched grave markers.

Lina felt a chill despite the midday sun's warmth. They'd stumbled across a burial ground that was obviously visited regularly. A strange fear had her turning and running back towards the men.

"A graveyard!" she told them, pushing back her dust-coated hair with an unconscious gesture. They followed her to the spot, stepping carefully around the stones that marked each grave.

Jay motioned and the other men fanned out slowly, moving silently over the grassy terrain. The formerly idyllic spot had now become eerily foreboding.

"Do you think it's the signal jammers?" Lina asked Jay, feeling as if eyes were watching her from the hills. Instinctively, she grabbed his free hand, gripping the callused warmth as she scanned the hills apprehensively. His blunt fingers closed around her slender ones, and she realized what she was doing. She quickly pulled her hand back, embarrassed.

"Perhaps," was all he said in response to her question, but his gleaming gaze told her he was amused by her actions. Amused and a little pleased.

2

Marcus spent the day after their return meeting with Ramus and the Technology Research Group at the Training Grounds. Initially he had been furious with himself for not killing the Southern Empire spies when he had the chance; for giving in to Aerina's pleas to spare Lina. Weakness had no place in a leader's heart, and he still had a job to do, regardless of Aerina's place in his life.

Considering the matter on the drive back to Alba, he had now come to the conclusion that it wasn't such a great loss, after all. The Southern Empire would have kept returning for the Technology. Their size greatly exceeded Alba; eventually they would have overwhelmed the small city-state in sheer numbers.

Now that they had the Technology, he could see how things played out. To the Empire, Alba was a small player in this emerging political landscape he was slowly uncovering.

Marcus had access to a few things that gave Alba a big advantage: the notes of the creators of the Technology, who also were the founders of Alba, and the brilliant minds of the many engineers who had descended from the original genius inventors that had established the city.

"I need to know why the Southern Empire has become so desperate to get the Technology. From all accounts, they may have known about it for years and been content to just steal bits and pieces of our other innovations. There must be something, some pressure, driving the leadership to act so rashly," Marcus told his second-in-command. Both watched the tech team they had assembled running more tests on the Technology.

Ramus considered this. "Their main enemy, the Northern Coalition, was destroyed nearly eighty years ago. Do you think the European Alliance has regained power?"

"That or the Terror States survived." Marcus paused, the computer in his mind accessing the control system. He turned the lights off in the test chamber and set off the water and smoke defenses. He watched one recruit focus intensely while the rest panicked, trying to run to the nearest door. He sensed another's access to the control system. The lights came back on and the smoke and water stopped. He nodded slightly. "Or perhaps a new player has risen to power. It has been nearly a hundred years. A lot can change even in just those few generations. Look at Alba. Most of our youth don't know what the outside is like, and they weren't raised on the horror stories of the Wars like we were. They will be an entirely new generation; a generation more like Aerina. Bold, curious, unafraid."

Ramus gave a faux shiver. "Serenity save us from an entire population like your partner."

Marcus' mouth quirked at the corner in his version of a smile. "We'll need people like that when war returns."

Ramus became serious, nodding his agreement.

Marcus turned away. "Keep up the good work," he called as he left. "The young woman with the red hair…she's the one to move on to the next tests. And give Simon an injection. I could have used someone with his hacking skills today."

He left the Training Grounds, returning to the Capitol for a meeting with the Senators that he was dreading. They weren't aware he had returned, and he wanted to catch them off-guard.

His plan worked.

"Then we'll take a vote on Caius as the new Consul—?"

"You would elect a new Consul without me? I'm

crushed." Marcus' lethally quiet voice interrupted the vote. Eight heads swiveled quickly towards the door where Marcus stood, legs braced and arms hanging loosely, as if ready for a fight.

"Trent. We didn't know you were back!" Senator Jessup, Population Control, spoke quickly.

"I can see that."

"You had said we could elect a new Consul..." Cauis began, only to sputter out as Marcus began pacing slowly forward.

"I don't plan to stop you," was all Marcus said, sitting in the chair at the head of the table. His choice wasn't lost on any of the Senators gathered. The Consul's chair.

Charged silence fell over the room. "However, I do request a little time to present my own candidate. The Senators can then vote as always on the best candidate."

After another long pause, eight "ayes" filled the room. Agreeing to his condition. Marcus said nothing, his dark eyes watching the six men and two women squirm in their chairs.

He had known they were going to be a problem. They didn't like his power, and they wanted him out. The Senators were highly educated in their respective fields, but none were capable of running Alba in a state of war. Of taking their technology and turning it into a weapon. Into a defense system.

It was time to mix things up. Time for other castes to be represented here. Not for some altruistic, sentimental principle about how everyone deserved representation. No, Marcus didn't care about ideals; he dealt in realities. Appointing additional Senators would be the best way to keep these eight from gaining too much control. The best way to keep Alba safe.

3

The attack came without warning.

Lina focused on putting one aching foot in front of the other. The only sounds were the quiet clomping of the men's feet, and the occasional displaced rock. The earthy smell of river water filled her nostrils.

Why had she helped them fix their locator?

The question had continued to plague her. She'd had a chance to ensure it was permanently unusable, delaying their departure and possibly giving the Albans the chance to overtake them.

Because you don't want anything to happen to Jay. She couldn't lie to herself. As much as he'd hurt her, as much as she should hate him, she couldn't wish him dead. And she wanted him to look at her differently. *Admit it, it bothers you that he thinks you're a naïve, sheltered girl.*

She knew how most people thought of her. *Don't tell Lina* was a common joke. She wasn't very good at subterfuge. She liked things simple and honest when dealing with people. Computers, electronic devices, technology…she understand how they worked. But people—emotions, mind games, subtle meanings and manipulation—it was exhausting to her. She hadn't really worried about it.

Until now.

Lost in her thoughts, she missed the opening shot. A nearly silent whoosh was followed by a low grunt and suddenly James was collapsing to the ground in front of her.

Lina froze, staring dumbfounded at the arrow protruding from his neck. The late afternoon calm exploded into battle as the men began firing back with their EMWs in the general direction of the attackers.

Stix grabbed Lina's arm as he charged past her, pulling her from the state of shock that had kept her rooted in place.

She ran beside him, another arrow thunking off the rock behind her.

The wiry man was surprisingly strong, dragging her along with him as he ran and fired. He shoved her behind a large boulder, crowding in beside her.

Thomas and Royce crouched together behind a boulder several feet away. The men alternated shots with their EMWs to keep the unseen enemy at bay while trying to determine just what they were up against.

Lina glanced around, desperately trying find Jay. Where was he? Then she saw a quick movement up the mountain. Her panic subsided slightly as she recognized his familiar form pressed against another large rocky outcropping. He was headed for a rectangular opening a hundred feet above him.

"Cave dwellers?" she murmured to her herself.

Stix heard. "Bastards can't be too primitive if they are the ones jamming our signal."

The loud crack and pop of the EMW sounded again, and then Lina heard Stix cursing. She glanced over, her back pressed tight to the sharp rocks, fear making her oblivious to the pain. James had crawled behind a boulder, but blood was now pumping freely from the wound in his neck.

Stix shoved a weapon in her hand. "Cover me!" he called, heading towards James' position in a low crouch. Lina stared at the unfamiliar weapon in her hand. What was she supposed to do with it? She'd never held a weapon before, much less fired one.

Lina watched helplessly as Thomas and Royce fired repeatedly to cover their comrade, but an old-fashioned ballistic weapon struck Stix in the leg and he went down hard, his EMW skittering out of reach. He stood quickly, but his leg immediately gave out and the small man collapsed again to the ground.

Lina glanced over at the two men to the right still firing rapidly. Jay was closing the gap between himself and the entrance to the dwelling above them. James was slowly bleeding to death.

No one could help Stix.

Fear made her breathing shallow, but at the same time, adrenaline pumped through her body, making her feel nearly invincible. Without giving herself time to think, Lina dashed forward, grabbing Stix's foot and dragging him back towards their boulder.

The minute and thirty seconds it took felt like barely a moment, passing in a blur. The panic made her vision a tunnel with only one goal: get back behind the safety of the boulder.

Stix was cursing her as she released his leg, and she realized in her blind panic she had grabbed his injured leg. Without apologizing, still a little in shock, Lina helped him bandage the wound. Glancing up, she saw that James was now unconscious, the blood flowing more slowly from the wound in his neck.

He was going to die.

Lina felt nausea rising in her throat as the chilling realization spread. She looked back over at Thomas, who was also looking at James. She saw the same realization cross his blunt features, saw the moment cool concentration became angry desperation.

Thomas charged across the open space, firing his EMW in rapid succession. An arrow slit the air, embedding itself in his shoulder, but it didn't even slow the large man.

He made it to his brother as Stix and Royce continued to keep the attackers pinned down. Lina watched distantly as he slowly lowered his brother down, his hand pressed to the younger man's neck to staunch the flow of blood. Stix tossed the med kit he had in his pack towards the two, and Thomas caught it, ripping it open and pulling out the wound sealant and stapler that would hopefully close the wound.

It was probably too late, Lina thought fatalistically, the blessed numbness of shock settling on her shivering form. The ground around James was red with his blood, and the unconscious man was pale, his lips tinged blue.

Jay had disappeared, perhaps inside. Perhaps dead.

Lina felt hysterical laughter bubble up in her throat. She'd never survive without Jay. Had she survived the Southern Empire only to be killed by primitive cave dwellers and their arrows?

Stix tossed his EMW on the ground as it slowly recharged, pulling a second one from the strap crisscrossing his chest. He looked over at the Royce, holding up his hand, and the other man nodded.

Silence stretched.

Thomas had begun pumping his own blood into his brother through a field transfusion kit. Lina looked away, her stomach turning.

Were the attackers waiting patiently for one of them to foolishly raise their heads and look? Were they even now slowly approaching their positions, weapons ready to maim and kill?

Lina took deep breaths, trying to focus on an image of her Serenity Pool at home, imagining the cool water gently lapping against the marble edge.

It did little to help.

An explosion interrupted the silence, making her start violently. Lina looked up to see Jay half running, half falling down the hillside. The large entrance to the cave had collapsed, no doubt under one of Jay's hand-held explosive devices. But it was obvious now that the large opening hadn't been the only point of attack, and many of the assailants were spanning the hillside.

Firing resumed, arrows and bullets raining down. Lina's heart froze as Jay went down, rolling several feet before regaining his feet and flinging his large form behind an outcropping.

Lina opened her mouth to ask Stix what, if any, plan they had when a loud whistle and boom echoed across the rocky terrain. An explosion, larger than the first, lit up the hillside with fiery sparks and raining rock.

Jay used the diversion to descend another hundred yards, hiding himself in thick shrubs.

Another boom, this time with the familiar pop of an EMW, echoed across the mountain. Artificial lighting danced over the terrain, followed again by the sonic boom.

Lina scrambled close to Stix, looking to the source of the attack. Did their attackers have weapons behind them? Then her panicked gaze fell on the two black-clothed men further down the hillside.

Virmortus from Alba. Relentless, skilled Reapers.

The two Alban assassins began firing again on the hillside, giving Jay the opportunity to join his team. "Let's go!" he called, helping Thomas hoist a still-unconscious James.

Lina hesitated. Should she try to stay with the Albans? They would continue after Jay and his men, anyway. They had come for the Technology, not for her. She might be safer staying with Jay's team.

She certainly felt safer with Jay.

Hurrying after them, she took one more look back at the Alban warriors. They seemed to be holding their own against the still-unseen attackers, and were covering the Confederate's retreat, whether it was intentional or not.

Lina couldn't help but feel that her decision to stick with Jay had been a turning point for her. At this moment, she wouldn't worry about it. She would just be thankful she had survived this far.

One thing was certain: no one in Alba would believe what she had been through. She barely believed it herself.

4

Lina sat beside Stix in a large, thick grove of trees near the river. They were well-hidden from the old interstate, with

Royce standing guard atop a small ridge. She couldn't see him, but knew he was laying perfectly still on his stomach, a long-range weapon clamped in his dark, slender hands.

The knowledge did little to comfort her.

They were a sad-looking group. Thomas had cracked the arrow off and pushed it through his shoulder, bandaging the wound efficiently. She had been unable to look away from his precise, quick movements. Jay, too, had cleaned up the many abrasions resulting from the explosion and tumble down the mountainside. They acted as if it was routine to be injured after overcoming near-death. Just another day as a spy.

Now they were waiting to find out if James was going to live.

Jay and Thomas watched as Stix again tested James' blood pressure and other vitals.

"Better, but he's still on the edge. We can't move him yet."

As he packed away the med kit, Stix glanced at Lina from beneath shaggy eyebrows. "Why did you save me?"

Lina was surprised by the question. She shrugged, not even certain herself. "Better the enemy I know...No, that's not true. I suppose I just don't want to see anyone die. Even someone as unlikable as you," she finished with a half-smile to let him know she was kidding. Partially.

Stix grunted in response. "Thanks," he said gruffly, his eyes still downcast.

"The old coot just said thanks," Jay called out.

Thomas grinned half-heartedly at Jay's attempt to lighten the mood. "I suppose we'll see pigs flying next," he replied. Jay slapped the large man's back as he passed, a man's way to show affection, Lina supposed.

"It is a good thing the Albans were there to save your ass again," Lina added. Her choice of words, spoken in her well-modulated voice, had three pairs of eyes turning in surprise. She smiled, pretending to be busy rewinding the unused gauze.

Stix got over his surprise first. "That was hardly a challenge. We'd've had it under control in a few more minutes, even without those novices."

"Damn straight," Thomas added. Jay just grinned at her over the weapon he was re-checking.

Even while joking, they were preparing for the next battle.

"If you were so impressed by those feeble soldiers that call themselves Reapers, why didn't you stay with them?" Stix asked.

Lina paused, looking over at Jay. He seemed very intent on his weapon, but she sensed he was waiting for her answer. A strange urge overcame her; the urge to make him squirm. To feel as if she held the upper hand for once. "I considered staying behind with the Virmortus that saved us, but then I thought I'd better stay with Jay. In case there are…consequences from our indiscretion. I'll know for sure in about nine months."

Jay's tawny head, which had become somewhat shaggy, lifted quickly, the sardonic gleam completely absent. For once, his normal cocky expression was completely absent.

"Albans have a mandatory anti-pregnancy vaccination." Jay's statement almost came out as a question.

"Do they?" She pretended to be busy adjusting her sadly mangled shoes.

"You had the shot, right?"

"You're the expert on Alban society."

"Lina…" The men laughed at Jay's white face and pleading tone.

"Can't you see she's messing with you, man?" Thomas finally had pity on Jay, although he continued to grin, a real one this time, at his leader's expense. It was a much-needed moment of levity that relieved some of the tension. Lina allowed a small smile, which Jay returned.

"Don't joke with a man about something like that." He

came closer, settling beside Lina as the other men busied themselves setting up camp for the night.

Lina refused to meet Jay's eyes. The daring impulse that had pushed her to join in on the teasing had fled, leaving her feeling self-conscious and a little ashamed. *Nice girls don't talk about feelings, and they certainly don't talk about indiscretions.* Her mother's words played in her head, a constant reminder of her short-comings.

"Lina." Jay waited patiently until Lina finally raised her head to meet his gaze. His face was tanned, the blonde stubble covering his squared jaw only serving to make him look a little more dangerous; a little more handsome. Her heart skipped, in spite of herself.

"If you had been... if you really did become..." he couldn't seem to even mouth the words. Lina watched him with fascination, surprised at his unusual hesitance. He started again. "What happened between us, as much as you don't want to believe it, was separate from this. And if something would have come from it, I would have taken care of you."

Lina felt a flush spreading across her face, despite her attempts to stay cool. She wanted to believe him, but she wasn't sure what to think anymore. He had always known what words she wanted to hear, and was good at offering them. Was this all it was, lip service to keep her amiable? *She won't give us any trouble.* His words came back to her, and she stiffened.

He was watching her, waiting for a response. She nodded, looking back down at her hands to avoid his knowing eyes. They were covered in cuts and abrasions, and raw from exposure to the elements. No longer were they the soft hands of a lady; of a Patrician.

Jay's hand closed over both of hers for a moment, sending an unexpected spark through her body. The chemistry was still strong between them, even with the distrust and anger. Perhaps because of it.

Then he was rising, going to help the men finish preparing the concealed camp for the night.

They were close to the extraction point in the old city of Reno, but with James being injured, they needed to wait until he stabilized more to continue.

She watched the sun slowly set behind the trees, the calming rush of the river making her think of home; of the muted roar of the ocean that had lulled her to sleep each night.

What would Alba be like when she returned? *If* she returned. Changes had already been happening, although she had paid them little attention. She'd been so wrapped in her grief, in herself, she hadn't thought much for the city that was her home. Shame spread at her selfishness.

The world was much bigger now than it had ever been for her. It had consisted of Alba and the Capitol Terrace; her petty goals for a future as a Patrician in the Technology Sector and perhaps a husband and two kids. Exactly like her mother. Like every other Patrician before her.

It was what good Alban girls were expected to do. What was expected of a Patrician. All her life she'd tried to be the good girl her mother needed, and her father demanded. To avoid making waves that would cause even more discord in their family. To be more like the brother she'd idolized.

But that life was gone forever. Would she ever be able to go back to being just a Patrician again? Did she have the courage to be something *more* than just a Patrician?

Sighing, she looked back at the men and was startled to see Stix smiling. It was an unexpected sight on the gruff man's face, and it made her curious to know what had caused the expression.

Moving closer, she could see he was looking at something on his hand-held device. Nudie pictures? Bawdy jokes? What else could get that uncouth little man to loosen up?

He glanced up quickly, meeting her curious gaze.

"My kids," he told her, turning the screen so she could see the silent video of two youths playing in a stream. She wouldn't have guessed he had children so young. Or that he had children at all. He seemed like more of a loner than a family man. Long, straggly hair streaked with grey lay around his slight shoulders. Several scars crisscrossed wrinkles on his leathery skin, tanned from the constant exposure to sun and elements. Another scar on his neck made her think the raspy voice was acquired at some point in his career.

"I haven't seen them in over nine months."

"Is that normal?" she asked despite herself, glancing up from the images of two young girls waving. Stix's normally aloof brown eyes were still fixed on the screen, soft with affection.

"Yeah. Some missions go on for some time. But it's a good job. And the Lord knows I ain't good at nothin' else."

"Have you been with Jay for a long time?"

"Yeah, I got assigned his unit on his first mission as Agent in Charge. Before he was the Wolf. He was just Jayden then, although many of 'em who didn't know what he could do called him Junior. Mockery, you know, cause of his father." Stix spit, then seemed embarrassed, wiping his mouth with the back of his hand. Lina looked away, pretending not to notice.

"His father?" Lina had a hard time following his colloquialisms.

"That's right, you Albans wouldn't know about Jayden Kane March, Senior. He's a legend in the Empire. A top agent. A real ladies man. Jay is just like him." Stix leaned back, surreptitiously pulling a nicotine stick from his pack. "Kid hates being called Junior, tho. Guess he wanted to make a name for himself. And he damn sure did that. They call him the Wolf. Top agent now, although some still say it's only because his father is gone."

"His father is dead?" Lina didn't want to ask about Jay; didn't want to know more about how great he was at being an agent and seducing women. After all, she already knew that.

But she couldn't seem to stem the insatiable curiosity about her captor.

"Yeah, he was killed about ten years back, on a mission. Still have parades in his memory, even after—" he stopped suddenly as Jay returned from a brief reconnaissance of the area.

Lina glanced back at the screen. The video was ending, the girls waving goodbye to the videographer. The mother? Stix reluctantly shut off the device, looking surprisingly melancholy. Sympathy flooded her soft heart, threatening the walls she'd been trying to build.

Even enemy spies had families they loved; someone who worried if they would come home.

Someone who would grieve if they didn't.

Her gaze moved to where Jay methodically went through his pack, taking inventory and checking that everything was in order.

He looked up, raising a brow in question as he caught her watching him. His mouth was held in its normal grin, making a completely inappropriate warmth spread through her. She looked away first, shaking her head as if to deny any attraction, at least to herself.

Did Jay have someone at home, worrying about him? Waiting for him to return, watching the door to see if he walked through it?

She had once flirted with the idea of being that someone, back when she'd thought he was an Aggie. It had seemed so unattainable then, when they had been on the same side.

Now it was impossible.

5

"I had dinner with my father today. The Senators are not happy." Aerina moved a chess piece, her shadowed blue eyes on Marcus' blunt features.

"I don't have time to keep them in line and deal with the Southern Empire." Marcus' eyes followed her move, but his mind was not on their game.

He hadn't told Aerina his decision to appoint new Senators. While he trusted her, he knew she was trying to rebuild a relationship with her father, and he didn't want to force her to lie; to come between them more than he already did. And he certainly didn't want the Senators discovering his plans before he was ready.

Emotion and relationships were tricky things to maneuver. It was true what he'd told Aerina; life had been more straightforward before her. He'd rather face a group of armed men in a dark alley than deal with "relationship issues". He hated any uncertainty or lack of control. And when it came to Aerina, sometimes he felt completely helpless and out of his element. But he wouldn't change it; he couldn't imagine a life now without her in it.

"I know you need to be in control right now, but the Senators are well-known and trusted. I just think it isn't a good idea to antagonize them further—"

The muted chimes of the doorbell interrupted whatever Aerina had been about to say. *Helen Vanderbilt*, the electronic voice quietly announced. Marcus rose with relief at the unexpected visitor so late in the evening. He never thought he'd be happy to see someone besides Aerina at his door. At least he wouldn't have to suffer the still-unfamiliar pangs of guilt he felt over keeping things from Aerina.

"Helen!" Aerina hurried over to the door as Marcus stepped aside to let the petite blonde woman enter. She hugged her friend, surprised at the thinness of the other woman's form. Helen had always been slender, but now she was almost sickly. Aerina felt her heart twist. Lina had also been losing weight after Stephen's death. "How have you been doing?" she asked gently.

"That is what I'm here about. There is no point in ignoring the truth any longer. I'm pregnant," Helen stated in her normal no-nonsense tone.

Aerina's jaw dropped, and she had to work hard to close it. "Is it…?"

"Yes, it is Stephen's. I wanted to tell Lina first, but her mother doesn't seem to know where she is. Which is surprising, since she always has had Lina under her thumb."

Aerina met Marcus' eyes. "Lina is getting help for her…depression," she lied. They'd kept the attack and Lina's abduction quiet, not wanting to worry everyone and cause mass panic. She knew Helen would keep quiet about it, but the other woman obviously had a lot to deal with already.

Marcus quietly gathered his gear and left through the kitchen door. No doubt heading for the Training Grounds to check on the Technology Project, as it was being called. He'd been spending as much time there as possible lately.

For someone who claimed to be inexperienced with emotion, he had a great grasp of how to handle an emotionally charged situation.

Leave, as quickly as possible.

Aerina focused her attention back on the subject at hand. "I hesitate to ask this, but how…"

Helen sighed. "I was ill, and taking medication. I know the recommendation is to use additional protection because some medications can counteract the shot, but, well, you know how it is."

Aerina nodded sympathetically.

"I don't regret it. In fact, I'm happy. Happy to have a part of Stephen still here." Her voice cracked slightly, and Aerina gripped her hand, letting her own tears fall. Helen took a deep breath, bringing herself back under control.

"I wanted to tell you, because I knew you of all people would understand the position I'm in. Being pregnant and unwed is going to be difficult as a Patrician. Not only is it the height of irresponsibility, it will probably make me unmatchable. But I am not going to terminate."

"I'm glad," Aerina told her friend simply. "I know my own position is tenuous right now, but I'll help and support you however I can."

Helen's eyes grew misty again, and she coughed to clear the thickening in her throat.

"These hormones are ridiculous. But thank you."

6

The absolute darkness of night away from the city was still startling to Lina. It was also much colder at night, bitterly so. A fire would have stood out like a beacon to their enemies, and so Lina sat shivering in the dark, listening to the night sounds around her.

A small heater produced enough warmth for them to huddle around it. Lina held her blanket tightly, leaning back against a boulder that seemed to seep the warmth from her bones one moment at a time. James lay closest, his face pale and breathing heavy. He still hadn't regained consciousness. Thomas didn't leave his side. No one had said the words aloud, but she didn't think he could survive the night.

"Why does the Southern Empire want the Technology?" Lina asked, finding the long silence unnerving.

"That is privileged information for the President to divulge," Royce responded in his normal quiet, serious tone. He would have made a great Patrician, so proper and obedient.

"Ask Jay, he's got a special relationship with the

President," Thomas said baitingly, his eyes on the broad back of his leader. Jay was on watch, continually scanning the blackness for any sign of movement. Probably listening for any unusual sounds. Lina wondered what Thomas meant. Was Jay involved romantically with the President?

Jay finally answered, his low voice carrying over the rush of the river. "Are you familiar with the history of the Wars? The European Alliance backed the liberal northwest and eastern states during the Second American Civil War. But the terrorist state in the Middle East had grown powerful, more powerful than anyone knew, and used the opportunity to spread destruction across Western Europe. That is what gave the Southern Empire the ability to rise to power. Otherwise the Northern Coalition would have crushed the disorganized militia that began our nation.

"The European Alliance has re-emerged, however, and the President is worried about old alliances and wars rekindling. She wants something to give her a hold over Europe in case an upcoming meeting goes sour."

"Why wait this long to come after it?"

"I don't think they knew about it, not until recently. We've been...borrowing Alban technology for years. Like Royce said, your technology is the most advanced anywhere in the world, at least that we know of." Lina heard Jay shift and a few rocks tumble, but she could barely see his form in the black that surrounded them.

"You've been spying in Alba for that long, undetected?" Lina was shocked. How had they remained hidden from the Virmortus for so long?

"We had a contact; a very influential contact. She kept us supplied with technology and intel."

Lina opened her mouth to ask who the contact was when Jay interrupted.

"We need to keep our silence. Sound carries. Get some rest, we'll be up early and tomorrow will probably be another long day."

Lina lay down on the thin pad that constituted her bed for the night. She never expected to sleep, with her filthy scalp itching, the cold night air, and the hard ground. But every night she fell into exhausted slumber. She hoped tonight would be no different.

Lina awoke to the sound of harsh whispers. She sat up quickly in alarm, her eyes scanning the inky blackness to finally find focus on the small headlamp of one of the soldiers, shining on James' pallet.

The man was breathing slowly, with great heaving gasps. Lina shrunk back, fearing death was looming. An image of Stephen's gray face and large brown eyes open, glassed over, staring at a smoky sky rose in her mind, filling her with terrified sorrow. She didn't think she could bear to witness death approaching. She didn't *want* to witness it.

A tiny trickle of rocks on the hillside behind her sent new fear throughout her aching body. It traveled up her spine to the back of her head, every hair standing on end as she strained to listen.

The headlamp flicked off. Only the rushing of the river and night creatures filled the silence. Then a scuffing, closer now.

"Stop where you are or we will fire." Jay's low voice carried on the night air from somewhere above. A long silence followed his command.

A placating feminine voice rose above the rush of the nearby river. "We mean you no harm. We witnessed your battle with the Pumas and mean to offer assistance. May we approach?"

Another long silence.

"Drop your weapons. Send one representative. Anyone else who moves, we'll shoot," came Jay's harsh response. "I'm locked on several of you now."

A rasp and then a tiny flickering flame appeared, growing brighter as the individual must have lit a lantern.

"I'm approaching your camp now," the female voice again came from the location of the light, still soothing in tone. The woman obviously understood the adrenaline high that made trigger fingers jumpy.

Lina forced herself to sit still and not shrink back into the shadows as the woman approached slowly, holding the lantern high. It illuminated their small encampment, shining on first James and then Lina.

Lina glanced around in bewilderment. The rest of the Confederates had melted into the shadows, unseen. The slight woman waited patiently, her eyes moving over the area curiously. Her clothes were the color of the tan rocks around them, and her hair was cropped around her delicate head, her face narrow and thin.

Dark eyes of an indeterminate color fell on Lina, and the woman smiled hesitantly. Lina returned the smile, her own heart pounding heavily as she waited for what would happen next. Was this a trick; a trap to draw the men out? How many were out there, unseen?

Where *were* the men?

James' loud breathing reached her, each breath sounding more painful than the last. Lina shuffled over to him carefully, afraid of making any quick movements. Sitting down beside the wounded man, she did the only thing she knew to help.

She held his hand.

Another dimly lit figure stepped into the limited circle of light. She recognized Jay and her heart slowed slightly.

"Explain who you are and how you came to be here."

The woman turned to face Jay, her features unreadable.

"I am from a town south of the river. My people are the Mustangs; the ones who attacked you are the Pumas. We've been enemies for several generations. I—" The woman broke off as James' gasping became louder, each breath laborious.

"He doesn't have much time left. There is air in his chest cavity that has collapsed his lung. I know how to help him; I come from a line healers."

Lina gripped James' icy hand, his labored breathing painful to hear. She couldn't see Jay's expression in the dark.

"If he dies, you die." When he finally spoke, his words and tone sounded alien from the normal easy-going drawl she had become accustomed to. Right now he was not the soft-spoken Aggie or the sarcastic Southerner. He was the deadly agent, and she had no doubt he would do as he promised.

"May I ...?" The woman indicated something she'd left behind.

"Lina, get her bag." The barked command made Lina jump, and she gently set James' hand down, hurrying to do his bidding. She stumbled several times in the dark before seeing the brown bag, like an old world briefcase, resting against a boulder. It was surprisingly heavy. She hurried back, handing it carefully to Jay.

He kept his weapon trained on the woman as he pawed through it quickly, handing it back to Lina and nodding. Lina offered it to the woman.

"Thank you, dear," the woman said absently with a half-smile, accepting the bag and walking slowly towards James' gasping form.

Lina smiled slightly, as well. The woman couldn't be more than ten years her senior, but acted as if she were much older. Lina hoped she would find the same sense of control that this woman exuded by the time she reached thirty.

The woman worked quickly once she reached James, pulling tools out of her bag and setting them down carefully.

"I'm Lina. The injured man is James." Lina glanced for a moment at Jay. He could introduce himself. "Please tell me if I can assist you in any way," Lina offered quietly, unable to remain silent any longer. It just felt terribly rude, and her breeding would not allow it. *No matter the situation, there is never a reason to forego good manners.* Her mother's words; her first teacher.

"Thank you, Lina. I am Tikka Krumb, of the third

generation. You can call me TK." The woman's voice was soft and soothing as she continued to work.

Before Lina could look away, TK had inserted a straw-like protrusion into James' chest. Lina closed her eyes tightly, turning her head as her stomach rolled. Jay shifted slightly behind them, no doubt ready to stop the woman if she did something he didn't like. She could still hear the woman working, releasing the air from the chest cavity.

"Lina, could you hold this, please?" Lina opened her eyes with dread, but was relieved to see the straw had been removed and TK was holding a bandage in place over the small wound. Lina placed her hand over it as TK indicated, following her instructions carefully as she finished.

When the woman pulled a needle and thread from the bag, Lina finally spoke up.

"We still have liquid skin. I believe it would be easier," she offered, eyeing the needle dubiously. It seemed barbaric to actually sew someone together like a piece of fabric.

"Oh, I believe I had heard of such a thing, even in the Time Before. Please, I would be happy to use that instead." TK carefully replaced the needle and thread. Lina hesitated for only a moment, glancing at Jay's immobile form, before reaching into Stix's medical bag and pulling out the bottle.

She showed the woman how to apply it, watching as the synthetic skin bound the edges of the small wound tightly together. Lina then placed a bandage she had taken from the bag over it carefully.

James' breathing had slowed again, and he seemed to be resting more peacefully.

"Ah, wonderful," TK said with a smile, her narrow face transforming with each relaxing of her features. Lina couldn't help but smile back, feeling a surge of accomplishment at her small role in this. And that she hadn't vomited the last pitiful excuse for a meal she'd consumed.

"He's going to need rest. His blood oxygen is undoubtedly low. I could send a few of my cohabitants—"

"No," Jay interrupted rudely. "Your help is appreciated, but we don't want or need anything more. Except information."

TK nodded, packing away her things, her bony fingers caressing each piece as she tucked it away neatly into the leather case.

"What do you wish to know?" she asked, her voice still even, soothing.

"Tell me about your people, about the people in the caves, and if there are any other crazies around here we'll have to deal with."

"'Crazies?' Yes, I can see how one of your technological world would view us in that light. I myself wonder how we have come to this point in a mere hundred years," TK said musingly, folding her hands. The lantern continued to flicker, seeming even brighter now that Jay had turned off his headlamp, used during the ministrations to James. Lina found the woman's calmness in this charged situation a little strange. Was she used to this? Was she just mentally unstable?

The slight woman *had* saved James' life, so she couldn't be a complete lunatic. Her gaze traveled nervously to Jay's shadowy features. It was almost impossible to see his expression in the darkness that pressed in from all sides. Jay hovered at the edge of the tiny circle of light, his normally relaxed figure taut and ready.

"How did your people come together after the wars?" Lina asked to fill the silence.

"We were already together; we lived in the same small town we do now. A few new inhabitants trickled in after the war, but we've kept to ourselves. Our small numbers helped keep casualties low after the EMP blasts took out everything electronic.

"The Pumas lived in the neighboring town. According to the stories passed down to me from our elders, our towns, like many across the old US, lost many able-bodied adults to the war. That left behind the young and the old to rebuild.

"The old had knowledge, and the youths were brave. But impetuous." TK shook her head in the dark as if she remembered their actions personally. "They started the battle with the Pumas that still lingers today."

"How so?"

Lina started at the unexpected question from Jay, engrossed in the strange woman's story.

TK sighed deeply. "Our towns were rivals for years in the Time Before. Enemies on the field became enemies *in* the field."

Lina was confused. "I don't understand. Enemies on the field?"

"Football," Jay answered. "An old world game played by most small towns across the US. Rivalry could be intense in some towns."

"Precisely." TK nodded approvingly in the dark. "Looking back, the beginning of the hatred was stupid teenage pranks that escalated. Arguments over food, cattle grazing areas, water…we could have worked together, but there was too much animosity. The wars let petty dislike escalate into a never-ending battle that has resulted in many deaths over the years."

"No offense, but that sounds ludicrous. And you've named your tribe after animals?" Lina was both fascinated and horrified by the tale.

"Yes, they were the symbol of our towns in the Time Before. Mascots, they were called."

Lina nodded, thinking of the white stag on Alba's flag, representing peace.

"I believe we are digressing. Where are these Pumas located, and what kind of threat do they pose?" Jay interrupted impatiently.

"They live in the caves in the mountain you just attacked. After the EMP strikes, they isolated themselves to conserve their resources. Every overture we've tried to make over the years has been rejected; our last scout was sent back minus one hand."

Lina felt her mouth drop slightly. Who lived like that? No wonder Albans were discouraged from leaving the city, if these kind of savages were running around outside.

"Will they seek us out and attack?"

TK nodded, her serene features becoming concerned. "I don't know what their numbers are, but the isolation, and possibly a few generations of inbreeding, have twisted their minds. Their children have been taught to hate technology in any form. It has become almost a religion, I fear. They will seek you out because you've brought strange inventions, and if I can find you, they surely will."

"Was the signal jammer theirs?"

TK's brows scrunched in consideration. "Possibly. They will do whatever possible to keep —"

A loud scream in the distant hillside had Lina jumping to her feet, tripping as she scrambled towards Jay, nearly falling into him. He grabbed her arm, pulling her upright and off to the side, keeping his weapon steady the entire time.

"Goddamn, woman, relax." Jay's hand belied his harsh words, running gently down her back as he released her.

Lina's panicked gaze went back to where TK watched her curiously.

"Just a cougar, dear."

Lina's heart slowed slightly as she nodded, feeling stupid. She moved away from Jay's side with reluctance. As much as she hated to admit it, even to herself, he made her feel safe in this terrifying new world she had been thrust into. This world full of strange people and frightening tales.

She'd never liked scary bedtime stories, particularly not now when she was in the middle of one. Settling back down, she pretended to check on James, letting her dark, matted hair fall in front of her face to conceal the flush staining her cheeks.

"Anything else useful?"

"We have a guarded bridge not far down the river; you can cross safely. They have never crossed the river, at least not as long as we know."

"And what do you want."

TK smiled in the dim light of the still-flickering lamp, revealing crooked yet white teeth. The light was getting slowly weaker as whatever substance they were burning diminished. "Yes, nothing is for free, hmm? We all have ulterior motives."

Lina glanced up at Jay. He would know that better than most, she thought bitterly. He didn't even look at her, his shadowed eyes fixed on TK as she sat calmly, hands lightly clasped. He was waiting, his poker face in place. But TK was a good match, looking as if she was just settling down for afternoon tea with a friend.

"We want your technology."

Lina gasped. How could they know about the Technology? She'd only just learned of it herself.

Jay finally glanced at her, his look warning her to remain silent.

"What technology?"

"Medical technology, preferably. Any weapons you would be willing to part with; even a communication device that might allow us to reach distant settlements. To learn more about the changing world around us."

Of course. They didn't know about the Alban Technology.

"We have very little on hand, and what we have, we need. You would have more luck with the Albans following us."

"Yes, they were quite impressive during the battle. Unfortunately they disappeared after you did and we have been unable to locate them. You were easier to find, with your injured man and…larger group."

Jay's expression was resigned as his gaze flicked over at Lina. She glared back. How dare he blame her? She followed each order; it was his fault for bringing a Patrician who had never left Alba with him on a hike across the mountains.

"Lina, give her your earrings." TK opened her mouth to protest as Jay continued, "You can use them to bargain with the Albans. Send a scout. It's only a few days trip from here. They'll add you to their outpost route, I have no doubt. They give their outposts electricity, access to clean water, Com devices they call holoreaders, and even protection. It'll be worth the trip.

"Just don't tell them you helped us escape," he added almost as an afterthought.

"How do you know all that?" Lina asked as she removed the simple gold earrings in a stylized *L*, handing them over to TK.

"You'd be appalled at what I know that you don't, *diosa*," he drawled, the familiar sardonic gleam back in his eyes. Lina narrowed her eyes in response, bristling at the endearment that seemed more of an insult.

Jay became serious, looking back at TK. He pressed the screen on his watch, swiping a few times before glancing back up. He must have signaled to the others, for a few moments later the men appeared just beyond the circle of light.

"We're following Miss Krumb here to a bridge. Stay alert."

"Oh, call me TK, please," the skinny woman murmured as she rose. Her calm, easy movements and quiet words seemed to relax the men slightly, but Lina now saw the woman's eyes were busy studying, watching, and cataloguing what she saw.

They quickly put together a makeshift stretcher for James, Thomas and Royce hoisting the unconscious man carefully between them. Stix was nowhere to be seen. Lina opened her mouth to ask Jay about the missing man, but he stopped her before she could get a word out, pushing her in front.

"Ladies first, *diosa*. TK." His gaze warned her to remain silent. She nodded, finally understanding. Stix must be hanging back as cover for them; a surprise element they might need.

Jay obviously didn't trust this woman, even though she seemed harmless. Lina was beginning to learn that everything was uncertain out here in the strange world beyond the walls of Alba. She supposed that survival did things to people; it made them act in bizarre and even inhumane ways.

Or it made them into their baser selves. Perhaps they were even more in touch with the animal within than their technological counterparts.

After her experience with Jay, Lina had learned that the illusion of trust was dangerous. She certainly couldn't trust her own instincts. Not when it came to people. Certainly not when it came to men.

Look where that had gotten her, after all.

Jay walked behind Lina, watching her stumble along the rocky terrain. The elegance of her curvy form seemed almost second nature, but it was all an illusion. The woman had no coordination. He stepped forward quickly, catching her as she slipped once again. He smiled at her quietly murmured "Thank you."

It was damn cute how she was so proper, no matter how scared or pissed off she was.

Pushing aside his foolish thoughts, he turned his gaze to their leader.

The woman who called herself TK walked in front of Lina, moving easily over the terrain, obviously used to traversing it.

He didn't trust her. She made too much effort to appear harmless and accommodating. Was she leading them to a trap? She obviously had her eyes on their weapons, no doubt to continue their war with the group they called the Pumas.

The last thing he wanted to do was get caught up in some petty battle between two meaningless groups out here in this godforsaken region.

He was already feeling the pressure to get the

Technology back. *Your father would have left James behind*, a tiny voice sneered. He rolled his shoulders, shrugging off the thought. He only kept James because they might need him, and he had too much pride to leave a man behind on a mission.

It had nothing to do with the fact that Thomas was his friend, and against his better judgement, had talked him into taking his little brother along on this mission. James was eager and willing to follow orders, but didn't have the experience for this kind of mission.

Just another pebble of guilt to add to his growing mountain.

He glanced down at the heat tracker scope on his weapon. The two other unseen people who had been with TK continued to shadow them. TK had briefly introduced the young man and woman, both armed with only a crossbow. Those archaic weapons were no match for their modern arms, but if caught off-guard, they might be able to take out one or two of his men, particularly with James hurt and Lina to protect.

He checked again. Stix was still in position, just behind the two.

Jay thought he caught a glimpse of the fabled bridge ahead, a dark spot against the pale sheen of water under a nearly full moon. He motioned to his men to be on alert as they approached, his own eyes continually scanning the blackness around them. The men walked slowly, barely visible in the single headlamp Jay wore to illuminate their hike.

The scuff of a foot and a tumbling rock had all weapons swinging to the left, Jay instinctively moving to step between the unseen threat and Lina's frozen form.

He stood unmoving, listening. Lina's slender fingers gripped the back of his camo, but she remained silent. She was a survivor; he never would have guessed from the girl he had known in Alba that she'd make it this far so well.

"Jinx? Is that you?" TK called softly.

"Yes," a reply finally came from behind a grouping of rocks.

"It is safe to come out. These people are with me. I've promised them safe passage. Jill and Timothy are behind us; they'll wait with you until your shift is over."

A boy slowly stepped out from behind the rock, probably about fourteen. In the tiny glow from his headlamp, Jay could tell this boy had seen a lot in his short years. His face was thin like TK's, almost gaunt, deep shadows giving evidence to the deep hallows of his features. The boy's eyes gleamed in the light as Jay studied him for a long moment, wary and watchful.

These people were scrappy survivors. A little desperate, which made them dangerous and unreliable. The feeling of unease elevated to genuine concern. If they were going to make a move, it would be soon.

Jinx led them slowly down the embankment to the bridge, a small wooden structure only large enough for a person to cross single-file.

Clever, Jay thought as the boy lifted both flags that were in the posts on either side of bridge, waving them in an intricate sign language. Jay guessed they changed their signals regularly to keep their enemies from learning them.

They waited, and a second figure appeared, returning the signal.

Jinx motioned them to cross. TK thanked him, walking onto the bridge and motioning them to follow.

Lina hesitated, her eyes wide and luminous in the light from his lamp.

"Go. I'm right behind you," he said in a low voice, gently giving her a push. He motioned to Thomas and Royce carrying James to go first, then Lina followed. "We've got one more man coming. Let him cross. He'll give you the code 'Condor'." After the boy nodded his understanding, Jay clicked his light off, waiting a moment for his eyes to adjust to the darkness before following.

They were all on the bridge when the Mustangs made their move. Jay had been anticipating it, and wasn't surprised when TK stopped at the bridge's exit, turning with a knife raised to the thick ropes that bound it to the posts.

"I'm very sorry," she said in her kind, careful tone. "But my town is in desperate need of supplies and technology to help us combat the Pumas. We just can't fight them, losing a few people every year. We're slowly becoming extinct. I'm going to have to take all your weapons and supplies, or cut the bridge."

Jay sighed. Damn. He'd hoped they could pass through peacefully.

Nothing was ever as easy as it should be.

He glanced around quickly, cataloging the situation and determining his course of action. Stix would be getting into position now.

"Sure. We just need to pass through and get to our meeting point," Jay said reasonably, keeping his voice even. He could see Lina's white-knuckled grip on the rope railing even in the dark.

"Don't touch any weapons," TK warned, her voice getting a little sharper with each movement Jay made. Two more figures stepped out from behind the wooden wall built along the other bank. A quick glance had him dismissing the two guards as a threat, each armed with only a long bow and several knives. They, too, had the look of hunger about them.

Jay kept his hands out to the side, not wanting to scare them into shooting.

"This is your last chance to back down," he said quietly as TK motioned Jinx to come and begin taking Jay's weapons. Jinx hesitated at the lethal tone in Jay's low voice. His hand moved forward slowly again.

"Don't do it, kid, or you're dead." Jay glanced back at the kid, knowing the moment he touched one of Jay's weapons, Stix would fire.

"Please stop," Lina spoke up quietly, her eyes wide with panic. "You don't understand. You can't win here."

TK's gaze faltered, the knife in her hand shaking slightly. They were terrified. Jay pressed his advantage.

"She's right. She's a captive from Alba. You don't want to get involved in what is going on between the Southern Empire and Alba right now. Trust me, stealing from us will not solve any problems, it will just create new ones."

"Yes." Lina affirmed everything he said, the pure desolation of her tone another pebble of guilt in Jay's ever-growing collection. But it also got through to TK, and she slowly lowered her knife, nodding to Jinx. The boy stepped back, and a moment later, a quick arc and pop charged the air, the blast hitting first Jinx and the woman holding the long bow at ready.

"No!" Lina gasped, her anguished eyes meeting Jay's pleadingly.

"They're not dead," Jay told her, letting his voice carry to the others. "But everyone will be if you don't all stand down."

TK dropped her knife, putting her hands in the air. The others still standing all followed suit, their gazes ranging from fear to helpless rage.

They made it across without incident. The Mustangs remained frozen as they crossed. He didn't realize he was holding his breathe until he stepped onto the other side, the tension in his neck alleviating slightly as they moved behind the sad excuse for a blockade.

Thomas and Royce lowered James, checking his pulse.

"Still weak, but steady."

Jay nodded, looking to TK. "You made the right choice." He wanted to say more, but instinct warned him to move on quickly.

TK's serene features were pinched, and Jay motioned to his group to keep moving. Where the hell was Stix? He didn't want to give these people any more time than they already had to organize another attack.

Lina watched him, her own eyes going quickly to TK's sour expression in the low light from the single lantern hung in the guard post. Was she considering them as possible rescuers?

Another glance at her features, aristocratic lines emphasized by the deep shadows, told him she was just as nervous about these people as he was.

But she obviously couldn't help feeling sorry for them. He shook his head, knowing what she was going to do even before she did it. Reaching into her pack she held out several of the remaining protein bars, as well as her light that had a renewable energy cell.

"Thank you. I'm sorry we can't offer you more." Her voice was quiet; sad. TK met her eyes, nodding slowly, her features softening slightly. She took the offering and stepped back.

Lina didn't look at Jay as she followed the men with their burden between them. She walked beside James, and Jay was surprised to realize she was attempting to shield the injured man's body from a possible attack.

Turning back, he cursed with relief as he saw Stix coming across the bridge, fast and low.

"They're comin'; those barbarian sons of bitches found our camp and high-tailed it here. Right behind me and closing fast," Stix muttered to the small group, his eyes on the pitiful guard post and poorly armed guards manning it.

"Better cut your bridge now," Jay told TK as Stix headed after their small group. He hesitated, knowing they were unlikely to survive a battle tonight because of their wounded.

Not my problem. They had their own motives. They took a calculated risk and it might cost them.

Unconsciously he rolled his shoulders to shrug off the guilt, his father's training still clear in his mind. *Kindness can leave you open to manipulation. It is a weakness you can't afford...*

He turned away, staying watchful as they melted into

the darkness that would soon lighten as morning approached. They weren't far before he heard shouts and saw a small fire slowly growing. The guard post, no doubt.

Lina stopped, her gaze fixed on the fight behind them.

"Keep moving," he murmured, grabbing her shirt as he passed, pulling her alongside him.

"Jay, they helped us. We can't just—"

"They made a choice. The Technology, my mission, is my only responsibility."

A quick intake of breath told him Lina was about to argue, but she remained silent, dispelling the air slowly in a sigh. He almost wished she would argue. Her silence was more damning than any protests he could have logically refuted.

He pushed her ahead of him, probably a little harder than necessary, rolling his shoulders again to relieve the twinge he could never seem to shake.

He was his father's son, all right. He'd have made his old man proud today. The knowledge did nothing to lift the heaviness in his chest.

Kindness is weakness. And he couldn't afford to be weak.

He stopped, listening to the distant shouts from the uneven battle being waged behind them. His eyes stayed on Lina as she glanced back continually, her expression hidden in the darkness. He didn't have to see her expression to know what she was thinking.

Condemning him. Worrying about the people she'd only just met.

"Goddamnit," he muttered. He couldn't disappoint her; couldn't be the cold man everyone thought he was.

"Stix, come with me. The rest of you, keep moving. We'll catch up."

"Boss?" Stix asked quietly as they headed back towards the brightly burning guard post a half mile behind them.

"We're just going to even the odds a little bit."

"But you never get involved in local issues —"
"We are today."

7

The small group stood on the mountainside, looking down on the former city of Reno. Jay and Stix had easily taken care of the attackers, the element of surprise and their advanced weapons giving them the upper hand this time. They'd caught up with the group just before dawn.

James had gained consciousness that morning, although he was still weak. He was awake long enough for Thomas to jokingly tell him it was a good thing James' scrawny ass had been injured, because he wouldn't have been able to carry Thomas. James had smiled weakly, but pain shadowed his eyes.

The men had alternated carrying him between them, making the going slow. It was now late afternoon, and the day had warmed considerably. The scent of warm rock floated on the breeze.

"It's so...intact." Lina looked out over the city, the buildings lonely and vacant. The former concrete and steel had been overtaken by the green power of nature. But there was no damage here like most of the cities and towns they had passed. Some broken windows, rusted metal, and the wear of time was all that Reno displayed.

"Extraction is on the plateau to the left." Stix indicated a nearby rock formation. The hot breeze blew Lina's dark hair, and she impatiently brushed it back. It felt so gritty and disgusting, she wondered if she would ever feel clean again. "A few hours is all it should take."

Thomas and Jay settled a sleeping James at the extraction location. Lina sat in the sun atop the plateau, looking out over the land stretching below. Jay walked over, casting his shadow over her, making her shiver as the sun's warmth was momentarily eclipsed. He dropped beside her, eyes on her averted face.

"Still hate me?" he asked, tucking her rebellious hair behind a small ear, his hand lingering a moment longer than necessary.

"Yes."

He smiled at her response, a real grin that lightened his eyes without their normal sardonic edge.

"You wound me. After all my efforts to keep you alive, and see to your every comfort—" Lina snorted at that, her hand going to her bandaged side that ached, particularly after the long morning hike. "—I'd think you'd be over that little issue of me neglectin' to tell you who I was."

Lina waited for the fury to erupt in her breast, but could only muster a bitter pang. Either she was that exhausted, or the sharp sting of betrayal was beginning to alleviate slightly. Jay was an ass, no doubt, but there was another side to him that slipped out when he wasn't trying to be the champion everyone thought him to be.

"What is going to happen … when we get there?" she asked.

He followed her gaze to watch the men combing the ghost city for anything interesting. Or dangerous. "I'll bring your technology to the President. My mission will be completed. I'll go home."

"And me?"

Jay opened his mouth, then closed it. Finally, he said, "I don't know."

Lina nodded, unable to keep a single tear from trickling down her cheek. If she had been looking for reassurance, she'd get none from him. And she could face the reality of the situation; the reality that had been weighing on her since the moment she'd realized she was a captive of the enemy.

Once the Technology was safely in the Empire, she'd no longer be necessary as a shield against the Albans. Perhaps they'd kill her, or keep her prisoner indefinitely. Would she ever return to Alba? A wistful thought arose before she could stop it: *Had there ever been a moment when she'd been more than just a mission to Jay?*

Her pitiful thoughts were scattered by the sudden hiss of Jay's breath through his teeth. He didn't meet her gaze, his jaw clenched as he stood stiffly, large shoulders shrugging as if he needed to loosen up.

"Enough with the self-pity. Stop being a damn victim and take some ownership of your life," he burst out. Lina shrunk back at the unexpected attack. She *was* a victim here. A captive, pulled away from her home and family, used as a pawn in this dangerous game between battling nations.

How dare he question her right to feel sorrow? Her brother was dead, she was injured and abused, helpless…

Then the truth of his words hit her chest like a blow, stealing the indignant breath from her.

He was right.

She *was* feeling sorry for herself. Had been her entire life, in fact. For having an abusive father. For growing up in a broken family. For losing Stephen. For being a captive and leaving everything she'd known. For trusting the enemy.

He was right.

She'd been playing a victim perfectly, dismissing her ability to make choices—to alter the course of her life—without a second thought. By being a victim, she was forcing others to make the tough choices for her. It was an escape. Cowardice.

The bitter taste of shame again rose in her throat, but this time, she swallowed it down. No, she was done being ashamed.

She'd been stupid. Foolish. She alone had made these choices, and now she needed to fix it.

She might not have bold courage, or a persuasive tongue, but she was smart. Smarter than most people, including herself, gave her credit for.

The world around you is changing. Why can't you change, too?

She didn't have to be a victim anymore. The insecurities, the self-doubt, could stay here on this plateau. Her eyes followed Jay as he stood, the angry lines of his body moving him quickly away.

She didn't blame him. She was equally disgusted with herself.

She wasn't sure what her mother would tell her a proper Patrician should do, nor what someone like Aerina would do, but she knew what *she* could do.

Did she have the courage to do it?

Jay stalked off, his anger even greater because, dammit, he felt bad. He shouldn't have yelled at her. He knew she was scared, and none of this was her fault. She'd trusted him, and he'd used her.

And he felt like shit.

There. He'd admitted it. But it didn't mean anything. It wouldn't change anything. He was still going to complete his mission.

He never should have taken her. He'd tried to justify it, to himself and his men. The truth was, he could have left her behind. They didn't need a hostage; they probably could have moved faster without her.

But in the adrenaline high of the moment, when he'd had the Technology vial in his hands, and Lina unconscious at his feet, he found he couldn't leave her behind.

It was insane. Stupid. But he was done lying to himself. He'd told Lina to face the truth, when he himself had been hiding from it.

How could such a woman get under his skin so quickly? What was it about her that was so compelling he'd risked everything to keep her close?

She was attractive, but he'd been with better looking women. She was the opposite of the women he was normally drawn to—quiet, insecure, compassionate. He should feel nothing but disgust for her.

Only he felt a lot more than that.

He'd known that first night when he'd given in to the urge and kissed her that he'd regret it.

And he sure as hell did. He was surprised his men hadn't given him more shit than they did about bringing her. Stix had seen through his thin reasoning right away; he should have listened to his friend and left her behind in Alba.

His anger had carried him down to the base of the plateau. He looked up, seeing her forlorn, sadly battered figure still sitting where he'd left her.

Hissing a curse, he turned away.

She was more than what she'd first appeared. He could see the fire in her; the intellect she kept carefully under wraps. He didn't know how anyone could go through life being so full of the burden of self-doubt and the desperation to please. Not that it was his business, not that it should matter to him at all, but he wanted her to find some self-respect. Some confidence. She was attractive, obviously very smart, and she could be so much more than she let herself.

He took his time returning, walking through the abandoned city, weapon at ready. He almost hoped he'd encounter something that would require combat; he needed to let off some of the anger. His wish went unfulfilled. Each building, storefront, and housing unit was barren, long ago stripped of anything of value. He idly wondered why the city had been abandoned; why no survivors had taken up residence. The only residents now were wildlife, taking over the buildings as if they had been constructed just for them.

He saw the other men hiking back up the hill and followed, searching for the slender figure he'd left behind. Was she going to be furious? Weeping and hopeless? He dreaded seeing her gentle features twisted with sorrow and shame.

He would apologize for his earlier words, and offer to

return her home when this was all over. True or not, it might help lift her spirits.

What was one small lie on top of the many he'd already told her?

No, he told himself. Enough lies. She deserved the truth, no matter how difficult. She might not ever return home, but he would do everything he could to protect her.

Coming from the opposite direction, he cleared the rise before the men. The sight before him had his heart freezing in his chest, shock forcing his limbs immobile.

Lina stood before the gear he'd left on the ridge, the warm wind blowing her filthy, torn pantsuit around the curves she always tried so desperately to hide.

Except she wasn't trying to hide now. For once, her shoulders were thrown back, dark eyes focused, elegant features set with determination.

Her quiet voice carried easily on the wind. "I've been thinking about what you said. You're right. I've been a victim my whole life. Always waiting for someone to help me; for someone else to tell me what I should do. And look where that has brought me." She gestured towards the barren terrain and deserted city surrounding them with a humorless laugh.

"So I'm taking control." She lifted the syringe from the open first aid kit, the vial she'd removed from the cold box at the bottom of his pack already loaded. Before he could take more than two steps forward, the needle founds its way through the nearly translucent skin of her arm and into the dark purple vein. The amber liquid flowed eagerly into her arm.

Gasping, she let the empty syringe fall from her hand. She gripped her arm. Jay absently caught the empty syringe as it dropped to the uneven stone, his other hand going to grip her shoulder. Lina ignored him, flexing her hand, still holding her arm. Her teeth were gritted against the pain as the Technology flowed through her body, binding with her synapses, reading her signals.

Helpless anger filled him until he was nearly shaking, hurling the useless syringe over the plateau's edge. Grabbing a handful of her dust-coated locks, he wrapped them around his hand, pulling her head down.

"Give me one reason why I shouldn't kill you now," he hissed between clenched teeth, giving her hair a vicious jerk.

Tears spurted to the corners of her eyes at the pain, but she met his angry gaze bravely. "Because if you kill me, the Technology will become unusable. Your mission will be wasted. You will fail."

Jay scanned her determined features, disbelieving she'd been so bold. Who the hell was this girl? What happened to the shattered creature he'd left behind only an hour earlier? Shock mingled with outrage. His fist raised, the anger intensifying.

He'd screwed up. He'd underestimated her. And now she wasn't just an inconsequential hostage he could deal with on his own. Now she was important. Important to others besides him.

The entire game had just changed. He'd thought he had it all under control. And now everything had gone to hell.

His looked over at Stix. His friend and second-in-command looked away, not meeting Jay's eyes. He'd known Jay's choice in bringing Lina was stupid, and he'd let it go.

And now Jay was going to be forced to deal with the results of his poor choice. His selfish decision that might cost them the mission. And their lives.

Pushing her to the ground, he let the hand he'd raised drop to his side. In it, his EMW remained unfired. *I should have stopped her; killed her before she injected herself.*

"Oh Lina, I wish you hadn't done that." His voice was barely audible.

"Hell," Stix muttered.

"I wouldn't have thought she'd have the balls..." Thomas said in terrified wonder. The men all knew enough to have respect for the Technology that had altered the world once before. They also knew that she'd now compromised their mission, which put them all in danger. Failure was not an option for Agents of the Empire.

Lina stayed on the ground where she'd fallen, breathing deeply. The Technology was spreading through her body, burning its way through her bloodstream.

"Now what?" Royce asked quietly. "Is there a way to extract it?"

Jay just watched Lina slowly straighten, her dark brown eyes now seeming to gleam with an amber luminescence.

Kindness is weakness. She wasn't his problem anymore. And if he reminded himself of that enough, he just might start to believe it.

"We'll let the President worry about it."

Over an hour later, a quiet hum interrupted the charged silence that had fallen upon the group after Lina's shocking action. They had sat atop the plateau, waiting for the extraction. Lina had spent the time running through the gamut of emotions; euphoria to despair, triumph to regret. She kept clinging to the thought that she had made this choice. She was no longer a victim. Whatever happened, it was going to happen on her terms.

She was never going to be a victim again.

The hum grew louder, and the bee-sized dot also grew. Lina began to sense — no, see — the helicopter's internal computer; the system that ran the machine, the subsidiary controls, the weapons on board, and the network connecting the system to the home base.

She almost couldn't believe what was visible to her mind's eye. Was this possible? It was like she had developed a new sense; a computer sense.

Eyes wide, she accessed the simple back-up system where the passwords and logins were stored. A simple reset and she had gained control of the aircraft.

She held it, hovering, in the distance, the weapon systems locked out.

"What are you going to do, Lina?" Jay asked her quietly. He was the only agent aware of her full capabilities. She met his wary gaze.

"I don't know," she breathed, still in awe over what the Technology was allowing her to do. Her technological training, combined with this amazing Technology, made her feel like a god. A true *diosa*.

Was this how Stephen had felt? Could this be why he had been so eager to attack the enemy?

"What are they waiting for? We've secured the location," Stix grumbled.

"They're not waiting," Jay answered, his eyes still on Lina. "They can't move."

"What do you mean they can't—" Thomas trailed off, following Jay's eyes to where they rested on Lina. "Oh." The large, hot-headed man pulled out a knife and walked purposefully towards her. Even then, she couldn't seem to drum up fear. The awesome power flowing through her body, tingling in her synapses, made her feel invincible. Slowly, she turned on the side weapon of the helicopter, turning it in the direction of their group. It was charged, unlocked, and ready for her command.

"Stop," Jay said, his low command bringing Thomas to a halt. Jay walked forward until he stood directly before Lina, forcing her chin up so their gazes met.

"In this moment, you might have control. But even if you destroy the 'copter, and kill my entire crew, what do you think the Empire will do? Do you think they will tuck tail and run? No." Jay leaned even closer, his voice so soft it was barely audible. "They will come for you, for your city, with everything they've got. They'll destroy everyone and everything that is in their way. Perhaps they'll destroy the Technology, or perhaps they'll get lucky and find it. Either way, you lose. Alba loses. Do you want that on your conscience?"

Lina's eyes widened, the feeling of euphoria fading slightly as reality came creeping back.

"The kind of power you have includes huge responsibility. You're going to need to make some tough decisions, Lina. Are you ready to live with the consequences of your decisions? The results of your power?"

"I'm not going to be a victim any longer, Jay. I will protect Alba." Lina paused, collecting her thoughts. The helicopter humming, the armed men hovering, Jay's close presence…it was all so distracting. "You once said I could trust you. Will your President deal honorably with me? Will I be able to exchange the Technology for the safety of my State?"

The plateau was silent but for the distant whir of the helicopter as it hovered over the ghost city that was Reno. Finally, Jay spoke. "I can't promise anything on behalf of the President. She used to be fair and reasonable, but circumstances have changed her. I can promise that I will do everything I can to help you succeed. To keep you safe, and to keep your Sate secure." His large hands settled on her shoulders as he spoke, his eyes intent, urging her to believe him.

She wanted to believe him; to give over control and let him lead again. But she couldn't. She owed it to the people of Alba, to Stephen. To herself.

Hardening her resolve, she looked away from Jay's watchful eyes. Whatever happened, she would do her best to protect her nation. And be someone Stephen could have been proud of.

"I'll go with you. I'll speak with the President. But the moment I think Alba is in danger, I'll take as much of your Empire apart as I can before I'm stopped. And once I'm dead, the Technology in me will be useless."

Lina thought she saw a gleam of admiration in Jay's eyes as he stuck out one large, callused hand. She took it slowly, his fingers closing around hers tightly.

"We have a bargain."

Part 3 Change

No one truly wins in a war; no one except those who refrain from joining the conflict in the first place. But one truth remains: Mankind is never more brilliant than when devising ways to destroy one another. –From the Journal of Cecilia Delacroix

1

Lina sat quietly, watching in wonder at the Southern Empire passing below her. She knew from her schooling that the Southern Empire dwarfed Alba in size. Alba was, after all, a city-state. A small republic made up of a large city and outlying areas.

The Southern Empire was truly that: An empire. Farms and towns, small urban areas, and larger metropolitan areas passed beneath their aircraft. There was a vast difference between how the people lived; shanty towns sat only a few miles from what appeared to be vast estates surrounded by plush landscaping and manicured grounds.

Even in the segregated terraces of Alba, everyone had nice homes, access to the same quality of food and activities. No one wanted for anything. While her glimpse was brief, what she saw of the Southern Empire was much more like the pre-War states: vast differences in living styles and access to goods and services. Like plantations of the old world's history.

And near the cities and towns, she caught glimpses of their technology, the beautiful computer of her mind probing and exploring the vast networks and strangely familiar circuits.

"How do you fit into the hierarchy here?" she asked Jay, pitching her voice above the whir of the blades. She'd been overly aware of his proximity since he'd settled beside her on the padded bench of the large helicopter.

"The hierarchy?" Jay considered her question, his large form slouched in the seat, crowding her close to the window. She had to admit, if just to herself, there was an odd comfort in having his presence so close. It helped keep the terror of the unknown at bay.

Stix, who sat across from them, gave a half snort, half laugh. Jay kicked him good-humoredly.

"Shut up, you old fleabag." He turned back to Lina. "It's complicated."

Lina remembered Thomas' comment about Jay's special relationship with the President. Did they have a romantic relationship? She felt a frisson of panic, and a twisting in her stomach she refused to call jealousy.

What would happen if he had someone, someone like the President herself, waiting for his return?

She was too afraid of the answer to push further, so she changed the subject instead.

"Your capitol; it is built where old Charleston once was?"

Jay nodded, not looking at her, his eyes scanning the landscape below. His muscled arm rested behind her, the heat from it distracting. She wanted to lean back against it; to rest her head on his shoulder.

But that was impossible. He was the enemy, she a captive. She couldn't let down her guard or she'd be lost.

Be strong. You're just a means to an end for him.

She searched for another neutral topic, desperately needing idle chatter to calm her nerves.

"Do you have any brothers or sisters?" she asked, realizing that even when he'd been an Aggie in her mind, she'd never asked about his personal life.

How petty and selfish she had been. So absorbed in her

own world; her own problems.

Jay finally glanced down, the sardonic gleam back in the blue-green gaze. She was beginning to realize the mocking gleam was self-directed as much as it was directed at anyone else.

"Yeah, a few."

Lina tried not to take his short answers personally. Perhaps he didn't want to talk. She was sure he had a lot on his mind, such as how to explain her presence to the President. And the fact that she now *was* the Technology they had coveted.

Was he still angry about that? Another quick glance at his stubble-covered features convinced her he had other things on his mind.

Stix caught her eye and grinned, his yellowed, uneven teeth fully displayed. Her mouth quirked in response. At the very least, she'd earned respect from Jay's men over her actions. It surprised her to realize they'd been scared of the Technology; uncertain about its power.

She looked in the back where Thomas sat with James, who was again unconscious, now from painkillers fed to him through a drip in his arm. She thought it charming how Thomas was the quintessential big brother; worried about his younger sibling.

Like her own big brother. Her protector, defender, and confidant.

Lowering her head into her hands to hide the tears that caught her off-guard, she let the sorrow flow through her, a reminder of why she was doing this.

A large hand settled on her back, not rubbing, just touching. The warmth from it spread throughout her body, thawing the ice she'd been trying to build around her too-soft heart.

Jay was dangerous, able to easily get under her defenses. She had to tread carefully.

Swiping away the tears, she sat up. Jay still looked out

the window, but his hand remained on her shoulder, his thumb stroking the sensitive skin of her neck. Tiny frissons of electricity traveled from that spot to her entire body, taking her mind to a place she wasn't ready to go.

She should shrug it off; move away. But she didn't want to. Didn't want to wonder about his motives. For this moment, she would take the comfort she could get. Because she didn't know what the future would hold for her.

2

A large city soon approached, and Lina felt like a child on Peace Day, pressed to the glass in awe. Unlike the understated elegance of the Alban terraces, this city was a behemoth of technology and opulence. The Albans, particularly the Patricians, believed in disguising technology in beauty; in subtle touches. They also believed it was crass to display wealth, but instead thought everyone should celebrate experience and education.

The Southern Empire did not practice this. Their capitol screamed of excess. The name fit the city perfectly: New Glory was all about glorifying the Southern Empire and its success as a nation.

Elaborate architecture mingled with expansive gardens; statuary, hedges, and flowers all depicting scenes that Lina was unfamiliar with.

The vehicles lining the busy streets were themselves a testament of the inhabitant's obsession with the ostentatious. Each car was painted and decorated uniquely and quite brilliantly.

Too soon, they were landing in the center of what she assumed was the capitol.

"What is it with capitols and domes?" Jay must have heard her muttered question, because he grinned, the familiar flash of his even white teeth loosening the tightness in her chest. The massive gilded dome of the Southern Empire capitol put Alba's to shame. The entire Alban Capitol building could have fit into the Empire's dome.

As the helicopter touched gently down, Lina's heart accelerated. A greeting party awaited them. Soldiers dressed in the Empire's navy uniforms with the small star symbol of the Empire over their hearts lined on either side of the helicopter. In the middle stood a woman, not much older than Jay, dressed in a more feminine version of the navy uniforms. Surely this couldn't be the President?

Lina studied the woman as Jay helped her out of the helicopter. The woman had light brown hair and unremarkable eyes. Held in the slight moue of disapproval, as they were now, her potentially attractive features looked pinched.

The woman's disgusted gaze moved over the unkempt men and fell on Lina's own sad state of dress. Embarrassment crawled up her spine as the woman turned her nose up.

"I see you've brought back a *native*."

Lina's back stiffened. She could only imagine how she looked in her torn, filthy pantsuit, her hair unwashed with greasy strands hanging limply about her sunburnt face.

Jay grinned, resting an arm casually on Lina's shoulders. One large hand squeezed gently, as if telling her to relax.

Lina allowed the networks around her to draw her in, drowning out the contempt of the woman. They were always at the edge of her consciousness, tempting her with their complex structures and many access points.

"As much as I'd love to stand and exchange pleasantries, we haven't showered in days. We'll get cleaned up and meet y'all in the debriefing room." Jay's drawl had become more pronounced. Where before she had barely noticed the unusual cadence of his words, they now twanged from his mouth easily.

He's a chameleon, she reminded herself. Promises or

not, she needed to be careful.

"Fine, I expect you to be quick. You are already nearly a week behind schedule. The President will not be happy."

So she wasn't the President. Relief flooded in, relieving slightly the pinched feeling in her chest.

"Our esteemed leader rarely is happy. My deepest apologies for my tardiness." Jay's sardonic grin was firmly in place. That particular expression had been absent the past few days; had she been shown a glimpse of the real Jay, a quieter, more relaxed version of the man he portrayed now?

"Your apologies are noted," the young woman said stiffly, her hazel eyes sweeping over Lina one final time before dismissing her. "I'll take the Technology now."

Jay's grin widened, again showing his white, even teeth. "I think I'll just keep it with me. I'll deliver it to the President personally."

The woman's cool façade cracked slightly, her aloof disdain becoming anger.

"Listen to me, Jayden Kane March, keep in mind that I am now head of Defense—"

"Shh," Jay rudely interrupted, putting a hand to the woman's mouth to stop the flow of angry words. "We can talk later."

Pulling a confused Lina behind him, he motioned to his men to follow.

As they entered the massive capitol building, she heard the woman sputtering behind them.

Her eyes eagerly devoured the scene around her. Elegantly stitched rugs covered the floor; vaulted ceilings featured a massive, multicolored chandelier over a grand curving staircase. Rare gems and pre-war art adorned pedestals, carefully lit at intervals in each hall. At the same time, glass elevators hovered buoyantly in tubes, moving at high speeds throughout the building. It was a strange juxtaposition of old world grandeur and modern technology.

Lina still preferred Alba's elegance to this opulence. But

this did serve the purpose of awing the viewer; of making her feel small and insignificant next to the glory of this building.

The networks and systems that whirled in her mind's eye was what impressed her the most. She wanted to stop, close her eyes, and focus completely on the intricate programs, digging deeper to the code beneath.

A young woman approached, smiling genuinely. A bold red suit offset her dark skin and hair.

"Welcome back to New Glory, sir. Let me escort you to the hotel. Please let me know if there is anything you need." Her gaze included Lina in that offer.

"I don't suppose you have any clothes I could change into?"

"Of course, miss."

3

It felt heavenly to be clean. Lina felt as if she'd scrubbed a layer of skin off, but finally felt like a normal human being again.

She stepped into the room adjoining the bathroom. Its luxury matched the rest of the building: plush carpets, a large chandelier hanging in the center of the vaulted ceiling, and heavy furniture with intricate designs.

And the technology. Her mind tingled, and she practiced turning on lights, regulating the shower, even setting ambience of the room to sound like the ocean. Like home.

She wondered how far she could reach. Accessing an administrative login, she mentally wandered through the system, noting the structure; the strengths and weaknesses. The control panel was extensive enough that it would take her a little time to learn the commands, but it was well-designed; intuitive.

She adjusted the air temperature in the building to ten degrees warmer, keeping her own room at the comfortable seventy-two degrees. Then, she did the same for the entire city.

Each building and home, she noted, was connected to the network. She could enter each individual appliance control, or she could control them all at once through the central control panel.

Lina could have happily stayed connected to the networks around her all night, but a loud knock sounded at the door, dragging her back to the present.

Apparently Jay felt right at home, for he entered without waiting for her invite.

He stopped short when he saw her, his eyes widening. They moved slowly over her, and she felt a blush covering every inch of exposed skin in the revealing dress provided by the helpful assistant.

She stood awkwardly as he stared, unconsciously brushing her hair back. She'd seen her own image in the mirror. An unfamiliar face had stared back at her. Tanned, her dark hair with sun-kissed highlights, her curvy form more defined with the bit of weight she'd lost recently. The halter neck of the emerald dress dipped just low enough to reveal the curves of her full breasts, the waist cinching tightly with a wide, dark brown belt the same color as her hair, and following the line of her body to end just below her knees, a slit up her thigh allowing her to move easily.

"It feels strange to wear something besides white," she said finally to break the long silence. Jay managed to drag his eyes back up to hers. He still didn't say anything.

Lina gave a light laugh to hide her uncertainty. "What? Not used to seeing me without layers of dirt and smelling like a wet dog?"

"I think I kind of missed that bedraggled girl. She was damn cute."

Lina rolled her eyes, waiting for him to tell her what

was next. The truth was, without his solidly reassuring presence, she would be terrified and lost. He gave her confidence to face whatever waited outside of the engraved walnut door of her room.

He stood there in the doorway for another minute, tugging on the collar of his own clean dress shirt. Lina had to admit he looked good. Clean shaven, his hair combed back, muscular form in a tailored suit... Yes, her heartrate was up, and it wasn't just nerves.

"Shall we?" he asked, holding out an arm. She took it slowly, trying to ignore the familiar tingling sensation that spread through her at the contact. They walked quickly down the long hallway lit by crystal lamps.

"Is it getting hotter in here?" Jay asked suddenly. Lina smiled, noting the difference between her room and the hallway.

"I'm comfortable."

Jay looked at her, eyes narrowing. "Lina, be careful. The President will not take lightly to any perceived insult."

They had reached large double doors that separated the hotel from the adjoining Capitol. Just beyond the doors was a grand assembly room. Unlike the small meeting room for the Senators at the Alban Capitol, this room was monstrous. Rows and rows of plush chairs faced a tall podium.

Instead of entering the assembly room, Jay turned and headed further down the brightly lit hallway. The young woman that had escorted them to their rooms earlier waited at the open door, a smile still on her face. Her perfect white teeth gleamed against her dark skin.

Lina felt a moment of trepidation. She did not want to enter that room. Jay pulled her along steadily, not giving her the chance to stand hesitantly in the doorway, escorting her into the large office.

The interior of the room was as beautiful as the rest of the Capitol. It was decorated with artwork that was familiar to Lina from holofiles. Old world artwork. A large glass desk with golden edging gleamed near the open glass wall that overlooked the night-shrouded city far below. A cream rug with delicate gold threading offset the dark marble floor.

An older woman, tall and willowy, sat primly at the desk. Uniformed soldiers stood unobtrusively behind her. The pinched-faced woman that had greeted them first stood to the left, and a white-haired gentleman to her right.

"Jay, please introduce me to your … guest," the woman commanded. "I assume she is significant, or you wouldn't have dragged her across the country and brought her to this very important, private meeting." Though her voice was pleasant, Lina immediately noted the hard edge that even the slight drawl couldn't soften.

"Madam President, this is Lina Rhodes, a Patrician from the Republic of Alba. Lina, this is the President of the Sovereign States of the Southern Empire; her Defense Secretary, and General of the Empire's military." Jay made the introductions quickly, almost mockingly. Lina found his near-impertinence strange. Did he not like the President and her entourage? And what about the men's comments about Jay's relationship with this woman?

"Please sit," the President invited, leaning forward slightly. Her hair was pulled back in an intricate coronet, the high collar of her dress revealing pale skin at her throat, the tailored silk hanging elegantly on her slender form.

Jay settled into a gold-rimmed chair that automatically adjusted to match his large size. Lina perched carefully on her own seat, jumping as it moved to fit the contours of her body. The Defense Secretary's eyes glinted with derision. A gleam that was oddly familiar…

"Mona!" she summoned the woman hovering in the doorway. "Check the temperature settings. It seems as if it has gotten much too warm in here." The dark-skinned woman nodded, walking quickly towards the door, typing on a small, translucent device that reminded Lina a little of a holoreader.

"Where is my Technology, Jay?"

"Sitting before you, Ma'am."

"Explain," the President demanded impatiently.

"I have it," Lina said softly, drawing all eyes in the room. "I *am* the Technology."

A long silence followed.

"They've been injecting themselves? *Using* it?" The President seemed shocked. "None of your reports indicated this." Her voice was calm, cool, but Lina could sense the anger building behind the grey eyes that bored into Jay, ignoring Lina. She had the feeling not much caught this woman off-guard.

"That is a new development, I'm afraid." Jay seemed unconcerned over the President's rising ire.

"God help me, Jayden, if you don't start explaining…" The President stopped, composing herself. "Why don't you start at the beginning?"

Jay told an abridged version of the story, thankfully leaving out the strange relationship between the two of them. A relationship she couldn't begin to understand herself.

"So you injected yourself to keep the Technology from me?" The President turned her hard gaze on Lina, finally acknowledging her.

"I did it to protect Alba," Lina replied.

"If you think—" the Secretary began hotly. The President cut her off by raising her hand for silence.

"Your loyalty is admirable. Unfortunately, we still need the Technology you now house within your person. Tell me, my dear, what is to stop us from extracting it?"

Lina met the cold stare of President March with difficulty. Was successful extraction possible? Once bound to her neural network, was there a way to retrieve it? Certainly not without her death…

She needed to make a statement to protect herself, to protect Alba, or this endeavor would be pointless.

It didn't take more than a moment to travel the network and find their energy control. Shutting down the grid was embarrassingly easy. They really should consider better security measures.

The entire city went dark. To add to the effect, she set off their emergency alert system, sirens and alarms going off in the building and could be heard muted from outside the plated glass.

Then the fire defense system was activated, and water began to pour down. It felt good in the over-heated room.

To make sure she had their full attention, Lina engaged several anti-aircraft ballistics near the harbor, their fiery tales trailing behind as they took to the sky. It was an awesome sight in the complete darkness that had fallen over the city. She felt Jay's hands grip her shoulders with bruising force, his low voice in her ear.

"That's enough, Lina. You've made your point."

Lina stopped the impressive display of power, turning on the lights and halting the sirens and water in the same abrupt moment. The ballistics detonated high in the sky, the red-orange shrapnel raining harmlessly down into the harbor.

Lina focused back on the room, feeling almost intoxicated by her own power. It had been shockingly easy to locate each subfolder, to access the security codes, and to issue commands.

No wonder this Technology had nearly destroyed the world. In the hands of a clever sociopath, or a knowledgeable terrorist, it would be devastating.

Lina met the enigmatic gaze of the President. She sat still at the desk, watching Lina with interest, a strange light burning in her pale eyes. She seemed unfazed by the water still trickling down her elegant features.

"Alert the patrols; let them know the situation is under control. Tell them it was an emergency test."

The assistant at the door, who looked fearful and uncertain, turned away to speak into her device quickly. The Defense Secretary's device also began beeping.

"That was quite impressive, young lady," the President

said softly, her eyes going from where Jay still stood half in front of Lina, as if to protect her and threaten her at the same time. The General had his weapon at ready, although he held it loosely at his side. The soldiers in the room stood with their own EMWs charged and open, locked on Lina.

Through it all, Lina hadn't moved from her seat, except when Jay had half-pulled her from it to stop her. She now sat stiffly, her hands clenched to hide their trembling. She was a little shocked at her own capabilities. At her boldness. The Lina that had left Alba would have never dared to threaten a President. Exhilaration and awe pulsed through her, a strange elixir that gave her courage.

"The way I see it, we have three options. You can kill me and start all over trying to find the Technology in Alba. I assure you, it will be much more challenging this time, if they haven't destroyed it completely. Or you can try to extract it, and see how much damage I can do in the meantime. It would be a true display of the Technology's capabilities."

"And the final option?" the President asked, her gaze locked on Lina. She finally had the older woman's full attention.

"We can make a deal. We already share many devices and technology. I don't see why we can't create an alliance between our two nations." Lina was proud the words came out so smoothly. Stephen's face flashed before her, his blue lips and vacant eyes looking up at a smoky sky. The image was forever etched in her memory. Could she really make a deal with the people responsible for her brother's death? With this greedy, power-hungry nation?

"An alliance?" The President leaned back, her gaze flicking over to Jay. Lina also looked over at him, gauging his reaction. He'd sat back down, but she could tell he was stiff; ready to move again. Was he protecting her, or at ready to subdue her if she threatened the city again? Did he approve of her actions? Was he angry? His face was unreadable in the bright overhead lights.

"An alliance," the President said again, as if considering Lina's suggestion. "What authority, beyond the questionable power of the Technology, do you have to offer this?"

"I am certain the current leader of Alba would be willing to consider any option to keep the peace and defend our State." Lina met the older woman's hard gaze unflinchingly. She wanted to look to Jay; to try and determine his thoughts.

The kind of power you have includes huge responsibility ... Are you ready to live with the consequences of your decisions? Jay's warning ran through her mind. He wouldn't help her; he couldn't. She alone was going to have to live with the results of her choices here.

"All right, Lina Rhodes of Alba. I will consider your proposal and send an emissary to the Republic of Alba. Perhaps our two empires can finally become allies. In the meantime, I expect your cooperation. Mona, please escort Lina back to her room."

Lina nodded her acquiesce, rising slowly. She felt self-conscious in the wet dress that clung to her, shivering slightly in the still-warm room. Her eyes met Jay's. The sardonic glint she'd become familiar with had returned. He grinned, nodding his head as if to congratulate her.

Turning away, she followed Mona towards the door. She fought back the panic at being separated from Jay. She couldn't stop herself from glancing back once, meeting his knowing gaze. Straightening her back, she took a deep breath and left the room with as much dignity as her wet dress and slippery heels would allow.

4

"Aerina." Aerina started, turning quickly at the sound of her father's voice. She had spent the evening observing the

Technology Project, her mind still reeling with the information she'd tried to absorb. The power of this old Technology was impressive. She was beginning to see why the creators had hidden it away; how it had altered the world. But was it really best to bring it to light now? She shivered, thinking of such power in the hands of a superpower like the Southern Empire.

Mentally, she was exhausted, but had been unable to sleep. She'd decided to take a stroll to try and relax her overstimulated mind.

Her father stepped into the light of the nearest street lamp, his face more haggard and lined than she remembered. The war with the Southern Empire had taken its toll on everyone in the city. Particularly its leaders. She'd seen the same strain on Marcus' face.

"Father. How are you?" Aerina asked politely, her eyes watchful. Since moving in with Marcus, her relationship with her parents had been severely strained. Her mother refused to speak with her, and her father had distanced himself. Aerina had been doing her best to bridge the growing gap, but their relationship was still tenuous.

As long as she was with Marcus, it seemed they would be on opposing sides. The tension between Marcus and the Senators was well-known, and she knew it looked bad for a Senator's daughter to align with the Alpha Virmortus.

It made her heart feel heavy to know she had to choose between her family and her lover. Since her brother's death, they had never been close. But she'd harbored hope that one day, things would change. Now it seemed like an impossible dream.

"Why didn't you warn me that Trent was going to appoint new Senators?" Her father ignored her attempt at pleasantries, getting straight to the point. His face in the lamplight was tight; furious.

Aerina opened her mouth, speechless. Her mind worked quickly to assimilate the information. Marcus had assigned more Senators? He'd never said anything…

"I'm sorry Father, but I'm not involved in politics —"

"You had better start to concern yourself with politics, young lady, if you are with that Reaper. He's determined to destroy every ideal this State has held for the last hundred years. Did you know he was going to assign Senators from menial castes? He has assigned an Aggie to Society, for serenity's sake!"

Aerina just shook her head, trying to tamp down the anger that began to unfurl. Why hadn't he told her? This was a major decision; a huge change to their State. She had thought he trusted her; that their relationship was developing.

But he'd kept this a secret from her. *He still doesn't trust you*, an inner voice taunted. Trying to ignore the sinking weight in her stomach, Aerina turned away, determined to get the full story from Marcus.

"Aerina! I am not done speaking with you."

Aerina paused, speaking carefully past the lump in her throat. "I don't have any information for you, Father. I'm sorry, you'll have to take this up with Marcus."

"You are the direct descendent of Cecilia Delacroix, one of the founders of Alba and a creator of the Technology Trent stole from the vault. How can you betray your family, your country, for a killer?"

"He is more than a killer," Aerina answered quietly. "And he is our best chance for survival against the Southern Empire."

She walked back towards their villa — *Marcus' villa* — coming up with any number of reasons why he would have kept this from her. All the reasons came back to the same conclusion: He didn't fully trust her.

5

"There will never be an alliance with Alba," the

President told Jay coldly, pacing in front of her desk. Gone was the composed powerhouse. In its place was a damp, furious woman. Everyone had been excused, until only he remained, still seated in the damp chair.

Drying out all the buildings was going to a bitch of a job. He could only imagine the cost from the damages caused from Lina's little demonstration. The anti-aircraft ballistics alone were a huge expense to replace.

He had to give her some credit; her little maneuver had taken some guts. He was still having a hard time believing the insecure girl he'd befriended in Alba was the same woman who had just intimated the President of the Southern Empire, a woman feared by millions.

The little caterpillar was emerging from her cocoon and trying out her wings. He just hoped her newfound confidence didn't cost them all their lives. The President was capricious at best. And at her worst … she'd devour Lina and anyone in her path.

"How could you be so careless as to let her inject the *only vial* of Technology you managed to take?" The President wasn't done with her tirade. Jay settled deeper in the chair, debating about removing his damp suit jacket. The heat was still turned up, courtesy of the little monster he had created in Lina, and even in his wet clothes he was sweating. He could see beads of sweat on the President's nose.

"Why the hell is it still so hot!" she exclaimed mid-tirade, stopping her pacing and looking towards the closed door for Mona.

"Why do you think?" Jay asked, quietly amused.

"That little bitch. Who does she think she is, to try and *bargain* with me? Me, the President of the most powerful empire in the world!" The polite mask was off, and the real evil beneath was showing. This side of the President had usually been reserved for her family, and those who displeased her.

"That's debatable."

"What?" The President swung around, pinning Jay with her angry stare.

Jay sighed. "Madam President—"

"I told you not to call me that when we are alone."

"Sorry, I mean *Mother*, I know why you are so against an alliance with Alba. But Julius is deposed, possibly dead. Don't you think it's time to get over it?"

"That pitiful little civilization was responsible for your father's death. I would think you'd be a little more loyal to his memory!"

"He was a spy. He got caught. What did you expect them to do?"

"You know they didn't just kill him because he was a spy." Marcus' mother looked out over the bright lights of New Glory, her own damp clothes hanging on her thin form.

"I would think the real reason he was caught and killed would make you less inclined to hate the Albans. He was cheating on you with—"

"How dare you?!" She swung around, her arms stiff at her sides, fists clenched.

Jay knew it was time to pacify her.

"I'm sorry. I screwed up. I should have watched her more closely."

The acceptance of blame calmed her, as he knew it would. His mother's face grew composed again, her eyes flinty as she studied him. "She probably batted her big eyes at you, and all you could think about was screwing her. You're just like your weak, worthless father."

Jay sat up straight in his chair, anger rushing through him, but he remained silent. He knew better than to speak when she was in this kind of mood.

"But lucky for you I can take your screw up and hopefully work it to my benefit. Did you know that children born to Technology Users are also Users?"

Jay raised an eyebrow, afraid of where his mother was going to take this. "How do you know that?"

"I've been reading the original creator's journal, Cecilia Delacroix. Your father brought it to me before he was killed. His little whore stole it from the Alban Consul. A child has just as much power as the parent User." She pulled impatiently on the high neckline of her damp suit, pacing slowly to look out over the city that sloped downwards towards the harbor.

"I can bluff my way through the first meeting with the European Alliance, convince Lina to put on a display, and in the meantime, get her pregnant. I'm not certain extraction will even work; it's never been successfully performed as far as we know. But to have a completely dependent User... It will be much easier to run tests on an infant, to determine a way to reverse engineer this Technology. Then we won't need that Alban bitch."

Jay stared at his mother mutely. She'd always been volatile; difficult to please and harsh in her punishment of anyone who crossed her. But had she always been so soulless? His stomach turned to think he was the product of such a monster.

Unaware of her son's disgust, she continued. "I've seen how she looks at you, just like all the women always looked at your father. I doubt you'll have much trouble using that charm of yours to win her over. I'll have a syringe sent over that will counter the effect of the Alban anti-pregnancy vaccination." She studied her son's handsome features with a critical eye. "She shouldn't give you any trouble at all. Just keep her under control, impregnate her, and by next year, we'll be creating Users for our military. I know you'll do what's best for the Empire, just like your father."

Just like your father.

"And if I refuse?" Jay's voice was soft, disguising his revulsion.

"I'm sure I can find other candidates happy to use force, if necessary. She's a very attractive girl; very elegant, if a little too intelligent for her own good." The President's gaze was calculating. Jay tried to hide the burst of anger he felt at the thought of another man putting his hands on Lina. Since that night in the Alban park, she'd been his. Whether she knew it or not.

"Sure. I'll go along with your crazy scheme. But nine months is a long time. A lot can change in that time. And she's going to expect you to attempt to form an alliance."

"I'll humor her for now, and make her think she's getting what she wants. Just see that you do, as well."

6

Darkness had fallen by the time Jay returned to his suite in the Capitol hotel.

No matter how long he lingered in the spray, Jay couldn't seem to shower off the dirty feeling left from his discussion with his mother. Once dressed in dry clothes again, he walked out of the guest room in the Capitol to the one across the hall.

Every moment she'd been away from his side, anxiety had ridden high. He'd promised that he would keep her safe; to look after her.

And he was determined to do just that. Eager to just that, in fact.

Probably much too eager. But to hell with it, he was involved with her in this crazy situation they found themselves. And he didn't plan on going anywhere at the moment. Not without her right beside him.

He knocked lightly, opening the door with a swipe of his ID chip. His clearance allowed him access to most rooms in the Capitol.

The lights in the large room were off, but he could see the bed was empty through the open door to the connecting bedroom. This room was just as luxurious as the rest of the

Capitol, its intent to awe and intimidate visiting officials from other regions and the rare ambassador from other nations.

"Come in." Her quiet voice came from the chair near the window. Unlike the rest of the Capitol, the temperature in this room was comfortable. Lina sat in the large chair, her long legs drawn up under her chin, a light blanket thrown over them.

He walked forward slowly, fighting the familiar urge to take her into his arms. He knew he'd wrecked his chances with her; had known from the start nothing could come of the powerful chemistry between them besides a few mind-blowing bouts in the sack.

It was too bad they'd been limited to just one mind-blowing encounter before he'd made his move. Perhaps a few more times would exercise her from his system and allow his brain to start functioning properly again.

He sat in a matching chair adjacent to her, bracing his arms on his legs.

"Wanna break outta here?" he asked, his southern accent back and more pronounced than ever.

Lina looked at him quickly, her silky shoulder-length hair swinging around her shoulders.

"Is it … allowed?" she asked finally.

"You'll be with me."

"Ok," she agreed hesitantly.

Without waiting for her to change her mind, he grabbed her hand, pulling her to her feet. The blanket fell away and he stared at the skin exposed by the satin bed shorts and camisole she wore, stretched taut over her full breasts. Not hiding nearly as much at it revealed. He swallowed thickly, glancing away.

"You might want to put some clothes on."

"Oh." Lina flushed. "Mona brought these; I wasn't sure… I'll go see what else she put in the closet." She disappeared into the bedroom and Jay collapsed back into the chair, trying to find a comfortable position that would hide his obvious arousal.

Lina came back out a few minutes later in a light pink halter dress that floated around her knees. Jay stood, grabbing her hand again.

"I like you not in white."

Lina laughed quietly, shyly returning the smile. Her eyes scanned his light blue shirt and tan slacks. "I kind of miss your brown uniform."

"You just miss being my boss."

Lina laughed, full and throaty this time. "True."

The sound of her laughter warmed him in areas that weren't just below the belt. Places that he'd kept on ice for a long time.

He tugged her down long hallways until they reached an underground parking garage. It was filled with e-cars that were an example of the Empire's obsession with grandiosity, each color, design, and paint pattern more elaborate than the next.

"Isn't she a beauty?"

Lina stood beside him, looking dubiously at his pride and joy. A red Laferrari from the pre-war era. He'd rebuilt the entire thing himself.

"Does it run?"

He groaned at the question. "Of course it runs. A little high octane—"

"It runs on gasoline? Isn't that a petroleum derivative?" Lina's voice dripped disapproval.

"Just get in," he ordered, hitting the button to slowly lift the passenger door. Lina gingerly slid into the low car. Jay solicitously helped her, letting his hand linger on the soft skin of her upper arm before shutting the door behind her.

Anticipation lit his features like a graduate after Final Examinations as he slid into the driver's seat, his hands lightly caressing the wheel before pressing the ignition button. The car growled to life, the engine's throaty rumble idling for a moment. Lina looked over at him with a small smile, her brown eyes alight with amused resignation. She knew what she was in for.

They shot out of the parking space, slowing at the guard gate at the exit.

"Sir," the guard nodded respectfully at Jay while his eyes remained on Lina. "May I ask what you are doing?"

"Following the President's orders."

The guard looked again at Lina, then nodded, opening the gate.

Jay accelerated quickly, his turns tight and neat as they cruised out of the parking garage and onto the brightly lit streets of the vast metropolis that was New Glory.

Jay felt the familiar rush he always got from driving this beautiful old machine. Unlike the modern e-cars that were quiet, efficient, and could drive themselves, this machine screamed of power as he weaved amongst the slow-moving vehicles on the road.

He glanced over at Lina. She was looking at him as if seeing him for the first time, a smile still on her face. A flush spread on her cheeks and she looked away, biting her lip. Energy of a different kind crackled in the car, heating up the air between them.

"Your city is quite … impressive," she broke the charged silence, her eyes watching the towering skyscrapers pass by. They approached the ramp to a massive bridge that would take them across an inlet from the Atlantic Ocean. Warm air blasted from vents, fighting the cool night breeze that whipped through the open windows.

They zoomed over the steel bridge that provided both function and art. He slowed as they approached a gate on the other side, scanning his wrist for admittance. Lina rubbed her own wrist where the deactivated ID chip still sat. Jay caught the action, grinning at her. He held out his own hand, showing the small ID chip resting in it, attached to a chain.

"Took mine out the day I became an Agent."

He pulled through the gate, entering a much different

community. This street was wide, lined with trees and well-kept hedges. He turned into another gated drive, scanning the chip again.

He drove more slowly here, watching Lina's eyes widen at the vastness of the estate. The long drive wound through gardens, past a pond complete with multi-color fountain, and up to the massive house.

"What is this place?" she asked in awe.

"Welcome to my home."

7

Aerina paced the villa, the former exhaustion gone as her mind worked through different ways of confronting Marcus.

She was mid-pace when his quiet voice made her jump.

"I can see you already heard about the change in the Senate."

Whirling to face Marcus, Aerina' carefully planned words scattered.

"Why didn't you tell me?"

Marcus watched her, his dark gaze unreadable. Her anger rose another level at his silence. He stood just in the kitchen, thick arms crossed over his chest, legs braced apart. His battle-ready stance.

"Well?"

His eyes narrowed. She knew he still wasn't used to blatant disrespect from anyone, even her. Too damn bad. She was too angry—and if she were honest, too hurt—to remain calm.

"I knew you had a lot on your mind, with Lina still gone and Helen's pregnancy. I didn't want to put you in an uncomfortable position with your father."

"Did you think I would tell him?" she asked hotly,

unappeased by his answer.

"No, I didn't think you would tell him, and frankly, I didn't think you needed to know."

"You thought I didn't need to know?" she repeated incredulously, her anger rising another notch. Her hands curled into fists that she wanted to pound against his stubborn chest. "Why? Because I'm not involved in politics, which is a consequence of being in a relationship with a Reaper? Or because I'm just your lover; someone you sleep with, and not a trusted confidant like Ramus? Tell me Marcus, because I'd really like to know where exactly I stand with you." The pent-up insecurities poured out of Aerina's mouth. She watched Marcus' face tighten, his already unreadable expression becoming more distant with each accusation.

Part of her wanted to draw the words back, but greater was her need to bring everything into the open. She wanted a fight.

Marcus wasn't going to accommodate her. Without a word, he turned and went into the bathroom. A moment later, she heard the shower running.

Unable to stand another moment in the same villa, she slammed out the door, her angry strides carrying her quickly down the darkened streets of the Capitol Terrace.

An hour later, she was still too angry to return. She went to the one villa she knew would be open to her. Knocking a little guiltily, she waited. The door cracked open.

"Aerina! What are you doing here so late?" Helen's pale face scrunched with concern.

"I'm sorry to bother you, I just didn't … I didn't know where to go." Tears began to fall of their own accord. Aerina swiped them away angrily. Stupid to be so upset about this. She wouldn't blame her friend if she told her to go home and sleep in the bed she'd made for herself. But Helen opened the door wide and waved Aerina inside.

"We might as well be miserable together," she said. Aerina laughed through her tears, hugging her friend. Helen stood stiffly in the embrace, patting Aerina awkwardly. "You'll be the first person to sleep in my guest room."

Aerina glanced around Helen's new villa. She'd gotten it the same week she'd accepted the offer from the Senator of Law to become a representative for the Legal Sector. Just what she'd always wanted.

"Have you told anyone yet about the baby?" Aerina asked, following Helen to the small kitchen. She was glad to focus on something besides her own petty relationship issues. Helen selected tea for them both from the Dispensare, remembering Aerina's preference for honey and milk.

"No. I want to wait until … until it's a sure thing. I just started taking the hormonal injections that counteract the anti-pregnancy vaccine, and I wasn't sure if it would affect the baby." Helen's hand went instinctively to her still-flat stomach. "Enough about that. How is Lina doing with her treatments?"

Aerina hesitated, remembering her own anger at being left in the dark about important issues.

"To be honest, I didn't really tell you the whole truth about Lina. No one but Marcus and his team knows this…"

Helen nodded her understanding, her pale green eyes narrowing curiously as she waited for Aerina to continue.

"Lina was captured by a spy. They came for the Technology Marcus used to save us from the warship. Old Technology. But powerful."

"The Southern Empire?" Helen asked.

"Yes."

Aerina told her about what had happened the night Lina was taken, and how she and Marcus had attempted to stop them but failed.

Helen remained silent, sipping the hot tea to steady herself. She sighed heavily, shaking her head. "Poor Lina. She'll never survive as a captive. She's so timid and gentle."

"We know she made it to the extraction point in the old city of Reno. Marcus had a team following her. They saw her getting into the helicopter. Hopefully she's stronger than we think. Because now the Southern Empire has her and our Technology."

"Will that be the end of it? The end of the war?"

Aerina looked down at her hands clasped around the smooth tea cup, letting the warmth seep in. It did nothing to warm the coldness inside.

"I don't know. I wish we knew for certain what the Empire wanted with it. If they plan to use it as a weapon, it could spark another Global War. One I'm not sure we could avoid."

"The Senators have kept peace in Alba, but they couldn't control the rest of the world. I suppose it was only a matter of time until the population grew again, and humanity's thirst for power and exploration came here."

Aerina nodded. "Yes. I had always hoped the outside world would come to Alba; that it would open our gates again," she admitted guiltily. "But I never imagined it would be like this."

Helen's features softened slightly. "Don't feel guilty, Aerina. You wanted change; an adventure. I know you never wished for people to be hurt. Now," her voice became business-like again, "what is this Technology that you mentioned? That brought the Empire all the way across the continent to our little republic?"

"You recall the history lessons about the wars, and how the new technology was used in the Second American Civil War? The founders of Alba were the creators of this technology. They took the designs and the engineers who worked on the project and disappeared. After the world was destroyed, they created our society, and kept the Technology hidden here.

"I've never seen it, but Marcus tells me there was a journal written by Cecilia Delacroix, as well as the notes from the creators of the technology that detailed everything. Copies are kept in the Training Grounds, and the Consul has passed down the original to his or her heir."

"Cecilia Delacroix was the first Consul. Your great grandmother. Did your father know?"

Aerina nodded, feeling the twinge of betrayal once again. Always on the outside…

Helen watched her face. "He might have told you, Aerina, when you were older."

Perhaps, Aerina thought, although she wondered. She'd never been the daughter her parents had hoped she would become. But she appreciated Helen's words nonetheless.

"Marcus has been studying the Technology and running tests. They call them Users, which is how the old notes referred to them. Stephen and Marcus were both injected before boarding the warship. It was how they destroyed it." Aerina watched Helen's mouth tighten with pain, her green eyes darkening. Sorrow filled her own heart and she reached across the table, gripping Helen's thin fingers. "I'm sorry I didn't tell you sooner. I should have told you everything."

"I understand why you didn't. And it doesn't change anything. Stephen is still dead. And I'll still keep doing the job I am assigned." Helen squeezed her hand back, her voice thin with pain. "What about Lina? Why did they take her?"

"Protection, I guess. The agent that took her used her to force me to hand over the vial. He stabbed her," Aerina's voice cracked as she recalled the terrifying moments when she thought both she and Lina would be killed. "Two Virmortus have followed her to the Southern Empire to track the situation. But without any communication, we won't know what is happening unless they return. I just hope they keep her alive once they don't need her anymore. I feel so helpless, waiting on Marcus to decide what we need to do next."

"I know what you mean. And of all the people to be captured, Lina is probably the least capable of surviving. Poor thing," Helen said again. "She must be so terrified."

8

Lina shrieked as Jay pretended to toss her into the glassy depths of his swimming pool, which overlooked the dark ocean below. With a mischievous gleam, he instead stepped forward with her in his arms.

As the warm water closed over her head, Lina pushed away from Jay's solid form, kicking up to the surface.

After touring his impressive villa—no, *mansion*, she corrected herself—he had invited her to join him for a swim in the outdoor heated pool.

The water had looked inviting, but the banked heat in his eyes had warned her that she would be choosing to do more than just swim.

It seemed safer to keep her distance. The temptation to fall back under his spell was strong. He was being amiable and solicitous, making her feel like the center of his world. This was the same Jay whose spell she'd fallen under the first time. She didn't know how long she could remain strong.

Being true to the new Lina, she'd thrown caution to the wind. And now here she was, nearly naked with the irresistible enemy.

Jay surfaced beside her, sloughing water off his face. The underwater lights slowly changed from blue to the colors of sunset, turning his tawny hair red and making the grooves and hollows of his face more defined.

He didn't look like the enemy right now.

His face became unusually serious, his shadowy eyes meeting hers. Large, callused hands skimmed her sides, down to her hips, pulling her forward slowly, giving her time to move away.

She didn't. She'd known this moment would come since she'd agreed to his invitation.

She wanted him to kiss her; needed him to. *This is*

wrong, a niggling voice warned her. But she couldn't seem to pull away as his lips, wet with the salty pool water, lowered slowly to hover over hers.

"Lina?" He was asking for permission. Forcing her to make the decision.

She closed the gap, her body shaking with excitement and nerves. Her arms went around his neck, and their mouths fused. Desperate heat filled her, and desire pooled low, creating an ache. For a moment they sank below the water as his tongue explored the hollows of her mouth. Still holding her, he kicked towards the side, pressing her up against the clear edge that revealed the ocean below.

He sank down, his mouth moving slowly over her chin, her neck, and moving over the tops of her breasts.

"You're so beautiful, *diosa*," he murmured, his hands skimming the curves hidden beneath the water. The endearment made her back stiffen for a moment, although it didn't sound mocking this time. But as his hands continued to work their magic, the concern melted beneath the onslaught of sensation. She couldn't stop shaking, impatiently pulling him closer, wanting to feel his skin against hers.

The insurmountable concerns of the day faded as passion exploded around her like the weapons in the harbor.

He gave in to her urging, his hands becoming more urgent, his mouth against hers demanding. He removed the bathing suit in a few quick tugs, the strings giving way beneath his expert hands.

His experienced hands, a tiny voice warned. The thought cooled the ardor that had her core burning with need.

Was this part of his plan? Part of his mission?

His hands skimmed lower, brushing the exposed wound in her side that was still red and sore. More alarms went off in her mind, slamming the breaks completely on her desire.

Doubts and insecurities filled her, dousing the last flames of passion.

She began pulling away, pushing at his hands.

"Stop. I said stop!" she shouted at last when he seemed too absorbed to hear her first breathy request.

He shoved back, both breathing heavily.

"What's wrong?"

"I can't do this," she told him bitterly. "I can't let you use me again, no matter how much my body might want it."

His eyes widened slightly, and then she saw his face go blank. The desire, the bit of joy, was gone. The scornful gleam appeared.

"Yeah, I guess we've done this already. It isn't really my style to revisit something I've already had a taste of." The words cut as deeply as he'd intended, and Lina shrunk back into the shadows, grasping at the bits of bathing suit like a shield. Jay turned away, hoisting his large body from the pool in one easy movement. Water streamed from his perfectly sculpted form revealed by the swim trunks. Lina's stomach clenched at the sight, arousal warring with fear. Regret and uncertainty mingled.

What if she were wrong? What if he truly cared about her, just her? Could she enjoy the moment and not worry about his motives? Maybe she should give him another chance. Maybe…

But it was too late. He was already striding away, rolling his shoulders. Shrugging away the memory of this moment. Of her.

9

Jay's temper cooled quickly from Lina's rejection. Most of his anger had been self-directed. He wasn't even sure of his own motives anymore. Was he fulfilling his mother's instructions, or was he just using that as a convenient excuse to get his hands on her again?

Her reticence had been justified. She had every reason to question his intentions. He *had* betrayed her. Hell, he'd stabbed her to steal her nation's prized technology, kidnapped her, and dragged her across the continent. She'd be a fool not to be suspicious of his intentions. And while she might be a little naive and too kind for her own good, she wasn't a fool.

He was just tired of everyone, including himself, thinking he was like his father. A ladies man; an egotistical, self-centered ass.

He decided to mend the situation with Lina, wondering if he'd crushed her tender heart with his parting comment. He felt a rush of panic when he found her room empty, heading back to the pool in long strides. His heart slowed when he saw her tucked under a blanket on one of the outdoor couches overlooking ocean.

"Can I join you?" he asked quietly, making her start. She looked back at him, every emotion she felt clearly communicated by her expressive eyes. Hesitancy, hurt, and desire all warred in their depths.

He felt a rush of triumph that desire won out, and she nodded, moving her legs to make room for him. He slid next to her, close but not touching.

They sat in charged silence, looking out at the dark ocean.

"Don't you ever feel guilty about having all this, while some people in your country have almost nothing?" she asked, her eyes on the impressive yacht anchored not far from his private beach.

He shrugged, dislodging the blanket. He carefully tucked it back around her as he answered. "That's the beauty of capitalism. I can rest easy with the knowledge that I, or someone who supports me, has earned all this. I worked hard for every Empire Credit to my name." His tone was cynical; a little self-mocking. She wondered if he truly believed that.

"Why did you bring me here, away from the Capitol?"

Jay was quiet for a moment. "The President isn't

trustworthy. If I'm going to keep you safe I need to keep you close."

"She's your mother, isn't she?" Lina looked at his shadowy face as she asked, searching his eyes.

"Yes," he answered. "How did you know?"

Lina shrugged against him. "She looks like you, and some of things your men had said… And the Defense Secretary—"

"Is my sister," he finished for her. "Yes, even though this is supposed to be a democracy, there is raging nepotism. My other sister heads the Empire Credit management, and my brother was… Well, it doesn't matter. Democracy is a joke, mostly on the lower classes."

Lina said nothing for a long moment. "Yes, Alba is a little like that, although the lower classes are more equal. No one ever wants for anything. The Patricians don't approve of excess; wealth is considered crass. Balance is very important."

"Yes, I gathered that," he told her. "Even as an Aggie, I couldn't complain. If it wasn't for your mother's roses, I might have liked gardening."

Lina laughed lightly, the sound a gentle balm to the bitterness thoughts of his family engendered.

"What about your brother? You never said…"

Jay didn't want to talk about his brother. Hell, he hated thinking about his family at all. But his brother…

They should have been close, had been so similar in so many ways. Perhaps if he'd been closer, his brother would still be alive. Perhaps he could have stopped it…

He felt a cool hand touch the fist he hadn't been aware he'd been making and he forced his hand to relax, gently tracing the new cuts and calluses on her small, soft one. She shivered beside him, and he knew it wasn't from the cold.

He was burning up, himself. Memories of the unconsummated passion from earlier threatened to steal his concentration, and he shook his head to clear it. He focused on the dark ocean as he answered.

"My brother, like me, was an agent. He never came back from a mission. A west coast mission, actually."

"I'm so sorry. It must have been hard to lose both your father and brother that way."

Jay's mouth quirked in a smile that didn't reach his eyes. "They died heroes, serving the Empire. Mother couldn't have asked for a better campaign slogan if she'd planned it. She was elected that year."

Lina's eyes went wide, and he could tell she was uncertain what to make of his statement. What was he doing? Spilling his guts to this girl like some infatuated youth?

He shrugged his shoulders again, pulling his hand away from hers. "It was a long time ago; nearly a decade. He was on his first mission and probably screwed up. There's not room for mistakes in this career. My father would have been the first to tell him so."

Lina stayed silent, and he refused to look down at her upturned face, keeping his eyes fixed on the coastline below his estate. The estate bought with blood money; from his many successful missions and his mother's power.

Lina finally looked out over the water again, the only sound the light breeze rustling the garden plants and bringing the sound of the ripple of waves on the beach.

As if sensing his discomfort, she changed the subject. "My family and friends must be worried. Not just about me, but about your country and the threat it poses. Will your mother honor her agreement?"

"She sent an emissary to Alba," Jay answered shortly, grasping at the subject change like a drowning man. He turned to look at her, his eyes intent. "I can't say beyond that. Just know that no matter what happens, I'll protect you."

But can you protect me from yourself? Lina asked silently. Jay posed the biggest threat in this moment; not just a threat to her life, but a threat to her heart.

Despite repeated attempts to harden the soft heart that had caused her so much trouble, his words wormed their way in. She wanted to believe him; to let herself trust again. It was so alien to be at odds with anyone; to look upon another as an enemy. Even the feeling of betrayal, that terrible wrenching pain that had twisted in her gut during their journey, was beginning to slowly alleviate.

Was that wrong; disloyal to Stephen and Alba?

She just wasn't sure *what* to think anymore. She felt so confused. Her life had changed too significantly for her to absorb everything.

All she was certain of was that she couldn't keep waiting for someone else to fix things; to save her and protect her.

Stop being a damn victim and take some ownership of your life.

Jay's words echoed in her mind. She would do everything she could to protect the people of Alba. To keep what happened to Stephen from happening again.

And if she needed to trust Jay to do that, even just a little, she would. "Why didn't you tell me about your family; about your mother?"

Jay shrugged, the now-familiar roll of his muscled shoulders rippling beneath the t-shirt he wore. "Just used to downplaying it, I guess. Enough people think I got this job because of my parents."

"They must cast long shadows," Lina murmured thoughtfully. "I got a different impression of your father from what your men said. That he was a…"

"A womanizer? An egotist with complete disregard for women? That was him. He wasn't exactly known for his family values." Jay shifted slightly, the lines of his body taut. Lina resisted the urge to touch him; to try and soothe whatever demons seemed to be raging inside. "But no one here cares about that. He was famous, good-looking; a celebrity. That he was a terrible father and husband didn't matter to anyone. This isn't Alba with its emphasis on family and responsibility as a way to maintain balance in society."

"Well, not all families are balanced, no matter how well they hide it on the outside," said Lina with a touch of her own bitterness.

Jay glanced down at her, settling back a little into the couch, his arm coming down behind her. "Yeah, your parents were separated. Not everyone is relationship material." The comment seemed to be directed inward.

He must really believe what everyone says; that he is just like his father, Lina thought. Not too long ago, she would have agreed. But now she was beginning to wonder…

"My mother just got tired of his control and abuse," Lina said. "He would have been fine living with us, as long as we followed his rules."

"Couldn't she report him?" Jay asked in surprise.

"And ruin her image? Embarrass her parents, who arranged the match? No, she preferred to just live apart, and he let her. He knew she could hurt his reputation if she told what he did, and nothing was more important than that to him."

"Our fathers seem surprisingly alike for being born to two different cultures a continent apart."

Lina nodded, sharing a glance with Jay filled with understanding. If felt good to be in agreement for once. Almost as if they were on the same side.

10

Aerina woke with a start, disoriented. The view of the Serenity Garden from Helen's guest room reminded her of where she was.

Did Marcus worry when she didn't come home? She felt a moment of guilt. Perhaps she should have told him where she was staying.

Slipping out from under the white sheets, she walked

quietly out to the kitchen. The sun was just casting its forerunners across the horizon. She made a cup of tea and went to sit in the garden, watching the shadows shorten as the sun began its slow ascent.

She heard Helen moving around in the kitchen, and her friend soon appeared, her own cup of tea in hand.

"I need to go in to the office today," she told Aerina. "Are you going to be ok?"

"Yes, of course," Aerina answered. "I should be asking you that."

Helen waved off her concern. "I'm fine. Nearly every woman is pregnant once in their life. I can survive it as well as the next one. Will you be here when I come home?"

Aerina hesitated. "I don't know. Do you mind…?"

"No, of course not; stay as long as you like."

The door closed behind her friend, and Aerina rose, bringing her cup into the kitchen and putting it in the dishwasher. Helen had changed since Stephen's death. Before she would have never allowed an outcast like Aerina in her home, worried about how it might affect her own standing. Now her friend was on the verge of becoming an outcast herself.

Aerina sighed, stopping to look at a holophoto frame that slowly changed the projected pictures. Images of her, Lina, and Helen at the beach, at the Graduation Ball, at the theatre all flashed slowly past. An image of Stephen playing handball appeared, his olive skin, dark eyes, and high cheekbones — so like Lina's — were intensely focused on his task. It was the same expression Lina got when she was working in the lab.

Turning away, Aerina breathed deeply to contain the tears that threatened to spill forth. Normally Lina was the watering pot. She needed to keep herself together. To find some way to help get Lina back. She owed her friend.

Should she go to the Training Grounds? She'd been spending the last few weeks there, helping with the research, watching drone footage to try and learn about the lands surrounding them. Hoping for news of Lina from the Virmortus traveling to the Southern Empire.

She wanted to see the progress on the airplane they had been developing, she told herself firmly. All week they had promised a test demonstration, but had kept pushing it back. She didn't want to miss it.

The aircraft, a recommissioned fighter jet using Alban technology enhancements, had been a low-priority project for several years. Marcus had just re-prioritized it. It was now the focus of the state's top aerospace engineers. Aerina hadn't even known they trained aerospace engineers. It was a good thing preparedness was one of the Virmortus virtues.

Unlike their value of secrecy, which Aerina was growing to hate.

Whatever happened between her and Marcus, she was invested in this. There was no way she was going to let him shut her out completely. He could keep his damn secrets.

Riding on the tide of self-righteous anger, she dressed and headed out the door. She took a taxi, scanning the ID chip now embedded in her holoreader to pay. After removing two of them, she was never letting another one be implanted anywhere on her person.

She entered the front, standing before the tiny camera until she was buzzed inside.

Nemo, one of the newer recruits, met her in the long white entrance hallway. He couldn't have been more than ten, although the way he carried himself made him appear older.

"Miss Delacroix. Please come with me."

Aerina followed him through the inner door, glancing down at the trainees in the Pit. The sight of their battered conditions no longer shocked her as much as it initially had, but she would never be able to dismiss the violent training as casually as Marcus could.

If being a Reaper were the only way she could gain Marcus' complete trust, would she be willing to do it?

She didn't know. She knew she could kill; she'd done it before to protect herself and Marcus. But killing in defense was different than planning and executing an assassination.

Aerina sighed as they continued down the long stone hallway to the elevator. Marcus would probably never allow her to join, anyhow. Not only at 21 was she too old, she'd never be able to get the whole obedience thing right.

The elevator beeped, indicating they had reached the lower level that housed the Technology Project.

A familiar face greeted her after exiting.

"Julia!" Aerina stood in shock for a moment before hurrying to hug her Pleb friend. "What are you doing here?"

Julia smiled, nodding towards Research Room 2. "Simon thought Jamia would be a good candidate for the Technology. I guess it works better on younger subjects. *Users*, they're calling them. And people with a natural skill for holocomputers are who they've started recruiting."

Aerina followed Julia's gaze to the viewing window, seeing Simon sitting with Jamia, gesturing carefully. The young Eurasian girl listened intently, nodding often.

"And you're ok with your little sister becoming part of this?"

Julia's mouth kicked up at the corner in wry amusement. "As if I had much choice. Jamia is meant for more than what a Pleb position will offer her. And this will keep her out of trouble. I hope."

Aerina smiled. "I suppose that's true. She was ready to hack into the Virmortus files without a second thought when I asked. We're lucky to be alive."

"When Marcus' team grabbed us from the tech lab, I thought those were my last moments," Julia agreed with a shiver. Then she cast a speculative look at Aerina. "Although now that I've seen you with your Reaper, I know he'd have never harmed you."

Aerina shrugged, saying nothing. It was true. She'd pushed Marcus far beyond the boundaries of what anyone would consider reasonable, and he'd let her. Every time. He must love her. But could love exist without trust?

He trusts you, you idiot, a tiny voice in her head scolded her. *Stop being so insecure. He's a man, after all, and certainly not a saint.*

Maybe she was an idiot. Relationships were much trickier than she had imagined. All those emotions muddled even the most logical of people. That thought had her casting an inquiring gaze at her friend.

"So you and Simon...?" Aerina asked as they both watched Jamia putting her arm out for Simon to inject the amber liquid. Aerina forcibly repressed the feeling of foreboding that overcame her as she remembered Stephen doing the same thing hours before his death.

Julia smiled widely as she answered Aerina's unspoken question. "Yeah, he's staying with us. He practically begged me to move in. After our State was nearly destroyed, and you sacrificed everything to be with Marcus, what excuse did I have not to? We love each other. I don't want to waste any more time apart, questioning his love and what the future may or may not hold for us. We might be from different worlds, and he's not perfect; he never will be. But in this moment, it is enough."

Aerina watched Jamia gritting her teeth against the pain of the injection. Julia was right. Marcus wasn't perfect, but neither was she. Why waste time being angry? If losing Stephen had taught her anything, it was that life was precious and short.

"Thanks, Julia!" She hugged her friend tightly again. Julia hugged her back, baffled.

"Thanks for what?"

"For telling me what I should do. I've got to find Marcus," she laughed. "Will you be here later?"

"For another hour," Julia answered, still looking confused.

"I'll find you soon, if not here, then at the theatre. I'll tell you all about it!" With a wave, Aerina hurried towards Marcus' office, hoping he was here today.

His time had been split lately between the Capitol and the Training Grounds. It was no doubt wearing him thin, trying to be both the political leader and the head of the military intelligence. And she'd only compounded his issues by blowing up at him, rather than supporting him. Damn, she really was an idiot.

She came to his office door, knocking gently before pushing it open. Inside, Marcus was at his desk, talking on his Com device. His eyes met hers.

"Good. Complete the test flight. I'll be down to look it over later."

He set the reader down on the table, raising his eyebrows in question.

Her earlier enthusiasm was curbed by unexpected nervousness. Was he still angry? Did he even want to talk?

"I'm sorry about last night," she said. "I'm sure you had a good reason for—" she broke off as he rose suddenly, coming around the desk.

Her eyes widened as he closed the distance between them, and then he was kissing her before pulling her tight against him in a rare hug.

"Don't ever leave me like that again," he ordered gruffly.

"I'm sorry," she said again, muffled against his chest. "I should have told you where I went—"

"I knew you were at Helen's. I didn't know if you were coming back." His low voice was stark. She rested her chin on his chest, looking up into his dark eyes.

"I love you. I'd never be able to leave for long. No matter how much you piss me off."

He lowered his head and kissed her again, gently this time. Stepping back, he motioned for her to sit down in the chair before his desk.

"I've been meaning to ask you... I am in need of a new

Emissary. Besides the Virmortus, who are obviously unqualified, you have the most experience outside Alba. Would you be interested in the job?"

Aerina's eyes widened in shock. Outside Emissary? Her dream job?

"But I'm so young. And I haven't even been recruited yet..."

"I've spoken with Ramus. We need someone with an open mind, who is willing to travel, and is eager to learn about the world outside Alba. All qualifications which our recently deposed Emissary lacked. I don't know anyone who fits that better than you. Change is here in Alba to stay. I need people who will embrace it." Marcus crossed his arms, waiting.

"You're not just doing this because I'm sleeping with you, are you?"

Marcus' mouth quirked in his version of a smile. "First you complain I don't tell you enough because we're together, and now you complain I'm doing you a favor because of it. You should know I'd never offer a position to someone who was unqualified. Do you want the job or not?"

"Yes, yes, yes," Aerina answered quickly.

"Good," Marcus answered. "And I have a mission already."

11

Aerina watched with barely leashed excitement as the fighter jet went through a second test flight overhead. She barely felt the cold of the misty morning that surrounded them in the field outside of Alba.

Soon, she would be inside that jet.

Flying.

A message had come on Marcus' Com device the

previous day. The Southern Empire was coming, but this time they wanted to talk. The President was sending a representative, and she hoped an Alban representative would return to meet with her.

Marcus wanted her to go as the Emissary of Alba and discuss a possible truce between their countries. She might be able to bring Lina home. Excitement warred with nerves at the huge responsibility. She glanced over at Marcus. He stood beside her, arms loosely crossed over his muscled chest, feet spread. The tenser he became, the more relaxed he looked.

"We are going to be fine," she told him quietly.

"I am fairly sure this is a trap, but it is our best chance to determine their plan. And to save your friend," he said. He turned to face her, his hands settling on her shoulders. "You need to follow my instructions exactly; there will be no room for error. Do you understand?"

"I understand," Aerina assured him once again. She couldn't help but wonder if he was regretting his choice to appoint her as Emissary. While the worry was like a small lump in her stomach, it also made her more determined to prove her ability.

Behind Marcus, a familiar figure hiked up the hillside, bringing her from her thoughts.

"Vick!" Breaking free from Marcus' hold, she rushed across the clearing to hug the eccentric mayor of Vicksburg, a little outpost not far from Alba.

"Aerina, you are more beautiful than the last time I saw you. How are you?" he asked, hugging her tightly, smiling widely at Marcus' dark look.

"I'm fine. What are you doing here?"

"Vick is coming with us," Marcus answered for his friend. "He was raised in the Southern Empire, and will hopefully provide some insight."

"Really?" Aerina looked at Vick in surprise. She had no idea he was from the Southern Empire. "How…?"

Vick waved off the questions about to pour from Aerina.

"It's not something I like to talk about." His normally jovial demeanor darkened for a moment, then he smiled and the darkness in his eyes cleared.

"So you've decided to join us?"

Marcus nodded abruptly. "Ramus can handle the Senators. I want to be sure the Southern Empire is no longer a threat."

Vick nodded his understanding. "When do we leave? I find I'm eager to return to my homeland and renew old ties."

"A few more final preparations, and hopefully we will be gone by tomorrow. We're scheduled to meet with their representative in two days." Marcus studied his friend for a long moment. "Are you sure you're up for this?"

Vick made a production of looking shocked. "What? After calling in that favor you've held over my head for the last decade, you're second-guessing yourself? Has the great Marcus Trent, Alpha Virmortus of Alba, actually developed a conscience?"

Marcus' face remained impassive, and Aerina stifled a smile as her lover answered in his normal low tone. "I'll assume that means you're ready."

Vick laughed, the booming sound drawing the gaze of nearby aviation engineers overseeing the test-flight. "I'd follow you to hell itself, my friend."

Marcus glanced at Aerina, and she could see slight discomfort reflected in his ebony gaze. It was the same look he got when she told him she loved him. The poor guy wasn't used to emotional displays, since he'd grown up without any.

Then his mouth quirked in his version of a smile. "That's good. Because I have a feeling hell might be where we are headed."

12

"Come in!" Aerina pulled Helen into her villa, excited to have actual guests for dinner. Marcus was a bit of a deterrent to most visitors.

"I didn't know you were having other guests," her friend said stiffly, her pale eyes fixed on Vick. Aerina followed her friend's gaze to where the large man lounged on the divan, his muscled form seeming to dwarf the piece of furniture the same way Marcus' did. He had showered and changed into clean clothes after his trip to Alba from Vicksburg, but he was still as furry as ever. His beard, although neatly clipped, covered his face, and his long brown hair was tied back.

Vick's face spread in his perpetual grin as he rose to greet Helen. If possible, the thin woman stiffened further as he approached. Aerina began to wonder if she made a mistake in not cancelling her dinner plans with Helen after finding out Vick would be joining them.

"Aerina didn't tell me such a lovely guest would be joining us." Vick took Helen's hand, engulfing it in his large one. He towered over the petite woman. Helen smiled thinly, her light green eyes flinty as she nodded slightly before quickly extracting her hand.

Her reticence was a challenge to Vick, and his smile widened even further, which Aerina wouldn't have thought possible. White teeth flashed behind the thin beard.

Taking her arm, Vick drew Helen towards the couch. "Tell me, what role do you play here in this great state?"

Helen's gaze flicked over to Aerina, as if to demand assistance. Aerina pretended not to notice, hurrying to get food on the table. Marcus would be back shortly from checking on the research progress.

"I work in Legal," she heard Helen answering Vick.

Vick laughed. "That would have been my first guess."

"Is that so?" Helen retorted coolly.

"Yeah, you seem to be the type that always has all the answers. Did you know in the pre-war era, lawyers were mostly regarded with disgust? Nothing like the high regard I'm sure you experience here."

"Is that so?" Helen's voice had grown even colder. Aerina refused to look up from the table she was setting.

Vick leaned forward, resting his forearms on his widespread knees.

"Yep, but in every society, we all have a role, no matter how distasteful."

"And what is your role, Mr. Vick?"

"Just Vick. We don't waste time with formality in Vicksburg. And I'm the mayor, security, and sometimes engineer in my humble town."

"Mayor?" Disgust was thick in Helen's voice. "How many people live in your town?"

"Five hundred and eighty nine. Almost ninety; a new baby is due next month."

"My, that is quite a responsibility. It must keep you very busy."

Aerina chanced a quick glance. Vick was leaning in, his smile still firmly in place, eyes twinkling. He appeared to be enjoying the exchange. Although it was hard to tell with him; he always appeared happy. Helen was the real surprise. Her friend's normally pale face was lightly flushed, her pale green eyes flashing. Aerina could swear her prickly friend was enjoying herself.

"Not too busy to visit someone special." He raised his brow suggestively.

"I'm sure someday you'll find someone willing to look past your, um, rough exterior." Her tone suggested that was unlikely.

"So you're saying there's a chance?"

Helen opened her mouth to respond, then promptly

snapped it shut. She stood abruptly, her eyes panicked. Vick instinctively rose too, the gleam in his eyes being replaced by concern, his body tensed; ready.

Just like Marcus when he braced for battle.

Helen raised her hands towards her mouth as vomit spewed forth, raining down upon Vick's dark pants and boots.

Aerina stood, frozen for a moment.

Vick broke the silence. "If the idea disgusts you that much … are you alright?"

"I'm pregnant," Helen responded bluntly, making her way to the kitchen for a rag to clean the mess. "Apparently the condition turns your entire body against you."

Vick opened his mouth, for once at loss for words. His hazel eyes went to Aerina and back to Helen's stiff back. Finally, he asked, "Aren't you required to be married before you can file to have the anti-pregnancy shot counteracted?"

"I would be married if the father wasn't dead," came her sharp retort. Aerina intervened before things escalated.

"Sit down, Helen. I'll clean it up. The food is getting cold. Let's eat, since it doesn't look like Marcus is going to be on time. Vick, I'll get you a pair of Marcus' clean pants."

Dinner passed quickly, Aerina carefully steering the conversation to neutral subjects. Vick's hazel eyes continued to study Helen as if he were fascinated by her controlled demeanor. They were almost done when Marcus finally returned.

He seemed taken aback to see the small dinner party in his villa, used as he was to solitude, and more recently, Aerina's presence.

"Thank you for inviting me to dinner," Helen said quietly, her eyes on Marcus as she rose from the table. "I am still not feeling myself, so I'll cut the evening short."

"I'll walk you home," Vick offered, jumping to his feet.

"Oh, that isn't necessary —"

"I insist." His calm voice didn't leave room for

argument. For once, Helen didn't press the issue, tolerating Aerina's hug and preceding a waiting Vick out the front door.

"What was that all about?" Marcus asked as the door closed behind them, Vick sending a wink in Aerina's direction.

"I'm not sure. It is hard to tell with Vick, but I think he might have some kind of interest in Helen."

Marcus raised one brow. "I can't imagine he would be attracted to that uptight bi — er — your friend."

Aerina smiled at his attempt to be delicate. She appreciated the effort.

"You can never tell what sparks chemistry between two people."

His mouth quirked at that, and he pulled her in for a quick, hard kiss as she passed him with her hands full of dirty dishes.

"You're the expert on people."

13

Lina woke to the sound of the ocean outside her window, the scent of the salty air filling her room. For a moment, she thought she was still in Alba. Then the unfamiliar blue walls and grey drapes blowing lightly in the morning breeze reminded her.

She was in the Southern Empire. With Jay.

As the sleep cleared from her senses, the continual pull of the networks around her began again. This strange new sense worked much like her others; she knew it was there and could focus on it, but could also filter it out.

Mentally instructing the drapes to open, she looked out at the scene below.

Great green gardens stretched below, meeting the tan sand of beach, backlit by the brilliant blue-green of the ocean far beyond.

Thoughts of the previous night came rushing back. A flush spread over her. She had been so close to falling back under Jay's spell.

Would that really be so bad? Her inner voice asked. What would it hurt? They were both single adults. As long as she was careful to not let him influence her decisions…

He's still the enemy. She thought of Stephen, and guilt descended, intermingled with the constant weight of grief. Even if Jay hadn't pulled the trigger, he had played a role in the events that led up to Stephen's death.

He was the enemy, and no matter what happened, she needed to remember that.

Dressing quickly, Lina left the room with new resolve. She needed to learn all she could about this world that was so different, yet strangely similar, to Alba.

She padded slowly down the long carpeted hallways of the second floor. The estate seemed huge; she wasn't even sure where exactly Jay's room was. Was such a large structure really necessary for one individual? Even the grandest of villas in Alba were miniscule in comparison to this. It must take an army just to care for the place.

Jay was already up, conferring with an older gentleman she assumed was household staff. Both men nodded to her politely as she descended the massive curving staircase to the first floor.

Heavy rugs created intimate living areas in the large, open main floor. The marble foyer spread into well-shined wood floors that were a work of art themselves, each piece a color chosen to create intricate designs.

High ceilings stretched up several floors, and her eyes were caught by the art that adorned the walls. Pre-war art and objects were carefully placed throughout the mansion, contrasting with the ultra-modern interior. She thought of the ancient car he'd rebuilt that ran on gasoline, of all things. She shook her head at his apparent fascination with the archaic.

The mansion was a busy place. Workers of varying ages moved about, performing whatever chores had been assigned to them that day.

"Good morning." Jay's deep voice reached her where she still stood on the bottom stair, no doubt with her mouth hanging open in awe.

She smiled at him, returning the greeting.

"What is that symbol; is that a cross?" she asked curiously, indicating a decorative skylight high above.

He nodded. "Yes, the cross and dove are a symbol of faith; of our belief in something greater than ourselves. My youngest sister made it when my father was killed. Although knowing him, it seem seems a little blasphemous," he finished, the sardonic gleam returning to his eyes.

"Your sister is very talented," Lina murmured. "Is she an artist?"

Jay just shook his head, dismissing her question and turning the subject. "No one really talked about religion in Alba, although I did see a cross on a building in the Aggie's town."

Lina fought the hurt over his continual secrecy. It seemed to further emphasize the distance between them; he a Confederate of the Empire, she an Alban. To cover her emotions, Lina answered precisely: "Albans did away with religion. It was considered too divisive, and the founders didn't want anything to disrupt their attempts to keep peace. Of course, no one was forbidden from practicing a religion, because that too would stir discontent. But the State will not recognize any faith." Lina shrugged. "I'm sure some people practice some kind of religion in Alba. The window is beautiful, though."

Jay nodded slightly, his eyes shadowing for a moment. Then he smiled and he held out his arm.

"How about some breakfast?"

"Yes, thank you," she answered, taking his arm hesitantly. As her slender fingers closed over the bare skin revealed by his casual short-sleeve shirt, she tried to ignore the way it turned her insides warm and made her heart skip.

Rather than leading her to some sort of dining area, he took her to a patio, the door sliding open before them. It was a beautiful morning. The sun was shining, and it was warm but not overly humid. Her eyes took in the elaborate landscaping hidden in darkness the previous evening; the plants were so different here. Large, beautiful flowers mingled with spiky palms, tall grasses, and fruit trees.

He didn't stop at the table on the patio, which she saw stretched around back to the pool area. Her stomach did somersaults as she again remembered the night before. Had she let things continue to their natural conclusion, would it have been like the first time? The same explosive sensation; the strange feeling of closeness? Or had that all been part of the illusion; the fantasy she'd created in her mind? Would she be able to take that same risk again, to trust someone with her body? With her heart?

She knew a flush tinged her cheeks, and she kept her head down as they descended the flagstone steps towards the boat house. The square, long shape reminded Lina of the villas at home.

When they reached the dock, a uniformed man met them. "She's charged and ready, sir." His eyes flicked to Lina for a moment before fixing again on Jay.

"After you," he told her, motioning to the gangplank set up to enter the large yacht.

Lina walked carefully across, Jay following close behind. On the upper deck, she saw a table set up with breakfast.

"Wow," she murmured. Jay grinned at her, his face lighting up with genuine pleasure. He was trying to please her.

Pulling out her chair, he settled her at the table before sitting himself.

The breakfast was wonderful, the morning sun rising higher in the sky as the yacht slid slowly through the blue-green waters, very like the color of Jay's eyes.

Jay sat back in his chair, studying Lina. His expression had turned serious. She had a feeling their idyllic morning was about to come to an end.

"What?"

"In a few days the President is hosting a state dinner, and she wants you to attend. She's going to expect you to display the power of the Technology before Congress."

Lina looked out over the sparkling water, squinting against the bright sun. Was everything he did for the President; his mother? Or was he really trying to help her get through this, like he promised. Did he care about her at all? Or was the Technology still his mission?

Questions whirled in her mind; questions without answers. She didn't know if she could handle the turmoil. What was she doing, trying to be someone important?

It was too late to back out now. *The kind of power you have includes huge responsibility.*

"Like turning things on or off? That kind of display?" Lina finally asked.

"Probably a little more complicated than that."

"I'm not much of a performer," Lina said ruefully. "Did you have something in mind?"

"I know someone who can help us."

14

Jay swiped the small screen embedded in the wall beside the doorway of a towering downtown skyscraper. He typed in a few numbers, waiting impatiently. A moment later, a distant voice answered through the speaker. "What do you want, Jay?"

"I need your expertise on a certain matter," he responded, blue-green gaze flicking to where Lina hovered uncertainly behind him. Her own eyes couldn't seem to stop moving, taking in the sights of the vast metropolis that was New Glory.

The lowest terrace in Alba, which was at sea level and stretched for miles along the Pacific coastline, was impressive in its own right. It was the home to over a million Plebs, and had its own tall buildings and crowded streets. But even the bustle of the city of Alba paled in comparison to this place.

Just the amount of vehicles here was shocking. Many of the Plebs traveled by foot or non-motorized vehicles, like bicycles or quadcycles. Here, it seemed every individual owned a vehicle, each more gaudy than the last.

A digitized voice interrupted her thoughts. "You have been granted entrance. Please proceed forward."

Jay pulled her into a small box, and she fought the feelings of claustrophobia that made her chest tighten as the doors slid closed, entrapping them in the eight by eight foot space.

As the door clicked shut, the walls suddenly became transparent, showing the outside of the building. They were moving upwards at a quick pace, the street receding.

"You have arrived," the digital host informed them as the box slid to a stop, the walls again becoming opaque. A door on the opposite side opened and they stepped into a small foyer, Jay pressing another button beside the door.

The door opened and a young woman stood before them, looking remarkably like the Secretary of Defense. Was this another sister?

"What do you want now?" the young woman asked, her eyes fixed on Lina suspiciously.

"I need your help, sister dear," Jay said sardonically, ruffling the woman's carefully coiffed hair, the same tawny color as Jay's. Her hands immediately went up to push his away, instinctively stepping back, which allowed enough room for Jay to push by her.

Lina hovered hesitantly in the doorway, uncertain about

how to proceed. It didn't seem like there was much love lost between these two siblings.

The woman turned blue-green eyes on Lina, pinning her with a direct, cynical gaze. It was an expression Lina had seen in Jay's eyes so many times, it made her heart turn over in unexpected sympathy.

With all their luxury and obvious success, they weren't happy. She couldn't stop the feeling of compassion that came over her as she looked at the two siblings, both carefully keeping a safe distance from one another.

"Lina, this is my baby sister, Chelsea. Chelsea, Lina of Alba." Jay made the introductions casually as he wandered around Chelsea's home, idly picking up objects and examining them. He held up one strange-looking device, eyebrows raising.

"Again, Chels?"

The young woman, probably the same age as Lina, flushed, hurrying forward to grab the object from Jay's hand. Lina had no idea what it was, but obviously was the subject of some contention between the siblings. Jay's expression hadn't changed much, but she could tell from the stiffening of his body that he was angry.

"A friend left that here. It isn't mine. I haven't touched the stuff since you locked me up in that atrocious clinic. They have nicer ones, you know." Bitterness spewed forth from the attractive girl's mouth.

"Yes, I know. But those are more like resorts, and the recidivism rate is pretty high. In fact, I think that is their goal: encourage their patients to return so they can continue making money. A good business model, actually. Nothing better than repeat clients, even in the rehabilitation industry."

"You're my brother. Not my parent or jail-keeper. I have rights—"

"No, you don't. Who is going to stop me?" Jay's voice had become low and dangerous, a side of him Lina rarely saw. This was the man who would stop at nothing to accomplish his mission. The man who'd unapologetically stabbed her to force Aerina to give up the Technology. She felt a twinge in her side at the reminder, her hand going to the nearly-healed wound. Jay's eyes flicked to her at the movement, and she read the frustration there.

He did care about his sister. He just didn't know how to show it. Except to protect her, even if it was from herself.

Just like he was trying to protect Lina, even though he'd been the one to endanger her in the first place.

"Don't worry, Jay. I won't tarnish the family's name any further," Chelsea assured him disparagingly. "Now tell me the meaning of your visit, or get out."

Jay gripped the strange device in his hand for a moment, his knuckles white. Then he relaxed, pocketing the device, the familiar cynical gleam in his eye.

"I need your playwriting skills for a little upcoming performance."

Chelsea looked taken aback. "Really? What kind of performance?"

Jay studied his little sister, as if debating how much to tell her. "Lina here needs to display some new Technology at a State Dinner in a few days. We were hoping you could help us make it a show worth watching."

The cynicism melted from Chelsea's face, her eyes lighting up with excitement. She looked younger with enthusiasm brightening her features. "A show before the Congress and Mother? Yes, I think I can come up with something suitable." Her blue-green gaze met Lina's, and she could already see the plans formulating. "When should we start?"

"Right now."

15

Jay left her alone with his sister, promising to pick Lina up at the end of day. He shot both women a dire look as he left, as if telling them to behave.

The day Lina spent with Chelsea creating a program for the State Dinner went quickly. She found the other girl to have an unexpected sense of humor, and an impressive intellect she kept disguised by her aura of ennui.

She also shared Jay's strange fixation with pre-war artifacts.

"Our father collected everything he could get his hands on," Chelsea explained as Lina studied an old Com device she had on display. It was quite heavy, and had a glass screen. A tiny apple with a bite out of it was etched in the corner. "That is one of the few old cell phones left that didn't have a broken screen. Daddy got it on a mission out west."

"Does it work?"

Chelsea nodded. "He had a charger built specially for it, since it runs on battery power instead of an energy cell."

"Why keep it?"

"Because it tells a story. Part of our history," Chelsea explained, her voice almost reverent. "Someone's entire life is saved on that phone. Pictures, videos, electronic messages… it is like discovering a tiny piece of the past."

"I'm surprised someone like your father would be so interested in a snapshot of someone's life from nearly a century ago," Lina said unthinkingly. She immediately felt contrite as Chelsea's face tightened. "I'm sorry, I shouldn't have—"

"No," Chelsea interrupted, "I know the things everyone says about my father. What Jay thinks of him. And perhaps some of them are true. But only because of *her*."

"The woman he had an affair with?"

"No, the President." Chelsea's voice was filled with disgust; loathing, even.

"Your mother?"

"Yes, although I refuse to call her such. She's a selfish, psychotic bitch and she drove my father to his death. And she'll do the same to Jay. And me," she finished quietly, looking down at the tiny marks between her fingers where Lina assumed she'd used narcotics.

Lina didn't know what to say. Before she could formulate a suitable answer, Chelsea rose, changing the conversation.

"Are you hungry? I'm not much of a cook, but I know a great taco bar just down the street. And they deliver."

Lina nodded with a slight smile, the other girl's words still running through her mind.

She's a selfish, psychotic bitch and she drove my father to his death. And she'll do the same to Jay.

Could Jay be wrong about his father? And could the President be more dangerous than even he knew? Or did he know, and not care?

Peace help her, she was terrified to execute her plan at the State Dinner. If the President was as horrific as everyone made her sound, that night might be her last.

16

"How did it go?" Jay asked as he chivalrously opened the car door for Lina later that evening. Tonight's ride was a little more understated and contemporary than the pre-war vehicle he'd driven before. She slid into the bucket seat and waited for Jay to enter before answering.

"It went great. We have a few things to finalize, but Chelsea helped me create a perfect program."

"Program?"

"I mean performance. Demonstration. Whatever," Lina corrected quickly, hoping he hadn't caught her slip. He looked at her quizzically, one brow raised. She smiled weakly, looking out the rain-streaked window as the city sped past.

"Lina, do you have something you need to tell me?" His voice was low, a little dangerous. Lina felt a twinge of alarm. She had always been terrible at keeping secrets.

"Lina." His voice was cold, demanding. The agent was emerging.

"I'm just nervous because of what your sister told me about the President," Lina burst out, letting her dark hair fall forward to conceal her face. Jay reached over to tuck it back behind her ear, turning her face towards him so he could see her eyes.

"I'll protect you. Just give her the display she wants and you'll be fine."

"I wish I could believe you," she answered truthfully, finally meeting his serious gaze. His jaw tightened slightly and he let his hand drop, instructing the self-driving e-car to return to his home.

"When this is over, you'll learn to trust me. I promise that." He spoke confidently, as if he was convincing himself as well as her.

I just hope you'll trust me, she thought.

"What do you want to do tonight?" he asked. "Swimming again?"

Lina laughed. "I don't know if that is a good idea. Besides, it's raining."

"That won't be a problem."

"Jay, stop, this is a bad idea." Lina pulled her lips from Jay's, her breath coming in great gasps. Her entire body ached to continue, but she was scared.

"It's a terrible idea, but I can't seem to care." He dropped his chin on her damp hair, his own bare chest heaving. She could feel the leashed power in his muscled form as he held her close.

The only sounds were their breathing and the rain falling on the glass ceiling of the pool room connected to the master suite. He ran his hands lightly up and down her bare arms, sending gooseflesh over her body. She shivered, but not from cold. The only barrier between their overheated bodies was the thin material of their swimsuit, and it did little to disguise his arousal, pressed to her throbbing center.

Inside, she raged a silent battle. She wanted this, but it felt so wrong. Like a betrayal.

How could she have such strong feelings for the enemy? It wasn't just desire, she admitted. And if she gave in now, how much more would it become?

He cursed under his breath, turning away in one movement and diving into the pool. Lina shakily sat down on the chaise, watching him stroke powerfully under the water to the other side, flipping and swimming back before surfacing. He ejected from the pool in a rush, the water streaming from across the bunched muscles and taut lines.

"If you don't want it, get out. Because in another moment it's going to be too late to say no."

Lina sat, frozen, indecision crippling her. If she stayed and he forced her, it would take the decision out of her hands.

No. That is what the old Lina would have done. She would make the choice. She was the one in control of her life.

He came closer, the pool lights gleaming off the corded muscles of his tanned arms and chest, the light hair tapering to disappear below his swim trunks. She followed the water droplets slowly running down, dripping onto the textured marble, before looking up to meet his blue-green gaze. The sardonic gleam was absent, but banked fires of desire made their shadowy depths blaze. He was waiting for her to decide.

She chose to stay.

Jay must have read her answer, for suddenly he dropped down beside her lounge, pulling her to the edge and spreading her legs slowly. The heat from his chest pressed against the ache of desire in her core. She couldn't stop the little moan that escaped as he leaned in closer, his lips hovering over her stomach.

"Are you sure, Lina? You know who I am. There's no claiming ignorance or betrayal this time."

It wasn't fair. Her body was screaming for the touch of his lips; the practiced skill of his hands. *Please don't make me answer. Just touch me, anywhere!* Her mind pleaded, but he waited, his lips hovering over the quivering skin of her stomach as she leaned back in the lounge. The ache between her legs had become a throbbing burn that she desperately needed relieved.

"Yes, I know who you are. And I don't care. I want you, want this—"

It was enough. He roughly pulled her up, his mouth slanting over hers in a kiss that was possessive and hungry. Then he moved down, tasting the wet saltiness of the droplets, following their path to the curves of her generous breasts, letting his hot breath tease the cool clothe of her swimsuit. Her nipples puckered and hardened, straining eagerly against the material. He took one his mouth, slowly, carefully. The sensation elicited another hungry moan from her.

His hands worked behind her until the suit fell away, and the heat of his mouth was now covering her breast, his tongue working magic she wouldn't have believed possible.

Then he moved lower, and she gasped as his hands gently stroked the smooth skin of her upper thighs, so close to the heat that was threatening to burn her alive.

Please, please, please…

And then he answered her silent prayer, gently sliding her bottoms down and tossing them aside, his fingers prodding the gentle folds that hid her most private parts.

"*Bella diosa*, I've been wanting to taste you since that night in the park. It wasn't enough, not nearly enough," he murmured against her flesh, and his mouth was replacing his fingers, his lips kissing and his tongue gently probing.

She felt mindless with the pleasure, everything else seeming to fade but this moment.

His tongue found the tiny bud of desire and played gently, wringing more gasps and moans from her parted lips.

He tucked a finger inside, then another. The delicious stretching sensation sent her over the edge, and she cried out as her climax overtook her, stealing her breathe away as her body pulsed its release.

He slowly moved up until his hardness was pressed against her. He paused a moment, touching her face until her eyes opened, and then he slowly entered, the fullness so much greater than his fingers that it sent new waves of pleasure.

"I can't wait," he muttered, pumping into her quickly, the fast movement rocking her body. Lina didn't care, clinging to his bunched shoulders, trying to match his rhythm. Her legs wrapped around his lean waist, pulling him closer with each thrust. With a final plunge, he groaned deeply, throwing back his head as he pulsed within her.

Lina stroked his sweat-streaked back as he collapsed on top of her, enjoying the crushing weight of his muscled body for a long moment. Finally, he lifted himself back off with a groan, kissing her quickly on the lips.

Lina smiled, basking in the warm afterglow of passion, letting it block out the worries that lingered just outside.

"*Diosa*, you are amazing. I thought the first time was a fluke, but that…" he shook his head, as if he couldn't find the words. "I'm glad you stayed. Damn glad."

"Me too."

He studied her face for a moment, as if seeing her anew. She bit her lip, her heart speeding up again, this time with an emotion different than mere desire. A strange nervous elation she was too afraid to name.

He grinned finally, not the sharp-edged crooking of his lips but a real smile that lightened his eyes and softened his features.

"I don't know what it is about you…" he murmured, as

if to himself. "I hope you know how special you are. How important. To...the Empire." He finished quickly, as if he had been about to say something else.

Rising quickly, he grabbed a towel, tossing it to her, and then picked up one for himself. Something fell from beneath it, clattering to the tile floor. It looked like a small tube; a syringe.

"What is that?" Lina asked curiously.

Jay scooped it up, casually tossing it into the trash.

"Nothing I'm going to need. Not anymore."

17

The day of the State Dinner, and Lina's performance, arrived much too quickly. Lina couldn't help the dread that filled her each time she thought of the upcoming event.

The night with Jay had been even better than she'd thought possible. He had been gentle, almost wary, in his efforts to please her, his impressive strength carefully leashed. She'd felt more than mere pleasure. A strange sense of understanding, of tenderness, growing until it eclipsed every other emotion. It had been both amazing and terrifying.

She didn't know how this would end, but she couldn't imagine any kind of happily-ever-after awaited them. No scenario she ran through her mind ended with them together.

A twinge of guilt rose, but she fought to crush it. She'd made her choice. It was one night she'd stolen for herself. In that pool house, they hadn't been an Alban and a Confederate; they weren't enemies. They were just a man and a woman.

But now she needed to get back to reality. Back to her mission; back to saving Alba.

Lina looked down at the dress Jay's assistant had supplied her with. She'd gratefully accepted the services of the beautician and hairdresser offered, but now she wondered if she would have been better off on her own.

The dress was white, as she had requested, but the layers and tufted satin had white chiffon flowers and feathers, of all things, interwoven with pearls. The tight bodice pushed her already generous breasts up until she was afraid they were going to pop out, cinching her waist tight. They'd tried to fit her with something called a bustle, which she'd flatly refused. Why try and make her rounded backside bigger than it already was?

The costume was a gaudy monstrosity and she felt ridiculous. That was without considering what they had done with her shoulder-length dark hair.

The hairdresser had decided Lina's hair was too short and added extensions until masses of dark brown hair lay in waves down her back. The thin man had then taken her new hair and proceeded to wind it up in some strange updo that trailed down her back, feathers and pearls interwoven with the new locks.

At least her make-up looked acceptable, if a little more overstated than her usual pastels. The deep greens and golds had made her brown eyes look huge and mysterious, with a slight slant at the edges. Bangs now fluttered over her left eye, even more obnoxious than the old hairstyle that had constantly blown in her face.

She stood staring at herself in the floor-length mirror in her guest bath, batting away the bangs.

If only her friends could see her now. She found it hard to believe women really dressed this way here. Up until now, the attire had seemed a little ostentatious but not that unlike Alba's dress.

This had to be a joke. There was no way she was leaving the house like this.

A perfunctory knock at the door interrupted her thoughts.

"Enter."

Jay opened the door, his eyes widening when he saw

her, scanning her form before getting stuck in the center of her chest.

"Wow."

"My thoughts exactly," Lina agreed darkly. Good, he thought it was ridiculous too.

"I can't believe Mabell West actually agreed to give you a design on such short notice." He couldn't seem to tear his eyes from her nearly overflowing bosom, and she resisted the urge to cross her arms over it.

"Mabell West? What...?" Lina had a sinking feeling she was going to be stuck wearing this.

"She's a famous clothes designer here. The feathers arc her signature, or so my sisters tell me. They will be envious tonight; they've been trying to get her to design them a State Dinner dress for years."

They can have mine, Lina thought. But she kept the unkind thought to herself, not wanting to offend Jay if he had asked this special designer for her dress. She sighed.

"I'm ready. Let's get this over with."

"That's the spirit," Jay said with the familiar twinkle in his eye. "I'm so glad to see you're excited about the evening ahead."

Lina said nothing, grasping handfuls of the costume and trying to exit the room gracefully. At least the voluminous skirts allowed her to wear low-heeled shoes so she wouldn't have to worry about twisting an ankle.

Jay looked impressive and not the least bit ridiculous in his own dark attire. The black suit was tailored to his muscular form perfectly, a white vest with crimson threading his only adornment. He was clean-shaven, which displayed his perfectly sculpted features, including the grooves that appeared when he smiled. Her heart fluttered in her chest, and heat settled in the pit of her stomach. Why did he have to be so handsome?

He's still the enemy, she reminded herself. Nothing had changed, regardless of the previous night.

It was getting more and more difficult to remember that.

A large black vehicle waited at the curb, the door held open by Jay's housekeeper. Nodding her thanks to the mature gentleman who had so far been very gracious to her, she climbed as gracefully as possible into the vehicle, dragging the dress with her.

Jay slid in next to her, glancing over at her as the door closed gently. He grinned. Lina narrowed her eyes.

"You think it's ridiculous too, don't you?"

He burst into the laughter he must have been holding back the entire time. "The dresses women wear to events are beyond ridiculous. It is like they are competing to be the most absurd. I've got to hand it to your people: besides the Patrician's obsession with white, they are much more practical."

"At least I won't be the only crazily-dressed woman there. Hopefully I can just blend in."

Jay knew Lina's wish would be impossible. It wasn't just because she looked beautiful, even in the impressive statement of a dress she wore. The very fact that she was Alban, and her talent in using the Technology, would make her exotic. Everyone would want to catch a glimpse of or meet her.

Jay cursed again the Technology that had made Lina so essential to the Empire; to his mother. His foolish wish of bringing her along as a "captive", and perhaps getting to know her better, seemed as naïve as he'd thought Lina to be initially.

He was an idiot. But he couldn't seem to stay away from Lina; to ignore the strong pull that had attracted him in the first place. She calmed him, and brought out the good that he'd been afraid didn't exist. He'd felt numb for so long, he'd begun to worry he was becoming his mother: Soulless, emotionless, and self-centered.

With Lina, he wanted to be different. He *was* different.

And he would fight with everything he had to protect her, and to keep her close.

The mission he'd given himself was nearly impossible, given her notoriety. She'd become an instant celebrity several days earlier following her initial display. There was nothing the people of New Glory, and the entire nation, loved more than a celebrity.

The President's press conference announcing their acquisition of powerful technology had created excitement throughout the nation. Lina didn't know it, but Jay's quick action in removing her from the Capitol's guest suite had sheltered her from the media frenzy that had followed, much to the President's frustration. She'd wanted to milk this media blitz of every drop of exposure for her upcoming campaign.

As much as he wanted to, he wouldn't be able to keep her under wraps forever; tonight she, and the Technology, would be making a public debut.

Confederates were very proud of their technology muscle, whether they flexed it or not. He figured just the announcement and reveal of the Technology's amazing capabilities would be enough to guarantee his mother a re-election when her five-year term was up. He was certain Lina didn't realize she had done the President a favor with her initial threatening display of power.

His black Masters V.2 slid to a stop beside the curb, the door opened by a black-clothed attendant. He nodded his thanks, swiping his ID over the man's wrist to leave a tip. The man nodded almost imperceptibly as he turned to help Lina from the car. Jay grinned as he heard her muttering about the dress, trying to gently smooth the ruffled feathers.

The gathered crowd went quiet as they turned towards the State ballroom's large entrance. A voice called out, "It's Jay and the Alban!" Then the mob erupted into shouts, startling Lina, her eyes going wide.

"Just smile and wave," Jay advised in a low voice. "The media reps are recording everything and will be replaying this on the networks later."

Lina immediately smiled, but Jay could see the strain on her face. Best to get her inside as quickly as possible. The real work was going to begin later.

He ushered her inside, politely refusing every request for interviews.

It wasn't much better inside. Congressman, celebrities, and other officials approached quickly from all sides, each wanting to get a moment of time with the Alban who had the Technology the President promised would guarantee their position as a world power.

"Can you give us a little preview of what this amazing Technology is?" one short woman asked, the scent of alcohol strong on her breath. The woman's dress was so full of ruffles and beading that it must weigh almost as much as the woman herself. Lina smiled widely, blinking. Her eyes went to Jay, and he felt her slender hand grip his arm tightly.

"She has something special planned for later. We wouldn't want to ruin the surprise," Jay said politely, pulling Lina along with him.

"Are you wearing the latest Mabell West design?!" A group of woman, dressed in strange and elaborate outfits like her own, approached. They pressed in close, giving her no room to retreat.

"Yes, I am very thankful to have received such a gift," Lina murmured. Jay squeezed her arm gently to show his approval.

"How is it you get to be her escort, Jayden?" Another woman asked slyly, her eyes going between the two."

Jay's smile definitely didn't reach his eyes as he replied, "I was privileged enough to escort Miss March from Alba, and continue to offer my protection and assistance in any capacity she needs me."

"I can imagine she's found your, um, personal protection to be quite satisfactory," a blonde woman said cattily. The group twittered. Jay raised an eyebrow at the classless comment, vaguely recognizing her as someone he might have had a brief fling with in the past.

This was going to go downhill fast.

They excused themselves, Jay forging a path through the throng without looking to either side. Lina's hand continued to grip his arm, the other dragging her dress along.

Suddenly Lina pulled him to a halt, turning quickly. To Jay's surprise, she hugged someone. Stix.

Stix seemed equally shocked. "You have no idea how nice it is to see a familiar face," she told him, clinging to his arms. "What are you doing here?"

"Security," Stix answered. "Jay asked me to help out in case … well, to look out…" he trailed off, his eyes looking to Jay for help.

"In case I get out of control?" Lina finished helpfully. Stix's leathery face flushed a shade darker and he nodded. Lina smiled. "Don't worry, I understand. I am not sure if I trust me with the Technology yet, either."

"My god, don't say that so loud," Jay begged, half-jokingly.

"Thomas!" Lina ignored Jay's comment, turning to the large man standing beside Stix. "How is James?"

"He's doing much better. I didn't think… I was a little worried there for awhile." Thomas cleared his throat and shrugged, as if trying to hide his emotions.

Lina smiled at him. "I'm glad. And Royce?"

"He's been reassigned. He's not normally part of our team. Jay treatin' you good?" Stix asked gruffly, eyeing the younger man.

"Yeah, she don't deserve the harassment the media'll give her. She's a real lady, man." Thomas added, his large hand coming to settle on Lina's bare shoulder. Lina felt warmth replace a little of the stark terror she'd felt since exiting the vehicle. Perhaps she was losing her mind, but in the past few weeks these dangerous strangers had practically become family.

Jay held up both hands as if in surrender. "She's become a force to be reckoned with. It's me you should be worried about."

"Jay, you're not monopolizing the guest of honor, are you?" The cool, refined voice was like a bucket of ice on Lina's warm feelings.

The President stepped forward with a wide smile that didn't match the ice in her eyes. Lina thought of the photograph in Jay's house of the dark-haired, swarthy skinned man whose white teeth gleamed in a wide grin. Jay might have his mother's coloring, but his appearance and demeanor seemed to be much more like his late father.

Thomas and Stix faded back into the shadows as Jay turned towards his mother. "No ma'am. Just making the rounds as expeditiously as possible."

"I have some people who are eager to meet her. Come." Without waiting for a response, the statuesque woman turned and walked into the crowd. Lina glanced at Jay, hesitating a moment. He grinned and motioned for her to proceed him.

The crowd of ostentatiously dressed woman in their plumage—apparently Mabell West was a busy woman—stood alongside the colorfully suited men. The massive foyer with shiny black marble floor and dark décor was a perfect backdrop to the brightly garbed crowd. Jay was the only man dressed in black, and Lina wondered at his disregard for the popular style.

It was hardly fair. She stifled a sneeze, a tiny feather drifting past her nose.

Lina dutifully followed the President and her entourage from cluster to cluster, murmuring the words expected of her, answering vaguely the questions asked. Her eyes continually went to Jay, who hung back, talking to the mob that wanted to curate his attention.

He talked easily with the people around him, his smile flashing again and again. It was the Jay she had met in Alba; the chameleon who knew what people wanted and gave it to them.

It scared her. She could see now this wasn't the real Jay. But who was the real Jay? She was convinced she had caught glimpses of him in their short time together.

Would it be enough? Would he forgive her what she was about to do?

The President had excused herself, but a younger version of the terrifying woman, the Defense Secretary, stuck close to Lina's side. The other woman couldn't have been more than five years older than Jay's own thirty years, but her pinched expression and reserved clothing made her appear older. And while the President carried with her an aura of cool disdain, her daughter seemed to exude bitter anger. The dislike that emanated from the woman at her side made Lina feel even more uptight.

As the evening progressed and the names and faces became a blur, Lina's nervousness steadily increased. Dinner approached, and she was the show.

Could she carry out the performance they had planned? She'd spent the entire day with Chelsea going over the brief performance, practicing what she would say, going back through the network to make sure she had the correct commands needed to display her talent. Had it been enough? Would Chelsea's plan work? The younger girl had seemed so different from her mother and other sister, it was hard for Lina to believe they were related.

Lina had felt a strange camaraderie with the other woman, laughing at her dry humor, relaxing in her eclectic home high above the city. But how much like Jay was his little sister? Could she trust the girl's motives; her help? Would the gathered crowd be impressed? How would they react?

What would Jay think of her performance?

Questions whirled through her over-charged brain, and the ever-present networks visible to her newly acquired sense threatened to overwhelm her.

Dinner opened with a dramatic rendition of the

Empire's national anthem, which was completed by the recitation of the audience: "For the glory of our Empire, our President, and our people."

Lina shivered in the still-overly warm room, the echo of the cultish words fading as a small band began to play the twangy music Jay had called Country Western ballads.

Jay was seated at the table next to hers at dinner, and her panic and uncertainty grew with the distance.

Chelsea hadn't been invited, still in disgrace over her recent stint at the rehab clinic, but she promised she'd find a way to watch the performance. Lina scanned the room, searching for her new confidant and friend.

Or perhaps the woman who had orchestrated her demise.

Doubt entered her mind yet again. What if Chelsea had her own motives, like Jay? Was Lina just a means to an end; revenge against the family Chelsea obviously resented?

She couldn't eat. Fears and doubts kept her stomach in knots. She spent the dinner staring at her plate, pushing food around, trying to politely answer the questions posed to her, although she barely heard them.

"Is Alba really divided into classes…?"

"How do the people feel about being legally segregated?"

"It seems so barbaric…"

She wanted to tell them their own country was obviously segregated, whether it was by law or not. That their unusual clothes and obsession with power seemed equally barbaric to her.

But she didn't. She quietly answered each question, dreading the approaching moment when she would be put on display like a wild animal in Alba's arena.

Jay's sister, the sour Defense Secretary, sat by her side. The other girl's light blue gaze, much like the President's own flinty eyes, rarely strayed from Lina's face.

As the dessert was being served by the silent, black-clothed attendants, the President stood. Lina felt her stomach drop. She nodded to Lina, indicating she was to follow the older woman up to the podium on the small stage.

Her legs felt wobbly as she stood, tripping over the voluminous skirts. Several hands moved to catch her and she thanked the faceless helpers absently, her mind whirling with what she was going to be required to do.

"Ladies and gentleman of our great nation, fellow Confederates, welcome. As you are all aware, tonight is a momentous occasion. After years of research, we finally have produced a technology that will not only change our States, but will alter the world. We will not need to wonder at our status as a superpower in the re-emerging global politics: we will be assured of our status." President March turned to motion to Lina. "I have with me our first test subject who is here from Alba, where the founders of this technology reside. She had graciously agreed to travel here and demonstrate how truly powerful this advancement will make the Southern Empire."

Graciously agreed?

Resounding applause broke out. Squinting against the bright lights, Lina looked over to where Jay lounged back in his chair. He did not applaud, his eyes watchful and dark in the shadows surrounding him. Did he suspect something?

This could very well be the end of their fragile relationship.

Your power includes responsibility.

She let her gaze scan over the room of expectant faces. It was time to shine, or to burn.

She closed her eyes, shutting out the lights and faces. Her mind opened, the new sense of the digital networks around her becoming clearer; brighter. The controls, commands, and inner workings all open to her. All tied together on a central network not unlike the one Alba used.

Program initiated.

The lights went out. The Com devices—she wasn't sure

what they called them here—began playing the Empire's anthem, Our Glory, as one. Each device then said a single word, spreading across the room, to form the phrase "Recognize the great power of the Technology before you. The Technology with the power to change the world. The Technology that once destroyed the world."

Gasps spread through the guests as each device then began showing historical images of destruction; of cities being leveled from bombs set off by unknown individuals with new and unchartered abilities. Of burning cities, looted and dark from electromagnetic pulse weapons used to combat the Technology.

The heavy drapes over the wall of windows on the north and east sides of the room flew open to reveal the dark harbor.

The city lights began to blink, and then went dark. The lights that went on in select buildings were in the shape of numbers, counting down: 3, 2, 1.

Like the first evening, antiballistic missiles launched from the harbor into the night sky, exploding in a hail of cascading fire that lit the harbor. A ship anchored off the military base began to sound its distant horn, and two aircraft lifted, coming fast towards the capitol in which the stunned crowd sat, fascinated. A few of the guests gasped in fear as the military helicopters approached, getting up from their chairs. The aircraft were now lit by spotlights from the roof of a nearby building, their lights blinding the inhabitants of the room.

The gasps turned to shrieks as the 'copters hovered just outside the windows, their blades screeching across the glass in a painful cacophony.

Lina's eyes opened, and she was unaware of their amber color that almost glowed in the dark room. She saw Jay sitting on the edge of his chair as if ready to lunge across the room and stop her. She knew Stix and Thomas, and no doubt other soldiers, were positioned around the edges of the room, waiting to hit her with an EMW blast that would steal her consciousness.

It would do no good. She had already planned and scheduled each event with Chelsea's help; it was merely running on the program she had initiated.

The grand finale was coming next. Hopefully Jay wouldn't hate her for what she had done.

The helicopters hovered outside the windows, and through their blades came the red laser of the mass EMW in the harbor, its aim centering on the President. A single blast from this massive weapon would destroy a small city.

Or a city square, such as the Empire's warship had done in Alba.

Jay was out of his chair, advancing slowly. Was he worried this was revenge? For Stephen. For Alba. For her.

A strange urge came over her. This was her chance. She could kill the President and the leaders of the Empire.

She could avenge her brother. End the threat.

"Don't do it, Lina." Jay's voice was close. He didn't make any attempt to touch her, but she could see the harsh lines of his body. He was ready. "Alba would surely be destroyed. And you would die for nothing. It wouldn't bring your brother back."

Lina met his blue-green gaze. He didn't look scared about impending death. He looked intense, concerned. Angry.

But it was never her intent to kill anyone. She just wanted them to know what kind of fire they were playing with. To remind them of how the world nearly ended once. It had taken a hundred years to get back to this point.

Were they willing to risk that yet again?

The blast, when it came, was deflected perfectly by the coated blades of the helicopters, flying horizontally for the brief moment required. The deflected electrical current struck and charred the artwork on display around the stateroom; hitting the myriad of chandeliers on the ceiling that imploded with the force of the energy; striking the drapery adorning each window.

Using the advanced weaponry of the Southern Empire, Lina's display worked beautifully. Fire erupted from each deflected strike location, triggering the water system which, for the second time in two days, rained down upon the gathering.

Screams and cries added to the cacophony of the helicopter blades and the fire alarm.

Lina looked over at Jay, his normal grin absent, lines of anger clear on his face.

"I'm sorry," she said quietly, knowing he couldn't hear above the noise. And she was sorry. Sorry she had deviated from their plan. Sorry that she was even in this position. Sorry they had to be on opposing sides in this.

Jay took the final step forward to close the distance between them, his hand going up to her neck. A painful, burning pressure began.

A moment later, blackness overcame her.

18

Aerina stood in back of the meeting room with Vick, both listening in to the Senators discussing the upcoming mission to the Southern Empire.

Discuss was probably too generous of a word. Argue was a little more accurate. Fight, probably closest to the truth.

As always, Marcus had distanced himself, merely observing the exchange between the gathered Patricians and newly elected members from a myriad of castes.

Aerina found the exchange fascinating, and she could tell from Vick's expression he did, too. She wasn't certain how Marcus had selected the new Senators, but they had a variety of personality types. Some were very vocal in their opinions, while others seemed a little intimated, even in awe, of the

Patricians and Marcus.

It was one of the silent, awe-struck Plebs who spoke into a moment of silence.

"Of course we must go. To sit and wait for what comes would not only be foolish, it would be a dishonor to the memory of those who died in battle."

All eyes in the room settled upon the slender man who spoke so passionately. He blinked owlish eyes that seemed to dominate his slender, effeminate features. Shaggy black hair was carefully curled and teased around his face, and his bright red clothing was carefully pressed.

Marcus' eyes gleamed for a moment, which Aerina would have missed had she not looked to him for his reaction. Obviously he had chosen this man for a reason, and was pleased with the results.

He finally took control of the conversation. "I will go with a small team. We will learn all we can of their motives and plans. We will decide how to proceed from there."

"What of a Consul?" Caius asked angrily.

"Ramus will have control until my return." Marcus' voice had become soft, an indication he was exerting careful control over himself. "I will present my candidate then for a vote."

"Another Virmortus in charge? It is ludicrous! You expect—"

"I expect you to follow my orders, and act in the best interests of our State."

Caius subsided into frustrated silence. Marcus could be more political, but he obviously felt that a heavy hand was necessary to scare the Senators into obedience.

And he was probably right. Divisive leadership now could mean the downfall of their State, and a complete failure of the research he had been overseeing of the Technology.

Marcus motioned to Ramus, who stepped in and began going through the meeting agenda. Vick and Aerina followed him out of the Capitol meeting room.

"We'll meet with the team who will be traveling to the Empire with us and go over protocol. It is risky. And it is probably some kind of trap."

"Then why are we going?" Vick asked.

"We don't have a choice. And I have a secret weapon."

"I hoped you'd say something like that." Vick grinned over at Aerina. She rolled her eyes. Didn't anything ever worry him?

She felt her own mixture of fear and excitement at the upcoming trip. To see the Southern Empire; to travel to the other side of the continent … it was more than she had ever dreamed possible. A year ago, this would have seemed impossible; like an alternate reality.

Now it *was* reality. It was both amazing and terrifying at the same time. She had no idea what the future held. For her, for Lina, for Alba. But she couldn't bring herself to regret anything she'd done so far.

"What about Lina?" she asked. Her friend was constantly at the forefront of her mind. She'd felt overwhelming relief when the message from the Empire had included a mention of the "Alban Patrician Representative" that was eagerly awaiting their visit. A veiled threat, but also hope that they could still bring Lina home. "Do we have a plan to find her and bring her back?"

"The Virmortus should be arriving in the Empire capitol soon, and will begin sending information. We should be able to learn more then."

We're coming, Lina. Just hang on a little longer.

Part 4 Free

In the end, technology is merely an extension of the greatest invention of all: the human mind. All possibilities and limitations start and end there. The sentient being – emotional, empathic, hopeful – has more power than any innovation.

– From the Journal of Cecilia Delacroix

1

Jay sat in the holding room where Lina was still unconscious, a myriad of emotions contained in his tense form. He looked at her unconscious figure, which he'd placed on the bed himself less than an hour earlier. He'd cut off the outlandish gown, tossing it carelessly in the corner of the steel room. She now lay in the wisps of cloth that passed as underclothes.

The cot on which Lina lay and the single stool were the only furnishings in the brightly lit, cold room. He'd placed a light blanket over her prone body to keep her creamy skin and tempting curves hidden from other eyes. From his own hungry gaze.

Even now, a few of the Confederate soldiers were tearing out the computerized lock and room controls, trying to replace them with mechanical security.

Anger over her betrayal warred with the pride he felt over the ingenuity and courage she'd displayed.

She'd obviously changed the script they had drawn up, no doubt with his devious little sister's help. He'd underestimated the delicate Patrician yet again.

No longer. The new Lina was obviously a force to be reckoned with. She was becoming accustomed to her new

power, and was learning how to hit the Empire where it hurt
most: their pride.

Why the hell hadn't she told him about her plan?

The door burst open and the President herself entered.
She'd changed from her wet, singed gown into pants and a
high-necked white silk shirt. Her hair was still damp from the
anti-fire system that had effectively put out the blazes.

"What the hell was that." The statement hissed from
between stiff lips, the President bristling with anger. Jay
turned on the stool, forcing himself to remain seated; relaxed.
He needed to calm her down before she did something rash.
Nothing angered the President more than being made to look
a fool.

"Didn't you appreciate the impressive display? I'm
certain the Congress, and the entire city, are now aware of the
Technology's power." As a final coup de grace, the entire
city's power grid had been shut down, keeping the city in the
dark. A code was required to reboot the system, which Jay
was certain only Lina knew. They had the best engineers at
work, trying to crack the intricate program that blocked their
access.

"I thought you had her under control!"

"So did I," Jay said ruefully.

"Is this humorous to you? The fate of our nation is at
stake here! If you cannot complete this mission, I'll find
someone who can."

Jay stiffened slightly. "I will complete the mission,
Madam President." His mother watched him, her gray-blue
eyes calculating.

"I think we'll try extraction. I can't waste any more time.
Due to your failure, I'll have to send another team back to
Alba to find my Technology. If they haven't destroyed it all by
now!"

Jay felt frustrated anger rising in his chest, and he forced
it back down. He had failed. But he was beginning to question
if maybe his mother was not the right person to get her hands

on the strange Technology currently housed in Lina. He'd always known she was a bit narcisstic and manipulative. But she was brilliant, ambitious, and he'd admired that. Now he wondered, how far would she go? Was she crazy enough to kill millions for her personal agenda?

She already has.

Leaning back against the wall, his expression giving away nothing of the doubt in his mind, he kept his tone calm and even. "Are you sure that is a good idea? Why not wait and see if they are willing to give you a sample of the Technology when they arrive?

"Give it to me?" she scoffed. "They will never part with it willingly. No, we'll just need to take our chances extracting it."

"I can't let you do that."

His mother's head jerked up, and she stared at him incredulously. What the hell was he doing? Lina had made her choice. She wasn't his responsibility. Acquiring the Technology was.

"'You can't let me'? Who are you to tell me what I can or cannot do?" His mother's voice had transformed into the angry hiss he remembered well. Anyone who didn't approve or agree with her was an enemy. Even as children, he and his siblings had learned to be careful about what they said to their narcissistic mother.

He needed to tread carefully.

"My mission is the Technology. I don't think extraction is a risk we can afford to take. I think we can still use her. Just give me a little more time."

Cold blue eyes studied him. "Perhaps you're right. We might need some leverage against the Albans. Although why they would care about this one stupid girl when their whole society is at stake, I can't imagine."

She turned, touching her damp hair with renewed irritation.

"I need to explain the situation to Congress. Damn

vultures are circling, hoping they can spin this to the media as a glaring mistake and oust me in the next election. When she wakes up, make sure you get her to admit publicly this was all her fault; that she was too weak to control the power of the Technology. I don't care how you have to convince her. But do it, or I will."

She exited the room without a backwards glance, confident of his obedience.

2

Aerina could barely contain her excitement as she watched the terrain speed by far below. Her nose had been pressed to the jet's window the entire flight, her heart racing, adrenaline pumping.

Marcus and Vick talked quietly, running different scenarios with the small team they had brought. Three Virmortus joined them, two of which were injected with the Technology. They watched Marcus run virtual scenarios on the holographic projection from his reader. Vick had worked with a cartographer to create detailed maps of the Southern Empire, where he had admitted to having spent the first twenty-two years of his life.

He hadn't volunteered further information, and Marcus was as close-mouthed as ever about the subject. Aerina's curiosity was like a slowly spreading fire within her, but she decided to bide her time.

"The rest of the Empire is weakly guarded, until we get to about here." Vick used his hand to draw part of the screen out, enlarging it. "This region is most important. The Capitol is located there. Most of their weapon storage is at the military base about sixty-five miles north of the Capitol. And their food supply comes from two main regions, the Great Lake Basin and the Southern Inland Preserve."

"What is this area?" Chessa, a female Virmortus not much older than Aerina, pointed to a large dark area in the north-eastern edge of the Empire.

"That was the rebel state. They tried to leave the Sovereign States of the Southern Empire. The current President was Secretary of Defense at the time." Vick's face had changed. Aerina turned to watch, her eyes widening at the stark tone and expression the normally jovially man wore. "She obliterated the entire region. Killed everything, burned every building, and razed entire towns. It was an amazing show of power, and it immediately stopped any rumblings of discontent among the other regions."

"How could the Congress allow that? The President? How could they allow her to do this to their own people?"

Vick turned to look at Aerina, his normal smile falling back into place, but his hazel eyes remained barren.

"She's always had a way of getting people to go along with her decisions; most are too afraid to disagree, or perhaps she's just that charismatic." Vick spoke as if he knew her personally, this larger-than-life President. Knew her, and hated her.

"The President is feared, but obeyed. She needs constant reassurance that she is powerful, brilliant, and becomes irrational when anyone disagrees with her." Vick pinned Aerina with a stare. "You need to keep your opinions to yourself. Don't try to reason with her; she doesn't care what anyone else thinks. And try to keep the sarcasm to a minimum."

Aerina grimaced. Keeping her opinions to herself was tough. She glanced at Marcus. His face was impassive, giving nothing away of his thoughts.

Subtlety had never been her strong suit. But she didn't want to let Marcus down. She was going to succeed at this; their lives, Lina's life, the survival of the entire State, depended on it.

Chessa and Lucien, the other Technology-injected

Virmortus, exchanged glances. Aerina stiffened. She had gotten the feeling that Chessa didn't like her, and figured it was because Aerina wasn't one of them. She had never experienced the harsh training or the extreme emotional duress that Virmortus underwent. Yet here she was, on this crucial mission, playing a key role. It must irk these trained killers to have a Patrician along for the ride.

Aerina listened as Vick went back to describing the layout of the Capitol and the technology used there, trying to commit it to memory.

How would they find Lina in such a massive nation, without any idea of where she might be?

She met Marcus' dark gaze and he gave a small nod.

She flashed a smile back.

Do what you can and let the rest go. The Medella's advice from the day of the Empire's attack ran through her mind. The health worker's words had helped that day as she saw injured and mutilated bodies of Albans. It had become a mantra she repeated and it helped relieve her self-imposed burden of guilt.

She was going to see the Southern Empire. And she was going to find Lina. Hope fluttered in her chest as she looked back out the window, growing until it became near-euphoria.

This was the life she was meant to live.

3

Before her eyes fluttered open, Lina could already see the virtual systems around her, beckoning to her. A tiny voice warned her to go back to sleep; to fight her body's awakening.

She ignored it, blinking quickly to adjust to the bright light of the room. The room was tiny, but never would she call it cozy. It was all metal, lit by bright overhead lights that were blinding to look at.

No windows, and the door was just a metal sheet that looked as if it might slide into the wall when opened. Almost absently she searched through the myriad of system commands for the controls of this room. Not knowing where she was made that difficult, so she dimmed the lights of every room in New Glory that was running on backup power.

The power I shut off. Obviously they haven't hacked my program yet. I must be better than I thought.

The relief was instant, her pounding headache aggravated by the bright glare softening slightly.

"Can't help yourself, can you?"

The sardonic voice drew her gaze to the single empty chair in the room, and the man standing just to the left of it. Jay leaned negligently against the wall, arms crossed lightly. His muscled form was still encased in suit pants, although he had discarded the jacket and dress shirt, wearing just a snug white undershirt. It delineated each well-defined muscle, making her swallow hard.

Despite his relaxed stance, she could see the anger burning in the blue-green depths of his gaze.

Lina felt at a disadvantage in her prone position, and tried to sit up. Her arms were caught, the clanging of metal drawing her panicked gaze to the strange manacles wrapped tightly around her wrists.

Handcuffs that were old and rusted were clamped tight, securing her to the bed.

"Where did you dig these up?" she managed to ask, trying to sound light-hearted even though panic was rising. She had known the plan would put her in this type of situation. But it didn't make her feel any less terrified.

"Pulled them from the museum, just for you."

He was furious. She was beginning to learn his tones; the sarcastic bite a sure sign of his anger.

"I'm surprised no one has gotten into my program," she said, attempting to match his casual demeanor. Inside, she was a quivery mess of fear. What was going to happen?

Jay pushed off the wall, approaching at an unhurried pace. She felt as if a mountain lion were approaching, stalking its intended victim.

He grabbed the chair, spinning and placing it beside the bed. Straddling it, he leaned close. "It might be a good idea to stop the program and reboot the power grid. Right now."

Lina didn't argue. She'd already proven her point, anyhow. It didn't take long to quarantine the program and use the back door she'd left open to stop the second-by-second password reset.

In a minute and a half it was shut down, the power grid rebooting.

"Done," she told Jay, her eyes not quite managing to rise above his square jaw. It was already shadowed with light stubble. How long had she been unconscious? As she stared, he pulled out a Com device, talking into it quickly.

"They confirmed the system is back up. Now, let's talk about you. More specifically, your future here in the Empire. Or lack thereof."

Lina's stomach sunk at his words. Was he threatening her? He was her one security here; the one person she trusted.

Trusted.

Did she really still trust him, after everything he'd done?

Yes, a small voice admitted.

Idiot, she told herself. But Jay's patience, his tendency to humor her, might now be at an end.

"What does that mean?" she asked.

"It means you've really pissed off the President now. And she's running the show. Democracy, penal system…it's all a joke. She is god here, and you've just incurred her wrath." Bitterness tinged his words, and Lina scanned his face, coming to a surprising conclusion.

He didn't like his mother. The President. The supreme ruler of this dystopian society.

She didn't know where she stood with Jay or how he truly felt about her. Maybe she was just a mission. A thorn in his side. But the new Lina wasn't going to play the victim here. And she wasn't going to let fear overpower her.

"I did what I felt was necessary."

Jay nodded slowly, his gaze on his clasped hands. Suddenly he stood, kicking the chair to the side in an angry explosion of movement. "Why the hell didn't you tell me you'd changed the script? You had plenty of opportunity."

"I knew you'd try to stop me."

Jay's jaw clenched and unclenched, and he unconsciously rolled his shoulders, frustrated rage bubbling to the surface, threatening to burst forth. What did she want from him? He'd looked after her, gotten her here safely; protected her from his goddamn psychotic mother. He'd kept his hands to himself as much as possible, though god knows he'd wanted more than just a single night with her. A lot more.

But he'd let her set the pace; be in control. He respected her, gave her time to work through everything, to learn to trust him.

And she still didn't. And that pissed him off. It stung his pride. And yeah, he admitted to himself, it hurt.

He glanced back to see Lina watching him, her dark eyes wide in her intelligent face, studying him. Curious, fearful, uncertain.

"Is it still because I mislead you in Alba; because I slept with you?" he asked, running his hands through his too-long hair in frustration. The tawny locks had grown out of control, and he was ready to go back to his normal buzzed hair that was much easier to manage. "I told you, even before you knew who I was, that the sex was different. Separate. I was an enemy spy, what the hell else was I supposed to do? I used you to get to the Technology, and you used me to thumb your nose at the Patricians."

Lina flushed, turning her head away for a moment before looking back at him. She looked so delicate and uncertain, it raised the protective instinct in him yet again.

Something about her made him want to be the hero; to have her look at him with adoration and respect instead of distrust and betrayal.

"We're still on opposite sides, Jay. What did you expect?"

"I expected you to trust me! I've done everything you wanted, tried to be a man you can—" He broke off before the forbidden words could burst forth; words that he'd never spoken and that would give her the upper hand.

He couldn't say them. He didn't even know if it was real.

"Jay, you lied to me. You used me—*stabbed* me, for serenity's sake. It isn't something I can just forget about. I'm not like you, able to put on a fake smile and ride through life like a surfer on a wave. I am a terrible surfer. Just ask my brother. But you can't ask him, because *your people killed him*!" Jay stared, surprised at her acerbic response. The scared little rabbit had grown some fangs, and he had to admit they stung.

His anger grew, mostly because he knew she was right and there was nothing he could do about it. He couldn't take it back; couldn't change the past.

But goddammit he would if he could. And that scared him as much as it angered him.

The anger felt safer, so he let it flow through him.

"Forget it. Forget trying to make amends for what I did. Because I can't. I'll never be able to take back what I've done to you. What we've done to Alba. You're probably right not to trust me. I'll just focus on completing my mission, and you can do whatever the hell you think you have to do. I'm done trying to be the good guy. I'm damned already, anyway."

Before his words fully registered, he leaned in and kissed her, his mouth hard and angry on hers.

Lina couldn't move, her head pinned to the hard cot beneath. He was so focused on punishing her for not trusting him, he didn't notice for a moment that she wasn't pulling away or trying to fight. His kiss immediately gentled at her acquiesce, his mouth changing from marauding to slowly exploring. Lina tried to raise her head higher, to get closer. She would have crawled in his lap, into his clothes, had the handcuffs allowed the movement.

Hope unfurled in his chest. Perhaps she trusted him a little; perhaps they weren't completely hopeless.

But now was not the best time to delve deeper, not with enemies all around.

Enemies. The word popped naturally into his head when he thought of his fellow southerners. What was happening to him?

He pulled back, and she instinctively tried to follow, brought up short by the cuffs. He turned away, leaning his hand against the wall, breathing deeply. Lina flushed, ashamed.

"At least your body is honest." His voice was low and harsh with restrained passion.

"Am I interrupting something?" The sardonic feminine drawl was so like Jay's, Lina knew immediately who it was. Chelsea leaned nonchalantly against the open door, knowing eyes going from Lina's flushed face to Jay's stiff back.

"How the hell did you get in here?" Jay's voice sounded more resigned than angry, as if he wouldn't have expected any less of his sister. He finally turned back, having got his body, and his anger, back under control. She's expected his anger, but was a little surprised at the reason behind it. He was angry she didn't trust him, as if he needed her to.

As if he cared.

"Oh please, I looked up how to pick a lock. What's with the rusty old deadbolt?" Chelsea's eyes went to Lina's cuffs. "Oh yeah. The great telekinetic."

Lina couldn't help but look on her partner-in-crime with affection. The tawny-haired girl with her blunt demeanor and sarcastic wit reminded her so much of Aerina.

And like Jay. Perhaps that was why she'd fallen so quick

for him; he was a male version of her best friend.

"Our show was flawless; bravo," Chelsea congratulated Lina, eyeing her cuffs again. "You predicted the ending, though. Damn. Sorry about that."

"I had a feeling you were involved," Jay said, pinning Chelsea with his gaze. "The President is furious. You'd better hope she doesn't learn about your involvement, or you'll spend the next decade or so in the rehab clinic."

Chelsea shrugged, her eyes not meeting Jay's. She was trying to look unconcerned, but Lina could see the tension in her face. The fear in her eyes.

It was familiar. The same look she'd seen on her own face in the mirror many times.

The walls she'd been painstakingly attempting to build around her heart cracked even further as she looked at this woman, born to a different world entirely, but still so like her.

Lonely. Insecure. Trying hard not to be a victim.

And Jay. How did she not notice that same look on his face before? He was much better at disguising the trauma left from his youth — at playing the easy-going cad — that she hadn't seen it until this moment.

She'd hurt him with her distrust, just as he'd done to her with his first betrayal.

"So now what happens?" Chelsea asked.

Jay looked over at Lina, who met the carefully banked embers of his gaze with new understanding. "The show's not over yet. Better start working on the script for Part Two."

4

"Let's set down here," Marcus instructed brusquely. The pilot nodded and the jet descended. They were inside the Southern Empire's radar, but their cloaking had held so far, Marcus monitoring the Confederate radar after Chessa had hacked into the network.

Aerina had only caught glimpses of ruins and the occasional vehicle which Vick referred to as "Mad Max style" after some ridiculous pre-war era film, a strange melding of materials from pre-war vehicles.

According to the map Vick had drawn up, they were in the south-western quadrant of the Empire, just above the Gulf. They'd flown over the northern part of Texico, which had been a mess of poorly constructed buildings, Mad Max vehicles, and settlements that looked straight out of the Dark Ages.

The jet settled gently onto a grassy clearing. Marcus and Vick exited first, weapons ready. Aerina noted Vick's new demeanor. Gone was the relaxed, jovial man she'd come to know. In his place was a man much more like Marcus: Composed, alert, dangerous. It told her a lot about his secret past.

Chessa carried a device with a limited-range radar so they would know what was within a mile radius. One of the other Virmortus had the map.

"You stay here with Vick," Marcus told Aerina in a low voice, the sounds of the forest slowly resuming as the wildlife returned to their interrupted activities. "We're going to do a little recon. I need to know what we're walking into."

Aerina opened her mouth to protest. She didn't want to leave him. But the look on his face told her that arguing wasn't going to matter; she wasn't invited on this little jaunt.

"How long will you be gone?" she asked instead, ignoring Chessa's sideways glance of satisfaction.

"I don't know. It depends if we can get a vehicle. I'd like to make it to New Glory and back. That's at least eight hours."

"Take Vick with you. He knows the terrain; he can help." Marcus was already shaking his close-cropped head.

"I need him here." To protect me, Aerina finished the sentence silently. When he was in Reaper mode, there was no arguing with Marcus.

"Will you look for Lina?" she asked instead. He nodded once, and she could see he was getting a little impatient.

"Isn't this dangerous?" She didn't care if this was a stupid question, her earlier excitement was beginning to be replaced with worry. She didn't want him to go. When she was with him, she had the irrational belief she could protect him.

"We have our old ID chips; with the Technology, we can have their scanner give whatever results we choose. We'll be fine. Just stay by the jet and you'll be safe. Vick is in charge. We'll return tonight, and then we'll all fly into New Glory tomorrow." His large hands settled on her shoulders, squeezing gently to reassure her. Aerina nodded, not wanting the others to see her growing fear.

Kissing her quick and hard on the mouth, Marcus turned away, walking into the dense forest without a backwards glance, Chessa and another Virmortus following.

Vick, two Virmortus, and the pilot remained.

"He's going to be fine." Vick's large hand settled gently on her shoulder. "We'd better get back on the jet, in case we need to make a quick getaway." Aerina nodded, her eyes still on the section of forest that had swallowed up Marcus.

Be safe.

5

They had been in the clearing for less than an hour when movement popped up on the radar just west of their aircraft.

"Damn," Vick muttered. "Locals." He studied the radar, looking out the jet's window at the area their visitors were approaching from.

"We could engage them," one of the assassins offered.

Vick hesitated, as if running through scenarios. "That

might be necessary. We can't leave without them detecting us at this point. I'll take the flank —"

"Wait," Aerina instructed sharply. Vick raised a questioning brow. "I have an idea. While you were all strategizing, I was studying the Empire's popular culture. Aircraft here are reserved for government officials and the very wealthy." As she talked, Aerina rushed over to the luggage they had brought, pulling clothes out until she found what she was looking for. "This was for any formal dinners, but I think it will do nicely." She stripped quickly, the fascinated group looking away politely. In a few moments, she was clothed in an elegant, if somewhat ostentatious, blue gown.

"We're stranded, and you're fixing the jet," she told the pilot. "Vick, you're my assistant."

"I'd love to play your servant, darlin', but I think I'd better keep my face hidden. Just in case," Vick responded, his eyes alight with humor. Aerina paused for a moment, giving him a quizzical look.

Who was he that he'd worry about some locals recognizing him?

Not wanting to get distracted, she saved that bit of information to review later.

"I'll be your assistant," one of the Virmortus offered. Aerina flashed him a smile of thanks.

"Better hide those weapons and lose the vest." He nodded, quickly doing as she instructed.

"If it doesn't work, we'll have to kill them," Vick murmured. Aerina nodded, hoping it wouldn't have to come to that. It wouldn't be the first death on her conscience.

An ancient truck rolled into the clearing several minutes later, an older man covered in grey hair driving. Several men, who looked like they could all be related, rode in the open back.

"An old Silverado. And it is in great condition. They must have replaced the fuel system with an energy cell. How did they keep it from rusting completely through?" Vick's voice was filled with awe. Aerina rolled her eyes. Vick and his obsession with pre-war antiques.

It was time for her to earn her keep. Pasting an annoyed smile on her face, she exited slowly, waving her "assistant" along behind her.

"Hello. I'm so glad to see this area isn't completely godforsaken. As you can see, my jet needed to make an emergency landing. My crew is working on fixing it."

The men in the pick-up stared at Aerina, jaws open. Finally, the older driver climbed out of the cab and limped over.

"Well, ma'am, I'm glad to see yer alright. We saw your airplane here land and hightailed it over to see what was going on. I'm mighty relieved to hear yer story. Was a little worried, to be honest." His friendly smile revealed yellowed, uneven teeth. Aerina's smile became slightly pained.

"Thank you. We should be on our way shortly. Right, James?"

The Virmortus took his cue. "Of course, miss. The crew is working as quickly as possible to resolve the issue. We should be airborne again shortly. We will be at our destination in plenty of time to prepare for your show."

"I knew it," one of the younger men burst out, hopping out of the back of the truck. "Yer Gloria Danes, the singer!"

Aerina smiled, turning her head coquettishly. "I really can't say. And please, keep this quiet. I'd hate to have this little incident appear in the news."

"We won't say a word, ma'am," another of the men spoke up.

"Can we be of any help?" the older man asked.

"Thank you, but no. My crew has it under control."

"Can I get an autograph for my wife? She loves your music."

"Me too!"

Vick watched from inside the jet as Aerina signed

whatever the farm workers provided, waving elegantly as they drove off in a cloud of excited dust to relate their tale.

What a woman.

"You do realize that they will tell the town that they saw us here," he commented when Aerina re-entered the jet.

"Of course," she said matter-of-factly. "But the story will just be another mysterious Gloria Dane spotting. It might hit a small-time news report but will quickly get brushed under the rug in favor of more popular news. Much better than the story of an unknown aircraft landing in the southwest province and missing locals. People, official people, would be much more likely to investigate that."

Vick smiled widely, his hazel eyes approving. "Marcus knew what he was doing when he appointed you Emissary, after all. And here I just thought you were that good in the sack."

Aerina wacked Vick in arm as she headed to the back restroom to change.

The engines rumbled to life, the low roar of air in the turbines increasing to a crescendo as the jet slowly lifted and sped forward.

"Where should I set our coordinates?" the pilot asked Vick.

"Marcus might kill me, if the Empire doesn't first, but let's head into New Glory. Head north first and then fly into their radar so it looks like we're coming straight from Alba. It will give Marcus and his team a little more time. And we might need the men on the ground. I'll let him know of the change in the plans."

6

"I'm going to kill him." Marcus' words had both the other Virmortus looking over at him curiously. They stood in a crowd in the city center of New Glory, waiting for the President to appear and make an announcement.

He closed his holoreader, clipping the tiny square to the weapon vest concealed beneath a Confederate police uniform.

Acquiring the disguises hadn't been difficult. Finding the location of the President had been even easier. She had a constant entourage of media and assistants.

"There's a change in the job. We've got to locate Lina Rhodes immediately, and then stay close to the President. The Beta Team is approaching New Glory now. We'll remain undercover and monitor the situation." Marcus' brusque instructions gave no indication of the angry fear that burned below the surface.

Vick was bringing Aerina in without him. He'd hoped to locate Lina and kill the President, making it unnecessary for Aerina to even approach New Glory. The bastard had made the decision and it was too late to turn back.

He'd keep Aerina safe. Or he'd die trying. He wasn't going back to Alba without her.

Aerina tried to calm her racing heart, her stomach churning. Their jet was slowly approaching the secure landing strip just outside of New Glory that they had been instructed to use.

From her seat near the window, she could see the motorcade of official-looking vehicles waiting below, all with the Empire's symbol, the star, emblazoned on the sides.

"You're going to do fine. Just follow my lead," Vick murmured beside her, his tanned, work-roughened hand resting lightly on her knee.

Aerina just nodded, afraid her voice would be unsteady and give away how truly nervous was.

The jet touched lightly down on the tarmac, the engines slowing until their roar was a dull hum, and then silence. The door opened, steps extending to the ground.

Vick went first, offering a hand to help her

descend. Aerina stopped for a moment at the top of the stairs, a slight smile pasted on her face, and took in the sight before her.

Soldiers lined the pathway towards the group of officials waiting to greet them, and many others were stationed around the otherwise-empty landing pad. An airport, she remembered.

"The President won't be here. She wants to be sure we know she is too important to fit her schedule to our arrival. We'll need to wait until she summons us." The unconcern in Vick's low voice calmed Aerina's racing heart slightly. They reached the bottom of the stairs and walked forward together, nearing the small group that was waiting to greet them.

Vick sighed deeply, making Aerina glance at him in concern.

"Brace yourself."

"Vicktor Lucas March. Do my eyes deceive me, or is it really you, back from the dead?" An older man walked forward, mouth hanging open. Aerina's eyes were caught by a sour-looking woman several years her senior that stared at Vick, white-faced. Murmurs began to spread through the small crowd gathered, and even some of the soldiers were stealing glances at her companion.

Who the hell was he?

"Vicktor. What… Where have you been? Are you an Alban now? How are you with their Emissary?" The woman stepped forward, questions flying from her mouth like accusations. The shock seemed to be fading and anger was taking over.

Vicktor stood, his hazel eyes going over the woman, studying her. He smiled, but Aerina noticed it didn't quite reach his eyes this time.

"I missed you, too, Jessica."

Questions whirled through Aerina's mind, but she remained silent. She would wait to ask him later, in private. And give him a piece of her mind for not telling her sooner.

"Aerina, this is Jessica March, the Secretary of Defense for the Sovereign States. Jessie, this is Aerina Delacroix, Emissary of Alba."

"Call me Secretary," Jessica instructed coldly, her blue-grey eyes barely scanning Aerina and dismissing her. Her interest remained in Vick.

The ride to the Capitol seemed endless. Jessica — excuse her, *the Secretary* — grilled Vicktor about his whereabouts for however many years he'd been presumed dead.

Frustrated with his vague answers, she finally gave up. "The President will be deathly angry when she sees you," she said with grim satisfaction.

Vick just continued to smile. "When has she been anything else *but* angry?"

"I'd be a little more concerned if I were you," she hissed back, apparently even angrier at Vick's lack of proper fear.

"Haven't changed a bit, have you?"

There was no time for Aerina to sneak a question or two of her own in. As soon as the door was opened by a waiting security guard, they were whisked into the Capitol. A smiling dark-skinned woman greeted them.

"Excellent, we've avoided the media. If you'll follow me right this way, I'll get you settled in a guest suite to freshen up before meeting with the President. She wanted to be there to greet you herself, but she's been so —" The woman's polite chatter stopped suddenly as she got a closer look at Vick.

"Hi Mona, you've certainly filled out nicely. Although I miss the pigtails," Vick commented, his eyes twinkling. Mona's mouth snapped closed.

"Vicktor? My god, it's been so long... I thought you were your brother at first. But he's never been so... hairy." She blushed after saying that, disconcerted. "I'm sorry, I didn't mean..."

"He always did like to look pretty for the ladies," Vick commented, but Aerina noticed his face had tightened at the mention of his brother.

"Yes, I um... I'll take you to your rooms," Mona finally said, dragging her eyes away from Vick to include Aerina in her statement.

Aerina wasn't sure what to make of the situation. She shot Vick a glance that promised retribution. He just smiled in return, politely taking her arm. As they followed Mona towards the guest rooms, another small group approached from the other side of the vast lobby.

"Brace yourself," Vick warned again under his breath as the statuesque woman leading the group surged forward. Then she was hugging Vick in a one-sided embrace as he remained stiff, his face gone blank.

"My darling son, you've returned! I've prayed for this moment for so many years, but I'd given up hope." The tawny-haired woman took a step back to study Vick, her hands on his shoulders. As tall as he was, she was nearly eye-to-eye with him.

"Madam President. You look the same as you did ten years ago when you saw us off." Vick's voice had gone flat, although his mouth was upturned in the facsimile of a smile.

The President's gaze was calculating as she studied Vick, and Aerina saw the same anger burning in her blue-grey eyes. Eyes that were a startling match to the Secretary of Defense. The President turned towards her entourage, her face changing. It glowed now as if she were overjoyed. She looked directly at the man holding a device that must be writing a holofile. The media, Aerina guessed.

"This is a day for celebration. My missing son, believed dead years ago on a mission for our glorious nation, has been found and returned." She turned towards Mona. "We'll officially announce it at the press conference concerning the Alban visitors." Her cold eyes traveled briefly to Aerina, cataloguing and dismissing her in the same way her daughter had earlier.

The President turned back to Vick, her smile thinning and her eyes slitting dangerously. "We have a lot to talk about, Vicktor. I look forward to catching up. And finding out what kept you from us this past decade."

The words were a threat. Aerina suppressed a shiver.

This was the President of the Southern Empire. Vick's mother.

And she was absolutely terrifying.

Several minutes later they were again alone, Mona and two soldiers their only escort as they headed towards the guest suites.

"I did not see that coming," Aerina murmured to Vick, holding tightly to his arm. Vick just continued to smile, shaking his head slightly. The hall was quiet, the only sound their footsteps muffled in the plush carpet. She got his message. Not here.

Aerina sighed, turning her attention to her luxurious surroundings. Unlike Alba, who restricted their usage of materials to what was available locally, the Empire obviously traded with other regions. The rich fabrics, the precious gemstones and metals that adorned the building were quite impressive.

The Empire itself was vast; the reality of it a little overwhelming. How were they going to find Lina? Was she being kept prisoner somewhere?

She looked over at Vick. His eyes were watchful, although he appeared relaxed as he walked beside her. She was glad he was with her.

It felt as if she had stepped into a different world entirely. Whatever happened, she wasn't leaving this place without Lina and Marcus.

7

Lina endured her captivity in the barren room by familiarizing herself with the Southern Empire's network. She had no idea how long it had been since Jay and Chelsea had left, or what was going to happen next.

A metal collar had been fixed around her neck, creating a feeling of claustrophobia as it locked into place. Jay had looked on emotionlessly as the soldiers sent from the President had secured it, and activated the remote.

"Just in case you get any ideas," one of them had remarked snidely. He had fallen silent after getting a glance at Jay's icy stare. A guard would hold the remote, which they had explained would immediately knock her out if she attempted anything. She didn't have the heart to remind them she could easily access the signal and deactivate the device. From Jay's face, she determined that he was aware and was happy not to say anything.

They were done playing nice. She was officially a prisoner now. She wasn't sure what that would mean, but she knew it wouldn't be good.

Getting lost in the code around her helped to take her mind from its fearful imaginings. And from the feelings of guilt over her deception.

He did the same thing to me, she told herself for the hundredth time. That just seemed childish, and did nothing to alleviate her remorse.

She felt so alone.

The door slid open, the unexpected noise after so much silence startling Lina. She watched with trepidation at who was about to enter.

Relief overwhelmed her at Stix's familiar face, accompanied by another soldier.

"Your presence is requested by the President," the soldier said curtly, undoing her handcuffs. Lina looked to Stix, rubbing her raw wrists. He nodded, indicating she should follow.

Chelsea had provided her with some fitted slacks and a blouse. They were probably loose on the smaller girl, but fit Lina snuggly.

Tugging at the clothes self-consciously, Lina stood and followed.

The hallways here were much different than the halls of the Capitol. The austere grey and blinding overhead lights were meant to intimidate, and it worked. Lina wrapped her arms tightly around herself, ignoring the urge to increase the temperature.

During her brief incarceration, she'd manage to identify the building she was being held in. It was called the Patriot Rehabilitation Center, and it appeared to be as eerie as the name suggested. It was basically used to brainwash citizens with anti-government sentiment. They had a live image feed from some of the other cells that she had accessed, and some of the things she witnessed had terrified her. She hadn't looked again.

An escalator took them to the main level lobby. The guard at the entrance scanned the soldier's ID. She thought there was going to be an altercation when Stix refused to scan his, but the guard finally stood down when he showed them his agent badge.

"He's the pilot for the Wolf," the soldier told the guard quietly. The guard immediately stepped back, nodding. A loud buzz was followed by the gate opening, letting them through.

An e-car was waiting in the turnaround. Lina hesitated briefly at the door, wishing Jay were here.

Her worry was alleviated slightly when Stix followed her into the car. The soldier climbed in the front seat, setting the destination in the autodriver.

"Where's Jay?" Lina couldn't contain the question a moment longer.

"He was called away for another job," Stix told her, his raspy voice holding a note of sympathy. She looked over at his grizzled face and read the understanding there. "He asked me and Thomas to watch out for you," he added, the words lifting the weight that had settled in her heart.

Perhaps he hadn't washed his hands of her after all.

"Where is your family?" she asked Stix, thinking of the images of the two young girls he'd showed her. That day seemed like a lifetime ago.

"They live about an hour west of here, in the low mountains. A little town called Asheville." His raspy voice softened when he spoke of them.

"When will you go home?"

Stix rubbed his beard lightly as he answered. "When Jay no longer needs me on this mission."

"I'll miss you," she said simply, meaning it. In a strange way, he reminded her a little of Stephen.

Stix appeared taken aback, then his face reddened.

"Well. That's awfully kind of you. You turned out not to be so bad, for a Patrician. You've got pluck."

Lina smiled, not quite sure what that meant but assuming it was good.

"What's going to happen now?" she asked quietly.

Stix shrugged, his eyes on the soldier in the front seat. "The President probably wants you to say something to the press. And perhaps the representative from Alba is here."

Lina's hand went instinctively to the collar on her neck, feeling a rush of excitement. Could her captivity be coming to an end? Then she thought of Jay. Going home would mean she would probably never see him again.

It's for the best, she told herself. But couldn't quite convince her heart.

8

Aerina pasted a smile on as bright lights shone in her face and people shouted questions at her, all holding recording devices. They stood at the back of a platform, waiting for the President to make an appearance and give a speech.

"This is ridiculous," she murmured to Vick, who stood beside her with a blank face.

"You're an instant celebrity. Most Confederates would kill to be in your shoes right now."

"But not you."

Vick looked at her for a moment, his real smile flashing.

"I hated every moment of being her son."

"I think you surprised her. I get the feeling that doesn't happen too often."

"She had me dead and buried, along with my father."

"What happened?" Aerina finally asked the question she'd been holding in since Marcus had casually announced Vick was a Confederate.

Vick opened his mouth to answer when the gathered crowd of media and supporters erupted into shouts. Another man had joined them on the platform, and Aerina couldn't keep her mouth from dropping open.

She looked between Vick and the man. Unlike Vick's long hair, tied back with a leather strip, and his close-cropped beard, the other man was clean shaven, his hair buzzed short. But otherwise they could have been twins, so close were their appearances.

"Is that…?"

"My younger brother. Jayden."

Jay turned to look at them, his eyes scanning Aerina and dismissing her. *I should be used to it by now*, she thought. Then the other man's gaze, an unexpected cyan green, met Vick's own hazel eyes.

He had obviously been forewarned of the identity of her escort, his cool eyes revealing nothing of his thoughts.

By the crowd's shouts and calls, Vick's brother was obviously very popular. He finally nodded, acknowledging Vick, and then turned to the crowd. He smiled, and Aerina was again taken aback at the similarities between the brothers. Jay's smile was the same false grin that Vick sported frequently.

This just kept getting crazier. And how dare Marcus not tell her? Vick was the son of the President of the Southern Empire, hiding in that dusty little outpost town just outside Alba.

"I can't believe you didn't tell me," she burst out softly, watching the crowd try to get Jay's attention, their interest in the Albans momentarily forgotten.

"I'd tried to put it behind me. But as long as she's alive, I'll never be free."

Aerina wondered what he meant by that. Her attention was caught now by another addition to their performance.

"Lina!" she gasped, rushing forward. Vick caught her arm, pulling her back.

"Careful. Play it cool."

Aerina nodded, anxious excitement burning in her chest. Lina was here. She looked fine, in fact she looked great. It looked like she'd been dressed and primped for this, her hair and make-up done, her dress an elegant white fitted dress with long sleeves and demure pencil skirt.

She looked every inch the elegant Patrician.

And she obviously had something with Vick's brother. His empty smile faltered upon her arrival, his eyes darkening with concern. He pulled her to his side, his hand remaining on Lina's arm. Aerina couldn't help but notice the protective way he stood beside her friend.

Lina felt overwhelming relief rush through her when she spotted Jay on the platform, Stix giving her a gentle shove to get her moving forward.

She didn't remember crossing the short distance, the noise of the growing crowd drowned out by the pounding in her head. She tried to take deep breaths to alleviate the anxiety, standing as close to Jay as she dared. The warmth of his hand on her arm helped. She glanced over at the other couple that waited with them, at first unable to believe her eyes.

Aerina stood with a man that looked like Jay's twin. Her friend was waiting for Lina to look, catching her eye with a wide smile, joy evident in her glowing blue eyes. Lina smiled back, unconsciously taking Jay's hand. His hand stiffened for a moment, and she thought he might pull away. Then it closed tightly around hers.

"What is Aerina doing here? And who is he?" Lina asked softly, glancing nervously at the crowd.

"She is the Emissary that Alba sent. And apparently her escort is my undead brother."

"Your brother? I thought he was killed on a mission years ago. Where has he been all this time?"

"That is what I thought. And the same question I'd like to ask him."

Lina wanted to run to her friend; to ask her what was going on, and why she was here.

"I can't believe Marcus let her come." Lina hadn't realized she'd spoken the thought aloud until Jay answered.

"She'd better hope the President doesn't find out her importance to Alba's current leader. And I wonder where he is," he added musingly, scanning the crowd. "I can't imagine he'd let her come without him, even if her companion is my brother."

Just then the Defense Secretary entered the platform, walking straight to the podium, holding up her hands for quiet. She looked neither to the left or right, ignoring the presence of both brothers.

"And I thought my family was dysfunctional," Lina murmured. Jay gave her hand a punishing squeeze but kept his eyes on his sister.

The crowd fell silent, eagerly waiting to hear the announcement.

"The President has an important announcement. Thank you all for being here. Your support is essential to our beloved leader. Please welcome the leader of the Sovereign States of the Southern Empire, President March!"

Thunderous applause broke out in the crowd that now filled the Capitol's expansive lawn and spilled into the streets.

The President herself appeared, dressed in a deep red skirt and blazer. She waved, her smile bright, her grey-blue eyes gleaming. Lina shivered. The older woman knew how to turn on the charm when it suited her.

Lina stole a glance at Jay, and then at his brother. Both men wore the same smirk that didn't reach their eyes.

The President nodded to Jay, as if including him in her wide smile, and then turned to Vick.

"My son," she said loudly enough to be picked up by the podium microphone. She walked to him, her tall figure nearly reaching his nose, and hugged him.

For a long awkward moment, he stood stiffly, staring straight ahead. His eyes met Jay's over her head, and then he slowly raised his own arms to return the embrace.

The crowd roared their approval of the display. The prodigal son, the hero, had returned to their nation.

The President stepped aside, greeting Aerina politely, then moved back to center stage, before the podium.

"Fellow Confederates, patriots of our glorious nation, I have exciting news. My first son, believed to be killed on a mission for our country, has returned home. He has done much for our nation in the intervening years, and we thank him for his service in the face of such trying odds.

"He has made it possible for the Alban Emissary standing before you to venture here today and discuss a valuable alliance between our nations. An alliance that will not only exchange valuable knowledge, but will span the continent, making us a force that the world will learn to fear."

She paused to allow time for the crowd to demonstrate their roaring approval, smiling in satisfaction. She seemed to become even more luminescent with each approving clap and admiring shout. Lina found herself unable to look away from the President's compelling gaze, wanting to believe herself that such an alliance was possible.

"Many of you witnessed the demonstration of the great power of the Alban nation, and the Technology they offer to share. In our hands, this Technology will make us the undisputed world power. It will become means to trade with other nations, and will once again unite the world in a global economy not seen in over a hundred years."

The air was heavy with humidity, and the dark clouds above began to slowly release their moisture. The rain was more of a mist, but Lina shivered nonetheless.

The President was unaffected by the rain, reveling in this moment, the culmination of her planning. The approval of the masses. The eye of the nation on her, their savior, and the re-creator of the global economy.

It was during one particularly loud applause that Lina caught a strange change in the networks around her. An alert that an unknown user was accessing the central system.

Before she could delve deeper, the world around her seemed to explode. In fact, the Capitol behind her burst into flames, so hot she thought her hair had been singed.

The crowd was frozen for a moment, then the cheers of approval turned to screams as the mob turned to flee. Lina watched the scene as if from a distance, shock taking over and cementing her feet.

A large hand connected with her back, knocking the breath from her while simultaneously throwing her off the stage onto the grass below. Then Aerina was grabbing her arm and pulling her. She glanced back to see Jay jumping off the platform with his sister tucked under his arm. The Secretary seemed unconscious or in shock.

They were running as more buildings ignited, some exploding, some smoking. Lina hesitates, watching Jay thrust his sister into the hands of a soldier, barking orders. Their eyes met for a brief moment, and then she was being pulled away. Aerina's hand gripped Lina, her friend's small finger's digging into the delicate bones of her wrist as she was dragged along in her wake.

They joined the mob that was fleeing the destruction, smoke and screams adding to the confusion around them. It wasn't until Lina recognized Marcus running alongside Aerina that she realized what was happening.

He had orchestrated this.

Dressed like an officer, he played the part well, directing people away from the blast and towards the waterfront.

Lina glanced around, wondering where Jay was. Was he ok?

The dark clouds and the billowing black smoke combined to create early darkness. Lina's heart raced, and she fought the urge to look behind her.

How many people were going to be injured from this? Were they going too far? One look at Marcus' stark features had her swallowing the question on her lips.

He wasn't too concerned about the havoc, at least not now.

As they neared the waterfront, Marcus suddenly stopped, slipping back between two towering buildings. The rest of the group followed, leaving the masses still fleeing the fires and reigning debris.

They paused beside a door, one of the 'officers' with them moving forward, swiping open the touch screen beside the door.

"Hurry up," Marcus said after nearly a silent minute ticked by, the crowd still loud and panicked outside the alley.

"I'm sorry," the man apologized, flexing his hands nervously and typing in another sequence.

"Password incorrect."

Lina finally realized what they were trying to do. Scanning through the system, she isolated the building on the security network, running through their commands. Finding the security release wasn't hard.

The door beeped, the panel shutting down.

"What the hell…" the Virmortus stepped back, glancing

at Marcus.

"Just open it," Lina told him, all eyes turning. "Their entire security system is down. It will reboot in about 27 seconds."

Marcus pushed through the door, holding it open and motioning the group inside, his eyes scanning the empty alley.

"Nice work," he murmured to Lina as she passed. She smiled slightly, nodding as she continued into the dark interior.

This was a service entrance. Small emergency lights lit the long hallways and they hurried down, passing laundry rooms, closets of cleaning supplies and a large lunch room. It smelled of laundry soap and lemon, so overpowering it cloaked the smoky odor that clung to their damp hair and clothes.

"Dock 23 is where Vick will meet us with the boat," Marcus told the group in a low voice. "We're going to split up and meet there. Aerina, you're with me. Lina, go with Chessa and Lucien. Ges and Thomas," he nodded to the last two. "Stay with the crowd as much as possible." He pulled work clothes from the locker room, throwing them to the women.

"Get changed."

Aerina and Lina hurried to do as he said, Lina ignoring the mild discomfort she felt at disrobing before the group. It helped that none seemed interested, busy listening to Marcus outline the best route.

"Be ready to take an alternate route. They'll be looking for us. The women will be harder to disguise from the facial recognition scanners, but they shouldn't have our features yet. Keep your heads down," he ordered the women.

Lina nodded as she struggled to button the plain blue shirt, tucking it into the white pants. They were a little big, but not nearly as baggy as Aerina's.

"Let's go."

Marcus opened the back door, and he and Aerina disappeared into the alley on the other side of the building, heading back towards the street. They looked like a police officer helping a worker escape.

"We're next," Chessa ordered. Lucien went first, pulling Lina behind him. Lina squinted, trying to get a glimpse of Aerina and Marcus, but the crowd had already swallowed them up.

Both Chessa and Lucien were dressed in the same police attire Marcus had been wearing, and a woman carrying two children immediately stopped upon seeing them.

"Please!" she cried. "My baby is still in the building." She pointed to the building a block up, flames and black smoke boiling from the base. Another building several blocks over began to topple, the heat of the fire too much for the supports. The woman screamed, her children clinging to her legs as she shrunk back.

"I'm sorry, ma'am. Keep moving, please," Lucien ordered softly, gently urging her away from the building that still held her baby.

The woman sobbed, pulling her two terrified offspring with her.

Lina put her hand to her mouth, sickness overwhelming her.

"We have to stop this," she told them, panic in her voice. "These people are innocent. That baby…"

"We don't have time for this," Chessa exclaimed impatiently, grabbing Lina's arm and pulling her along.

"Stop! We have to help them. We have to stop this!" Lina tried to dig in her heels, but her curvy form, tall as it was, was no match for Chessa's hard-earned strength. The smaller woman easily drug her along. Lucien followed, his pale eyes watchful.

I can't let this happen, Lina thought, her eyes on the woman and two children. The panicked crowd was pushing, trying to pass one another. In the chaos, the little girl got separated from her mother and brother. She began screaming, stopping. The mother was being dragged away quickly by the crowd, trying to reach back for her daughter.

The girl went down beneath the onslaught, and Lina ran forward without thought, finding the strength to break free from Chessa's hold. Grabbing the girl, she muscled her onto her shoulder, Lucien and Chessa both helping to drag both of them away from the mob.

Lina reunited the girl with her mother, the woman still sobbing.

Enough.

Lina ran through the controls, finding the cause of the explosions. A combination of the energy cells and the heating systems. She stopped the rest of the explosions set to go off, and then redirected the anti-fire systems, which malfunctioned after the energy cells imploded, to take energy from an offline back up system.

The smoke only seemed to increase as water began to combat the flames.

She'd done all she could. The rescue workers would have to do the rest.

Running alongside Chessa and Lucien, she saw the dark water of New Glory harbor stretching below. The street dipped sharply down to a long boardwalk for recreational use.

Boats were docked around the harbor, from small pleasure vessels to large cargo ships. Dock 23 was to the far south, forcing them to circle around.

They fought their way through the crowd that had no destination in mind, just trying to get as far as possible from the destruction.

Lina blindly followed Chessa, gripping the other woman's weapon belt when the crowd was especially violent. She was afraid that if she lost sight of the other woman, she would never get out of this hell that New Glory had quickly become.

They finally approached Dock 23, clearly labeled with a neat white sign.

Marcus stood at the gated entrance, arms crossed. If his police attire didn't deter the looters and desperate thieves, his very appearance would. No sane person would take on that man.

He stepped aside to let them pass, closing the gate behind them.

"You're the last."

"Sorry," Chessa replied shortly. "Someone slowed us down."

Lina ignored her, following Lucien onto the small pleasure craft. It had a small cabin, and seating in front and back. It was nothing like Jay's massive yacht.

"Start the motor," Marcus ordered, tossing the lines. Aerina hurried over and hugged Lina, pulling her into the cabin.

"I'm so glad you are alright," she told her friend.

"I can't believe... I never expected this," Lina replied, still in shock. Aerina's mouth quirked.

"Marcus never does anything in small measures. Although I have to admit, when the first building blew, I thought it was you."

Lina froze. "I wonder if they all think that. If Jay thinks..."

"Jay?"

Lina had forgotten for a moment that Aerina knew nothing of Jay. Of his role in all this. Of what he meant to her.

Lina shook her head. "It's a long story."

Aerina leaned back, propping her heel-clad feet on the bench opposite her and shoving the sleeves of her baggy work shirt up yet again. "We've got a long trip. Fill me in on your adventure."

She wouldn't exactly call it an adventure. But that was Aerina. To her, everything was an adventure.

Lina opened her mouth to begin her story with her first meeting in Alba. Before she could get the first word out, cursing interrupted her.

"Prepare to be boarded," came a voice over a loudspeaker.

A military vessel cruised up alongside them, weapons trained on their watercraft as hooks were deployed, connecting the two boats.

A large man swiftly descended the cutter's ladder, jumping the last few feet to land fluidly before them. Lina stifled the gasp as she recognized him.

Jay.

His eyes searched the group quickly, coming to rest on her. She thought she detected relief, which quickly became anger, and then icy blankness.

His dress clothes were blackened and rumpled, an ammo belt crisscrossing his heaving chest. The civilized man of the last week had again disappeared and the dangerous agent was back in his place.

He looked over at Vick.

"Leaving so soon, brother? Mother will be crushed."

Vick's hands rested lightly on the boat controls. He grinned, but his hazel eyes remained wary. "We'll have to catch up another time. I realized ten years wasn't nearly long enough to get over her attempt to have me murdered."

Lina wondered if Marcus and his team were at this moment identifying the boat on the network and attempting to gain access to its controls. Jay glanced back at the military cutter hovering ominously behind him, no doubt thinking the same thing.

"Hand her over and I'll let you leave," he finally said quietly.

"Forget it!" Aerina burst out, silent until now. She ignored the warning look Marcus shot her way. "Your mother is a psychotic criminal. No one, not even you, can protect her. And no one will be safe if she gets her hands on our Technology."

Jay looked at Aerina for a long moment, and then he met Lina's eyes. She would give anything to read what he was thinking, his familiar features blank, his eyes still cold.

Muted shouts, distant screams, alarms, and sirens filled the air around them. New Glory was in chaos, but the boat was silent. Lina met Jay's eyes, waiting to see what he would do next.

Unless Marcus's team could take control of the military cutter hooked to their starboard side, they didn't stand a chance escaping.

Had all this violence been for nothing? Lina knew Jay's devotion to his country; to his mission. He wouldn't let them go. He couldn't.

His eyes bored into hers as if seeking something; answers, perhaps. And then Jay turned away.

Swiftly ascending the ladder up to the larger cutter moored alongside them, he called up, "I was wrong. Nothing here. Release this craft and keep looking."

Lina watched his familiar form disappear over the side of the cutter. Their boat was released and the military boat was moving away. Vick didn't waste a moment starting up the motors, shooting forward in the quickly crowding waters.

The sight behind them was magnificent to behold. What must have been an awe-inspiring skyline was now the image of hell itself; all fiery brimstone.

"Wow. What was that all about?" Aerina finally asked in shock.

Lina tore her gaze from Jay's shrinking form, standing alone at the back of the boat, watching their smaller vessel escaping towards the open ocean.

"He must really like you to give up being the hero. There was nothing Jay liked more than saving the day." Vick's voice was thoughtful as he expertly manned the controls. Marcus continually scanned the surrounding waters, his face giving nothing away of his thoughts. But something told Lina he was interested in their conversation.

In the reason why Jay had let them go.

Lina had to admit, she was equally interested in the

answer to that question.

But in a way, she knew.

"He was being the hero. Our hero. My hero," she said softly.

Aerina smiled, understanding. "You and that agent, huh? He wasn't the one who…"

"Stole the Technology and kidnapped me? Yes, it was him," Lina admitted freely. "He was undercover as an Aggie gardener."

"Oh, Lina, a Patrician and a gardener? That is so…"

"Cliché?" Lina finished again. "Yeah, I know. Turns out, he wasn't really the gardener. Imagine my surprise." Her voice was deprecating, but it was all self-directed.

"Don't be too hard on yourself," Aerina said, looking back at the burning city behind them. "We've all done crazy things for love. And I'd say you did pretty good for yourself."

"Injecting yourself with the Technology kept it out of her hands," Marcus spoke, his low voice making Lina jump. "It was a bold move."

"The Technology in her hands would be another world war," Vick said grimly.

"Isn't she your mother?" Aerina asked.

Vick swerved around a buoy that marked the edge of the harbor pier. Everyone held on as the boat began to hop on the choppy water.

"In a biological sense. But the day she tried to have me killed was the day I stopped calling her mother. If it hadn't been for Marcus, I'd be dead because of her."

"How did Marcus save you?" Aerina asked.

"We were tipped on the relationship between the former Consul's wife and an agent," Marcus answered. "Caught him with her. We were also told the coordinates of his partner. It was my job to neutralize the threat. My first job as Alpha.

"I found Vick in his camp. We fought. During the fight, he told me how my boss was working with the Defense Secretary of the Southern Empire, and that was how they had the intel. How they'd gotten into the city so easily.

"I believed him. I let him go, and told him if I ever saw him again I'd kill him." Marcus cast a look at Vick, as if to say it still wasn't too late.

"We met a year later. I'd started Vicksburg with a few other homeless drifters. Thought Marcus was going to try and kill me. But we struck a deal instead. I'd give him any useful information I came across, and he'd share supplies and technology with me." Vick shrugged. "Worked great. But I knew I owed him. And now we're finally even."

"How did Jay fit into the story?" Lina asked quietly, bracing herself as the boat exploded over another large wave.

Vick sighed. "Jay and I were close as children. But as we got older, the President, our mother, began to pay special attention to him. It made the rest of us kids envious. Resentful. He was the favored child, and we were basically dog shit.

"She pushed him hard to be perfect, and the more she pushed, the more he succeeded. It was the same way with our father; he was always trying to make her happy. And she never was.

"I used to be envious of Jay. Now I just feel sorry for him. I got out, and had a chance to be free from her control. Jay is still under her thumb. Although, I'd say he's started making his own decisions, if today is any indication," Vick finished wryly.

Lina felt overwhelming sadness at hearing their story. She'd been so hateful towards Jay, blaming him for her misery. He'd been trying to play the hero, first for the people of the Southern Empire. And then for Lina.

He'd let her go. Sacrificed everything. For her.

9

Jay watched the small boat hit the edge of the harbor

and round the buoys, disappearing into the early darkness beyond.

Letting her go had been the hardest thing he'd ever done. But he knew he couldn't protect her here. Not as long as the President was alive.

Fulfilling his mission no longer mattered. The Alban Technology was just another tool the President wanted to make everyone around her suffer.

He finally looked back towards the city. His city. And he couldn't seem to drum up any indignation over the sight of New Glory brought to its knees.

Like the biblical cities of Sodom and Gomorrah, New Glory was finally reaping the reward it deserved.

When they docked, Jay disembarked.

"Sir, should we keep looking?" asked the captain.

"No, I know where the Albans are," Jay replied, walking away without a backwards glance at the confused seamen.

"Take me to the Congress Safehouse," he commanded the driver of a waiting military vehicle. The soldier nodded, taking to the crowded streets. Police and soldiers had slowly begun to restore order, directing citizens to emergency shelters, putting out the fires. The anti-fire systems that had miraculously rebooted had helped a lot to slow the spread of the fires.

He entered the safehouse, the soldiers stepping aside to let him pass as they recognized him. The Congress that had escaped sat around a large meeting table, shouting and arguing amongst themselves.

Some things never changed, even in a time of crisis.

"Listen up," he commanded, and the room fell silent. "I have a solution to our…problem."

"We're listening," the Congressional Head said warily.

Jay scanned the faces in the room. He didn't know why he'd waited so long to do this. They had all known this day would come; had seen the signs.

He'd just never really had a reason to care before; no

one to play the hero for.

And now he did.

10

The trip back to Alba was long but uneventful. They'd been forced to leave their aircraft behind, instead stealing a military tank to drive through the poorly guarded northern border of Texaco. The Southern Empire insignia on the tank had kept the bandits at bay. No one wanted to mess with the Southern Empire.

Lina was unusually quiet, making Aerina increasingly concerned. She knew her friend would be different; it would be impossible to go through such an experience and remain the same. But her friend was usually eager to share her thoughts and worries with Aerina. Now, she could barely coax a few words from her.

Aerina sighed deeply, adjusting on the uncomfortable bench seat. Vick and Marcus sat in the front, two Virmortus behind them manning weapons, and the rest of them sitting on the benches in the back for soldier units.

The tiny viewers didn't allow them to see much of the scenery that passed swiftly. Aerina strained to see the red-tinted rock hills of what used to be Arizona. The sun hadn't even broken the horizon yet, but its reddish glow preceded it, reflected off the hills around them.

"Kind of amazing, after spending our whole life behind Alba's walls, to see the entire continent in a month." She broke the long silence, glancing at Lina's pensive features.

Her friend had changed in many ways. Her gently rounded features had become more defined with the weight she'd lost on this strange adventure. Gone, too, was the awkward way she held herself, as if trying to disguise her height and curves. Now she was relaxed, finally comfortable in the body she was given.

Was the agent responsible for this change; the man who'd let them go?

"It's hard to believe all this has happened in such a brief time. It seems like a lifetime ago that we were surfing with Stephen, going to the Graduate Ball…"

Aerina put her arm around Lina, resting her head on her friend's shoulder briefly. They were both still clad in the work clothes stolen from the Confederate high rise.

"Now what?" Lina asked, her dark eyes on Marcus as he expertly maneuvered the vehicle across the rarely used road. A light dusting of snow covered it here.

"I don't know," Aerina answered. "I don't think the Empire will give up. So I suppose back to preparing for war."

"I had thought that perhaps… I was naive."

Aerina heard the weight of sorrow in her friend's voice. "No one could reason with their nation. But I hope they got our message. That the Technology is dangerous, and we're not afraid to use it."

"They underestimated us. They won't do it again." Marcus' voice was hard to hear above the muted roar of the motor, but both women nodded agreement to his statement.

This wasn't over.

11

Lina stood at the edge of the Capitol balcony, overlooking the ocean far below. The mist had cleared in time for the setting sun to cast its glow over the city.

She scanned her home with new eyes. The carefully planned terraces, each at different elevations, connected by the large tram the citizens called the Ferry, were functional and ascetically appealing. The Pleb city, at sea level of the coastal city, had always seemed large and chaotic to her. But after

New Glory, it looked urbane and orderly.

Her life had been different since returning. She'd taken over Stephen's villa, much to her mother's dismay. But rather than sinking into depression, being in Stephen's space had made her feel closer, and helped her heal.

She'd joined the Technology Project at the Training Grounds under Aerina's urging. Having a Patrician of Technology as part of the project had given it legitimacy, and Lina had agreed to speak with the Senator of Technology about gaining the support of more influential Patrician voters.

She loved every moment of the work. The participants came from a myriad of backgrounds, but all shared her fascination with the interface between mind and technology systems.

Jamia, the youngest recruit, was her favorite. The young, effervescent girl always lifted Lina's spirits. Lina could now see why Aerina had looked outside of the Capitol Terrace to create new friendships.

The relationship between Aerina and herself had also evolved. The childhood friendship that had existed before had taken on a new level of closeness; of understanding.

No matter how much Lina's life was progressing; how many new relationships she created and olds ones she strengthened, she still felt loss.

The loss of Stephen, certainly, but leaving Jay behind had been unexpectedly devastating. She hardly knew him, but in their brief time together, an unusual connection had formed.

And she missed that connection; that sense of understanding. The electric chemistry. She missed him.

The muted beep of her holoreader interrupted her morose thoughts. Shaking her head, she glanced down to see Aerina's image projected. Pressing the button, she opened the connection.

"Hi—"

"Where are you? I'm coming to get you. You need to be

here now!" Her friend's words tumbled over each other as she spoke.

"I'm at the Capitol, what—"

"Meet me out front, I'll be there in a minute." Aerina disconnected, leaving Lina concerned and confused.

Hurrying to the front drive of the Capitol, Lina waited. Her searching gaze soon caught the sight of Marcus' familiar black e-car cruising swiftly down the cobbled street, screeching quietly into the turnaround.

Aerina was driving, motioning Lina to get in.

"What is going on?" Lina asked as the restraint clicked into place. Aerina was already back on the road, heading towards the Training Grounds.

"You are not going to believe who Marcus' team captured outside the city."

Lina felt hope budding in her chest, but forced herself to be logical. Why would he be here?

"Shall I begin guessing, or are you going to tell me?" she said instead.

"For that answer, I'll make you wait and see," Aerina retorted with a laugh.

"Aerina. You can't just—"

"Ok, ok. I want you to be emotionally ready, anyway. Your agent lover, Vick's brother—"

"Jay." Lina interrupted Aerina's gleeful announcement quietly. Terrified anticipation filled her, making her heart beat faster. He was here, in Alba. But why?

Was he finally finishing his mission? Did he let them go for a reason?

Could he be here for her?

"I heard he drove right up to the gate in the Southern Empire vehicle, but I don't know if that's true. Marcus has him now in the interrogation floor."

"Is he…?"

"Hurt? No, at least not yet."

Thoughts whirled in Lina's mind, drowning out the rest

of Aerina's chatter. The short trip to the massive steel building built into the stone wall of the mountain seemed to take forever.

Aerina pulled into an underground garage. Lina was out before the car was off, hurrying towards the elevator. Aerina rushed after her.

They requested admittance to the interrogation floor, and Ramus himself met them as the elevator doors slid open.

"He doesn't want to talk until he sees you, Ms. Rhodes," the dark-skinned man with an impressive build informed her. Lina nodded, her eyes on the screen showing the two men facing off in the small chamber.

The size of the men made the room seem tiny. Jay was shackled to strange bindings, a square device sitting innocuously on the table between them.

A nerve stimulator, she recognized from her training. A clever interrogation device invented not too many years previously.

Jay looked tired, but the same as the last time she'd seen him. Unusually serious, slightly disheveled, devastatingly attractive. His hair was still buzzed, his square jaw covered lightly in stubble.

"You really should consider improving your security," Jay taunted idly, his drawl clear even through the speaker.

"I caught you, didn't I?" Marcus responded evenly.

"I let you. Do you think I couldn't have found a way in, just like last time?"

Marcus' jaw flexed, but he remained silent, dark eyes fixed on Jay's gleaming blue-green ones.

Aerina sighed. "Nothing good will come of these two alpha males challenging each other. Send Lina in."

Lina started at the sound of her name, her gaze fixed on Jay.

She still couldn't believe he was sitting right there, only a wall between them.

A wall and a world of differences.

Ramus pressed a button, and Marcus stood, nodding. The door opened, and Ramus indicated Lina could enter the small room.

Jay's back was to her as she entered, and she saw him stiffen. As if he knew it was her.

Marcus met her eyes. "Just talk," he warned. Then he left.

Lina felt as if her feet were rooted to the grey cement floor, afraid to move forward and face him.

"Lina."

Her name on his lips sent a thrill to her heart, and she found the courage to move. She walked around, sinking into the metal chair as her shaky legs gave out.

"What are you doing here?" she asked finally. His eyes moved over her, taking in the small changes. Her longer hair, thinner face, confident posture.

"I wanted to see you…" he began, his voice for once lacking its normal confidence. "I wanted to tell you personally that the President is no longer in power. She's been impeached and formally deposed."

Lina's eyes widened. That had not been what she expected, and secretly, not what she'd hoped. But still…

"How?"

"Congress finally found the support they needed to reveal her history of violence and mental instability, and her inability to lead."

"You did it, didn't you?" Lina leaned forward, placing her hands on his clasped ones. He turned his slowly, wrapping them around her fingers. A familiar electrical current raced through her, warming her.

"It was past time. She was a poison to everyone around her."

"Who is running the Empire?"

"Not anyone with the name of March," he answered drily, his gaze on their entwined hands. His finger rubbed the soft inside of her palm gently, making her breath catch.

A moment of fear replaced the pleasure. Was this another attempt of his to use her? To get something from the Albans?

Lina scanned his face, trying to read his features. What were his intentions?

"Why come here, Jay? Because I'm sure you're needed back home."

"Needed?" Jay's sardonic smile twisted, his face becoming bitter. "Yeah, I'm sure they could find a use for me. I'm a celebrity; the nation's golden boy. A posterchild for patriotism, success, and everything the Empire stands for. But I'm done with politics. I quit the Agency, sold the house and yacht... I needed a change. Needed to be free." He leaned in intently, as if willing her to understand.

Lina looked down again, unable to think while meeting his eyes. He was doing it again, pulling her under his spell. Was it the truth? Was he done with the Southern Empire?

"What are you going to do now?"

He leaned back, shifting his large form in the small metal chair. "You're different. Different from when we met." His eyes went over her graceful form, clad in a white blouse and thin pencil skirt. "And when did you become such a good interrogator, asking questions and giving nothing away? What are you thinking behind those big brown eyes, *diosa*?"

The familiar endearment was both alarming and affecting. He was speaking the words she wanted to hear, giving her hope she had no right to cling to.

"I've been rebuilding my life here, finding a purpose. Finding confidence in my abilities; actually using my skills and the Technology," she replied softly, her turn to give him a look that begged his understanding.

His hands released hers and clenched into fists. His voice was dangerously soft when he replied. "Are you telling me there is no place for someone like me in your life now? That if I did come here for you, I wasted my time?"

He was here for her? She tried to control the excitement

those words engendered. A combination of fear and euphoria was trying to take over.

Was the strange feeling love? Was it possible? Could she love him?

"Jay, I…" she wasn't sure how to say what she was thinking, painfully aware of the camera eye fixed on them.

"Forget it. I figured this was a waste of time. But I had to know. Had to see you and make sure you were…ok. I can see you're doing great. Better than me."

"Jay—" she tried again.

"Send the Reaper back in. I'll finish my business with him."

Lina finally lost her temper. "Fine. But I'm going to say something first. You turned my life upside down, dragged me across the continent, seduced me, stabbed me. But you also changed me. You forced me to take responsibility for my own life, to take ownership of it. To embrace who I am, and to hell with the rest of the world. To enjoy pleasure for the sake of it, because life is short." She leaned closer, no longer caring who was watching.

"I'm still figuring out who I am, and who you are, Jayden Kane March, but I think I might love you. You've got me so confused, I don't even know what—"

Jay didn't wait for her to finish, standing so abruptly his chair flew back. His manacled hands caught on the table as he leaned forward, his mouth descending on hers.

She closed the final distance between them, wrapping her arms around him, feeling the muscles bulging as he pulled against his restraints to get closer to her.

Distantly Lina heard the door opening, but for the moment, didn't care. This was where she wanted to be. Her arms went around his neck.

His mouth slanted over hers, the kiss both desperate and demanding at once.

"Get your hands off her." Marcus' low voice finally penetrated the haze that had fallen over Lina, and she pushed back. Jay hesitated a moment before slowly sitting back down slowly.

Lina slid off the table, taking Jay's hand to show her unspoken support.

Aerina hovered in the doorway, looking worried. Lina couldn't help the blush that spread. *I guess I'm not quite as avant-garde as I thought.* "It's ok," she said aloud. "I believe him. He's not here for the Empire."

Jay didn't look at her, but he squeezed her hand.

"We'll see," was all Marcus said.

"Check for yourself," Jay challenged softly. "Any media from the Empire will be covering the story of the President's impeachment and imprisonment in a mental hospital."

"And the Technology?" Aerina asked.

Jay directed his answer to her, but kept his gaze fixed on Marcus. "The current Congress and President agree that it is too dangerous and better left to the Albans to protect. I can't say they won't change their minds if Europe becomes a threat, but they are content for now to focus internally. The President was covering up a lot of issues; discontent is high, and killing people only holds it off for so long."

"We'll look into your claims. You'll need to remain here until it is either confirmed or refuted."

Jay nodded. "I figured as much. Take me to your best cell."

Lina opened her mouth to protest, but Jay silenced her with a quick kiss. "I'll be fine. Come visit me?" She nodded as the manacles opened, allowing Jay to stand to his full height. He absently rubbed his wrist as he followed Marcus from the room, winking at Lina before he disappeared.

She collapsed against the table, taking a few deep breaths to slow her racing heart.

"Are you sure, Lina?" Aerina asked softly, her eyes concerned.

Was he being truthful? Or was this another elaborate plot? The moment those fears entered, she rejected them. She trusted him. Life didn't have any guarantees, and some things were worth taking a risk.

"I'm sure."

12

Lina, Helen, and Aerina sat in the lounges around Stephen's Serenity Pool, which had now become Lina's. Lina carefully poured what remained of the amber-colored liquor from Stephen's desk into the glasses each of the women held.

"To Stephen, who would have approved of the choices we've made," Aerina said, holding her glass up.

"And to your child, Stephen's child, may he be healthy, strong, and as wise as his parents." Lina raised her own glass.

Helen smiled, her eyes misting. "Damn these hormones," she muttered, raising her own glass. "And to you both, heroes of our nation and women I respect, love, and am honored to call my friends."

Each woman sipped the liquid, thinking of how their worlds had so completely changed in the past few months.

Helen poured the rest of her drink into Lina's glass, patting her still-flat stomach gently. "This little person has had enough. I think we might retire early tonight."

"Vick's here," Aerina commented casually. "He's meeting with Marcus and Jay. I think he said something about stopping by your place later. To check on you."

Helen immediately sat back down on the lounger. "I might be too tired to make it home. Lina, would you mind making up the guest room?"

Lina raised her brows questioningly. "Did I miss something?"

"No," Helen snapped quickly before Aerina could speak. "I just find I have an aversion to that...that uncouth outsider."

"She's thrown up on him twice," Aerina stated gleefully.

"I think he likes her."

Helen rolled her eyes, shaking her head

"Chemistry can pop up at the most inconvenient times," Lina said.

"Chemistry? Or perhaps love?" Aerina asked, her blue eyes questioning.

Lina flushed slightly, still uncomfortable talking about her feelings for the former Southern Empire spy, and currently homeless man who was even now being interrogated by the Virmortus. Hopefully not too harshly.

"Yes, I think we could call it love," she finally admitted, meeting Aerina's amused gaze.

"Good luck," Helen said. "You're going to have a long road in front of you if you pursue that relationship."

"Some things are worth a battle," Lina said. "And Jay is one of them.

The war is winding down, not because people have changed, but because there are too few resources to continue to fight. We can't create a society free from war, but we will build one that will be ready to face any new challenges humankind or mother-nature sends its way. A society that embraces knowledge and kindness, but also is familiar with fear and respect. A perfect society? No, there is no such thing as long as humanity lives. But a society based on values of balance and peace is a place to start.

And so we are creating Alba, the Pure City, based on Greco-roman beliefs of equality, knowledge, and human rights. And we will keep the Technology we have created until the time is right. When humanity has evolved enough to equal the evolution of science…

– From the Journal of Cecilia Delacroix

Get an exclusive sneak peek of
Outsider, Book 3 in *The Secret of Alba Series* by visiting
www.lindseywinsemius.com/my-books

www.ingramcontent.com/pod-product-compliance
Lightning Source LLC
Chambersburg PA
CBHW070802200626
46811CB00023B/394